PENGUIN BOOKS
JACK PATEL'S DUBAI DREAMS

P.G. Bhaskar lives in Dubai with his wife and son. When asked what he does for a living, he somewhat sheepishly replies 'banking'. He loves cricket and is often found on his sofa staring intently at the television set mouthing profanities when things don't go according to his plan. When not watching TV, writing or banking, he puts together quiz questions in the hope of getting people to attend his quizzes.

'*Jack Patel's Dubai Dreams* is like a movie on paper. The *sur*, *lay* and *taal* of every situation fits perfectly as the characters come alive. There's a smile on every page. Little insights from the corporate world are beautifully interlaced with snippets from daily life to create a delectable situational comedy.'—Shankar Mahadevan

METRO
READS

# Jack Patel's Dubai Dreams

## P.G. Bhaskar

PENGUIN BOOKS

PENGUIN BOOKS
Published by the Penguin Group
Penguin Books India Pvt. Ltd, 11 Community Centre, Panchsheel Park,
New Delhi 110 017, India
Penguin Group (USA) Inc., 375 Hudson Street, New York, New York 10014, USA
Penguin Group (Canada), 90 Eglinton Avenue East, Suite 700, Toronto,
Ontario, M4P 2Y3, Canada (a division of Pearson Penguin Canada Inc.)
Penguin Books Ltd, 80 Strand, London WC2R 0RL, England
Penguin Ireland, 25 St Stephen's Green, Dublin 2, Ireland
(a division of Penguin Books Ltd)
Penguin Group (Australia), 250 Camberwell Road, Camberwell,
Victoria 3124, Australia (a division of Pearson Australia Group Pty Ltd)
Penguin Group (NZ), 67 Apollo Drive, Rosedale, Auckland 0632,
New Zealand (a division of Pearson New Zealand Ltd)
Penguin Group (South Africa) (Pty) Ltd, 24 Sturdee Avenue, Rosebank,
Johannesburg 2196, South Africa

Penguin Books Ltd, Registered Offices: 80 Strand, London WC2R 0RL, England

First published by Penguin Books India 2011

Copyright © P.G. Bhaskar 2011

All rights reserved

10 9 8 7 6 5 4 3 2 1

This is a work of fiction. Names, characters, places and incidents are either the product
of the author's imagination or are used fictitiously and any resemblance to any actual
person, living or dead, events or locales is entirely coincidental.

ISBN 9780143415268

Typeset in Bembo Roman by SŪRYA, New Delhi
Printed at Manipal Press Ltd, Manipal

*I dedicate this book to all the men, women and families who have been touched by the ups and downs of the world of investments. I wish them well.*

# 1

## COMING BACK HOME

With an ear-splitting wail, the train charged in—briskly, purposefully and seemingly full of energy. It was very different from the way I felt. The initial glow and excitement surrounding my recent engagement had passed. My immediate concern was to figure out how I was going to make a living and support a family. The one overwhelming thought was that it should be something far removed from the world of investments. I had yet to recover fully from the tumultuous events in my life in the last few months. The hustle and bustle around me did little to soothe my frayed nerves.

It was January, 2009 and I was at the Chennai Central Station. It had been five years since I had taken a train in India. A heavily loaded hand-cart zipped dangerously close, pushed by a frenzied youth. I hurriedly stepped back and almost came in the way of a fellow traveller who leaned to his right, tightened the muscles on his cheek, pursed his lips and expertly spat out in a stream, the juice from a paan . . . The pillar which he had aimed at, now bore a fresh, bright red stain.

Quickly, I shook myself out of the stupor I had fallen into. Get a hold on yourself, Jack, my boy, I told myself. You are back in India now. The country on the move. Out here, either you keep moving, or get trampled upon.

I started running clumsily in the same direction as the train, trying to avoid the hundreds of suitcases that were threatening to run over my toes like a modern juggernaut. I had no idea if I was

moving in the right direction—my compartment could well be at
the other end of the platform—but hundreds of others were doing
it and somehow it didn't seem right not to. I suppose this is what
'herd mentality' is all about. In the world I had just come from, this
psychological phenomenon results in a few people making money
and everyone else losing it.

A large family jostled and pushed past me. I held myself back,
irritated. If there was one part of me that was more British than
Indian, it was in this matter of queues. On the very first day of my
first visit to London many years ago, I had fallen in love with the
city primarily on the strength of the discipline of its queue system.
When would we Indians learn, I wondered, that queuing up means
standing *behind* one another and not shoulder to shoulder.

Meanwhile, a little fellow holding a sharp-edged wooden crate
tied up with nylon rope dug into my neck with his elbow. Politely,
I suggested that he take his place at the end of the line. 'What line,
no line!' he screamed. 'What you talking bloody English? You
think you big man, talking damn English? Lord Mayor of London,
you? Englishman all gone in 1947! I bought also *ticket*. I pay
money, bought ticket, understand?' He pushed his way in, still
muttering 'Talking bloody English . . .' I held back, nonplussed
and stunned into silence. Once everyone had rushed in, I followed.
I realized that part of their hurry was to find space near their seats
for their luggage.

Near me was a rather noisy family of five including three
children; a girl of about ten and two younger boys. They were
obviously Tamilians. Over the years, I have picked up a fair bit of
Tamil, though I still can't speak it fluently. Starting with swear
words taught to me in hushed whispers by classmates at school, I
have progressed steadily. While the couple spoke in Tamil to each
other, they seemed to deliberately speak only in English with their
children. 'Don't make unnecessary sound, da!' the father admonished
one of the boys. 'Okay, go and come,' the mother told the girl,
after she whispered something into her mother's ear. Then, as an
afterthought, as the girl proceeded towards the loo, she hissed,
'Don't *fully* sit.'

I shut my eyes. It was rather sudden, all this, coming on top of everything that had happened. Just a few months ago, I had been Jai 'Jack' Patel, a successful Financial Advisor, the fastest million-dollar revenue generator in the history of Myers York. I had had a loyal and happy fan following of wealthy, greedy clients. Yet, now, like the prodigal son, I was back home, licking my wounds so to speak, possibly about to do what my father had wanted me to do in the first place. Which was to help him manage the family business or get into tobacco farming in Gujarat. Or maybe run a farm and manage some plantations, like my grandfather used to do. I was now on the way to finalizing a transaction to buy land near a place called Brahmadesam. It had been strongly recommended to us by my friend Kitch's father. In another couple of months, I'd be getting married. My fiancée says she is looking forward to life on a farm. I am not entirely sure. But having botched my first independent 'venture', I guess I'll go with the flow. In any case, what's wrong with giving farming a chance? The world can't be full of money managers. One can do without a mutual fund but everyone needs to eat. I took a deep breath.

All things considered, it was good to be back home. Good not to be held responsible for uncontrollable, uncertain market forces. Good not to wake up in the middle of the night, drenched in sweat and plagued by confusion, fear and guilt. The only thing that was bothering me was an uneasy sense of defeat and a concern about my next move.

I looked out of the window again. A couple of kids were waving. No one waved back but they didn't seem to mind. They looked immensely happy and kept waving, chattering excitedly to each other. I pondered over this. Excitement and happiness. Could it be so easy? Then why is it that most of the world works so much and tries so hard to achieve it? Maybe it's best to simply be like these children, do something simple and pleasurable, expecting nothing in return. Just a happy wave moment, then a series of such happy moments . . . I took another deep breath.

The smell of sambar and chutney tickled my nostrils. I was born to Gujarati parents, but my palate is equally south Indian. Years of living in Chennai has induced a strong preference for local delicacies. I wished I had picked up something to eat at the Chennai station. I examined the side flap of my suitcase, vaguely remembering having seen something there. There was a packet of potato chips. I examined it, looking for signs to open it. There were none. I tried the top right, then the left. I turned it over and tried both ends. I tried pulling the two sides apart and then attempted to rip it across the centre. Nothing worked. I put it back in the flap with a mild curse. It might be a good business idea in India, I thought, to manufacture wrappers and packets that would open easily.

There was a swish of the curtains and a young girl thrust a plate towards me. I stared dumbly. A voice sounded from behind her. 'Please take.' It was the girl's mother. I needed no second invitation. I took. There was idli, sambar and two types of chutneys. I finished it in a jiffy and the girl, who was obviously a gifted mind reader, came back with a refill, smiling sweetly.

This can happen only in India, I thought. Where else would someone take the trouble to offer a meal to a perfect stranger on a train? Who else celebrate the event of eating on a train as much as Indians do? More often than not, travel in India is a picnic, or even a feast. More than the journey itself, many people look forward to the eating.

I got up and poked my head in. 'I loved it,' I told them, addressing the family at large. 'Thank you very much.'

'Welcome!' the lady replied with a smile.

I returned to my seat. The man asked his wife for a véshti, the staple 'below the waist' apparel of many Tamilians. She unzipped one of their bags and gave it to him, white and folded neatly. He unfolded it, draped it around his waist and then wiggled his legs to allow his trousers to slide down.

I yawned. The last few days had been such a rush. I was worried about the things to come. What lies ahead for Jai? The three kids were now singing Rahman's chartbuster 'Jai ho'. They were vague about the rest of the lyrics, but put enough gusto in those two words to compensate. '*Jai ho!*' So symbolic! I tried to think positively about the future. But, as I stared out of the window with unseeing eyes, only the past just kept coming at me. Everything that had happened in the last four years.

# 2

## THE 'STREET' BECKONS

Over four years ago, Myers York—among the largest investment firms in the world—announced its first-ever presence on Indian soil with a series of centre-spread advertisements that took Mumbai, the erstwhile Bombay, by storm. This was followed up by a television blitz. They were not just setting up a three-member representative office like most other institutions looking to get a foot-hold in the country. They had obtained a full-fledged licence and were rather making a point of it. As they proclaimed their communication, they were not just looking for an address in India. They were here to stay, to take root. They wanted to 'give the Indian investment world the international edge that it deserved'. Their office was inaugurated by the Chief Minister, no less, where a kurta-clad American Regional Manager broke the traditional coconut in full glare of the cameras.

This Wall Street colossus was a household name internationally, with a presence in fifty-five countries. This was number fifty-six. In its first two weeks in India, it launched four investment products. Its advertisements in the media had Bollywood star, Abhijit Shrivastava, telling the public that he always went in for the 'cutting-edge' to stay ahead of the rest. 'Cutting-edge film banners, cutting-edge technology and cutting-edge investments', he says in the advertisement, which concludes by his looking into the camera and saying 'I use Myers York to manage my investments. Myers rock. They really do!' before signing off with a wink and a thumbs-up sign.

I was all of twenty-four. I didn't just like this whole show. I *loved* it. I was mesmerized by it. And I wanted to be part of it.

India was doing phenomenally well, economically. Following a grave crisis in the early 1990s, the country's socialist experiment of several decades had been discarded and replaced by a kind of controlled capitalism that had more than doubled its economic growth rate over ten years. The lumbering elephant had long since awoken and was changing into a different animal altogether, something with significantly more spring in its step. Yet, it was reassuring in a sense, to have one of the largest investment firms in the world come down from New York to seek a permanent abode here. Over the years, the American dream had slowly but steadily also taken root in some young Indian minds. There may be some resistance to western concepts in India if it is pushed through or if it is seen to be accompanied by a touch of arrogance. But many western concepts, thoughts and ideas have filtered in quietly, naturally. Even if it is pushed through in a commercial form, we are ready to embrace it and lap it up, if the company behind it shows even a modicum of respect for local culture. McDonalds did this with a lot of understanding, when they substituted beef with chicken in their burgers. In fact, they went a step further and introduced *McAloo Tikki*. Likewise, Myers York while making no secret of their opinion that they were exceptionally good at what they did, showed humility in wanting to understand India, absorb local taste, soak in local culture and fall in line with Indian requirements. They were willing to spend, to be flexible and considerate. But they wanted the business. Even as they were telling us about their sophisticated technology, high salaries and plush offices with a library, gym and recreation room, they were giving their products Indian names and using Indian concepts to promote them. Like the bindi on the Hindu woman's forehead. Or names from Indian mythology. There was one advertisement about a product that offered a combination of five types of investment and insurance protection. To emphasize that, the ad drew upon the *pancha bhoota* (the five elements of nature) concept of Hindu philosophy, the five Ks of the Sikh religion and the number of times that a Muslim does his daily *namaz*. It went well. I, for one, was floored. Some critics derided it as typical American hype. Well, if this was hype, I decided I *liked* hype and I wanted a big chunk of it. This was exactly the kind of stuff I was looking for: a big respected international name, a career in investment and a great platform for a successful take off.

I was also tired of my job, of spending several hours on technical analysis every day and the painful daily train commute all the way from Borivli to the city and back. A company like Myers York would pay me twice as much. Perhaps I would even be able to afford to move to Bandra or Khar, or maybe even closer downtown where the office was.

I spent two days doing and re-doing my résumé. Then, in a sudden moment of madness, I made up my mind to just walk into the company's office and demand a job. That morning, I had accompanied a colleague to a client's office and had just convinced the client to give us a Rs two-crore discretionary portfolio. Initially, he seemed hesitant, but my technical charts and work on back-testing hypotheses worked on him in a way that no amount of tedious explanations and aggressive sales pitches could. 'This is very good,' he kept repeating. I came out of the building feeling like a million bucks. I realized we were just two blocks away from Myers' office. My CV was in my briefcase. While my colleague headed towards the station, I excused myself.

Even as I stepped into the brand-new Myers building, I was filled with a nervous energy that seemed to push me forward. Within seconds, I was at the reception, trying to remember the name of the Regional Manager I had read about, the guy who had broken the coconut. The lady at the reception was talking to a gentleman. She paused and looked at me, inquiringly. I took a quick breath to steady myself. 'My name is Jai Patel,' I said softly, trying to sound quietly confident. 'I want to meet James Ackermann.' In most circumstances, the lady would have asked me what it was in connection with. She would have then asked me to leave my

CV with her and told me they would get back to me. But this was one of those days where everything goes without a hitch. If I had written the script for the day myself, I couldn't have done better. The gentleman she was talking to looked at me and said, 'I'm James, how may I help you?'

Four days later, I was at a meeting with James Ackerman, Myers' Regional Head, Cyrus Irani, who ran their Dubai office, and Peggy Mitchell, Unit Head at the Dubai office,

The two years that I spent at IIM Bangalore and my subsequent stint at Mumbai had given me a new-found confidence. I was almost completely at ease. On the odd occasion when I was not, I think I managed to cover it up pretty well, leaning back, keeping my legs crossed, casually intertwining my fingers and looking them in the eye, a light smile playing on my face from time to time.

Everyone was formally dressed. I was wearing my best suit. Well, let's say the newer of the two that I possessed. A uniformed man came along with tea and coffee. All, except Mr Irani, took their cups. The waiter seemed to know his preferences and didn't even offer him anything.

'Cyrus doesn't drink tea or coffee,' Mr Ackermann told me, almost as if he owed me an explanation.

'No minor vices,' said Peggy and everyone laughed lightly.

'So, Jaykii . . .' Mr Ackermann began, staring into my card. 'May I call you Jack?'

'Sure'

'Tell me, Jack, what do you know about Myers York?'

I couldn't have hoped for a better start. I had spent much of the last forty-eight hours devouring their published financial statements and surfing the net for information about the company. 'I know everything that's in your balance sheet, Mr Ackermann,' I said, in a soft voice. I knew I was making a strong statement and I didn't want to sound brash. 'I know your assets, your liabilities. I know your revenue statement and your equity ratios. I know the company's public history over the last ten years. I know the movement of the share price from the time it was listed, the highs, the lows and the averages. And I know one more thing. I know that it's a company that I very much want to be a part of.'

'It's the company everyone wants to be part of.' James laughed, joined in by the others. I did too, though my laughter was tinged with nervousness.

'Jack, you might be under the impression we are meeting with you for a job at our India office. That's not quite so. We did all the recruitment we needed for Mumbai quite some time ago. But Cyrus and Peggy are looking for someone for their Dubai office. A young Financial Advisor to handle primarily the Indian community. We are already way behind in this race and we want to catch up. We have some half a dozen advisors at the Dubai office, but Peggy is looking for two more. We think there's still a huge untapped market within the Indian diaspora.'

I was dumbfounded. A consultant at Myers York's Dubai office? *Was this a dream*? Me, Jai Patel, still green behind the ears and just a year out of business school!

He seemed to sense what was going on in my mind. 'We are looking for someone who can grow with us, Jack.' His voice seemed reassuring, encouraging.

For a moment I remained tongue-tied. Then, I said, 'I want this job, Mr Ackermann. I would do anything to get it.'

'Your experience with managing investments so far has been only in India, Jack.' This was Mr Irani. Rather unusually, he was wearing a bow-tie. I don't think I had ever seen anybody wear one in real life. His somewhat bushy eyebrows made him appear a little intimidating. 'How do you think you will be able to cope up with international investments?' he asked.

I hesitated for a second. Then, I remembered something I had heard recently.

'Money speaks the same language everywhere, Mr Irani, doesn't it?' I said. 'People all over the world have the same emotions, fear, worry, greed . . . I am hardworking and I am willing to learn. I come from a business family. We have family and friends all over the world. Bringing business in will not be a problem. As a technical analyst at my firm, I have helped clinch several accounts. I am sure I can handle clients on my own. Besides, I know Myers have a fantastic training programme.'

'You're right about that,' said Peggy. 'It is the best and the most sought after in the industry.'

Some polite conversation and handshakes followed. Mr Irani asked me about quizzing, which I had put down on my résumé as one of my interests. I told them I had represented both my school and college at quiz contests.

'Well, let me see how much you know,' Mr Ackermann said to me, unexpectedly. 'What do you think are the chances of your becoming a Myers York employee?'

Then, even as I floundered a bit, he winked and told me to expect a call soon.

As I stepped out of the building, I was sweating and feeling weak-kneed. It was as if the divine force which had kept me calm and unruffled throughout the meeting had suddenly deserted me. I decided I needed some fresh air. I wanted to walk. And think. I stepped out and walked almost the entire length of Marine Drive and back. I was very excited and happy. But also tired, famished and soaked in sweat. I took a cab to the VT station, went to my favourite roadside eatery nearby and tucked into a plate of pav bhaji, complete with a slab of butter, spring onions and extra pav. Get ready to fly, Jack Patel, I told myself. It's your time now, on Wall Street.

Less than a week later, I got a call from a lady from Myers York's Human Resources department, telling me that she had received an offer letter for me from their Dubai office.

My years at Bangalore and Mumbai had been among the most fun years of my life. But I was now eager to taste some triumph. I wanted to achieve things. I was craving for a list of accomplishments against my name. I felt the need for success on a larger scale, a bigger canvas on which to express myself. I wanted more colours on the picture that was beginning to form. I was ready to let myself loose on the international investment world. As far as I was concerned, Myers York couldn't have 'invaded' India at a better time.

# 3

## THE INSIDE STORY

My name is Jaikishan Patel. Born on 29 February 1980, I am one of those select few who can celebrate their birthdays without any feeling of guilt only *once* every four years. My parents are Shantilal and Nalini Patel. I have a younger sister called Kinnari, a name that I've always liked. She herself hates it, however, and has always wished for a 'modern' name with fewer syllables. At home, we call her Kitty. My mother says it's because the first sound she made was like that of the mewing of a kitten. My sister doesn't care for that either. I can empathize—it can't be much fun going through life being called Kitty because the first sound you made sounded like a cat. I have no pet names myself. I've always been called 'Jai' by my family.

If something could be described as being simultaneously fragile and strong, it would be a pretty good description of my mother. She can weep buckets while watching a blind Bollywood mother lose her way in a jungle during a thunderstorm, yet remain completely under control and in charge during real-life crises. My father is a stoic, stolidly conservative and deeply religious man, who has always met any new, rebellious or revolutionary idea with the steadfast placidity of the buffalo that often dots Chennai's roads. Known to all his friends as Shantibhai, he started life in Uganda, where my grandfather was a prosperous businessman. Everything went along fine till 1971, when Idi Amin, in an apparently desperate bid to bolster his popularity, promulgated a law that required anyone without a Ugandan passport to leave the country. At that time, the Indian community in Uganda, they tell me, was very enterprising, well-to-do and were effectively running the economy of the country. Perhaps it was this that prompted Idi Amin to act as he did. My father says he did it to win support from the local people. Others say he was drunk with power and had lost his sense of balance. Anyway, it changed the course of life for my family. In 1972, my father, and his parents left Uganda for good and took the long ship journey to Gujarat.

Shortly after that, my father met and married my mother. No, not exactly, because *he* says he never met her before marriage. In traditional, Indian style, his parents chose a bride for him. They offered to show him a photograph, but he declined their offer. Anyone you choose has to be good, he apparently told them. The story contrasts slightly with my mother's version. She says my father definitely *did* see her picture and that he told her on their wedding night that she looked even prettier than in the photograph.

My father tried several businesses in Baroda, but didn't succeed in any significant way. He was probably too rigid, principled and straightforward in his approach to succeed in the India of the 1970s and 80s, where bureaucracy, corruption and the licence *raj*, as it was called, all reigned supreme. It was my uncle who persuaded him to shift to Madras then. I had just completed my first year of schooling then. My uncle convinced my father that better work ethics prevailed in south India and that he would do better if he were to be based there.

I am not sure if that line of thinking was correct or not. But whether for that reason or any other, the fact is that my father *did* taste success soon after the shift. My mother says it is because Goddess Lakshmi came into our house in the form of my little sister, Kinnari, who, I must say, has always been rather buoyed by this thought.

After initially doing well with textile trading, my father opened a readymade garments shop in 1988. By the mid-1990s, that had grown to three as the market for readymades among the young and the trendy increased substantially. Madras, which for decades had remained stubbornly traditional, rather like my father himself, was giving way to youth and fashion. The city's educated, English-speaking population attracted new business and enabled the city to take off. With that, our business did, too. Somehow, my own interest in the family business was slight. Sure, we were doing well and the success of this business had made life easier for all of us. But my heart simply wasn't in it.

Soon we moved to a better location in Madras, near the famous 'Music Academy', not far from the famous Marina beach and within walking distance from where superstar Rajinikant lived. We were definitely upwardly mobile, economically. What better sign of this than to live within sniffing distance of a celluloid hero?

But garments were definitely not my cup of tea. Nor was tobacco farming, which my father was also involved with. He owned several acres of farming land at Bhadran, our village in Gujarat, and spent a few days there, every month. Once or twice a year, we would all go there and also visit the Sri Nathji temple at Nathdwara and another of his favourite temples, the Jalaram Bapa mandir at Virpur.

Much as my father tried to coax me into joining him in his business, I was reluctant. Having seen the way my father had struggled and worked over the last twenty years, the life that he had led held no charm for me. Twelve-, sometimes fourteen-hour days, family holidays that were few and far between, workers often coming home on weekends with their problems . . . I didn't think it was worth it. Besides, it was mundane and unexciting. It didn't have punch. It lacked glamour.

My own passion was finance and investments. I applied for my first new issue of equity shares when I was seventeen. Three months later, I had sold it at a substantial profit. I was hooked. Trapped in the world of high finance! I completed my Post Graduate Business Management studies from the Indian Institute of Management in Bangalore, following which I spent a year working at the brokerage house in Mumbai. For the first few months, I had no specific work there. I usually ended up helping out with whatever the firm happened to be grappling with at that point in time. There was always some issue that we were fire-fighting. Then, I became the firm's unofficial technical analyst, partly because of my own interest in the subject and partly because the existing analyst left suddenly. The job involved a study of price movements and making predictions of potential future movements based on the patterns formed and on certain established theories.

That was when I fell in love with Rina, who doubled up as office administrator and secretary to my boss. She was a voluptuous girl and had a way of talking to me that made me feel very important and desirable. For several weeks, you could say I was practically consumed by her, firmly convinced that I had found my soulmate. One day, I happened to call her once from my boss' room. She started talking to me, assuming he was on the line. I discovered to my shock that she was having an affair with him as well. She even used the very same words of endearment! Love died midway through that phone call. In an instant, as if someone had switched off a light.

It's just as well that my father had no idea of this part of my life. Being a close-knit family and with all the factors of traditional family values and conservative family members coming into play, I didn't want to hurt anyone. Seen from my father's eyes, I was already the rebel in the family.

After this little business, I must confess I got a little worried about my own ability to decide what was best for me. Marriages in our family happened early. Most of them were still arranged by the parents of the bride and the groom. Of course, in all cases nowadays, they would meet—in fact, several times—and would get married after mutual consent. The men (or 'boys', as they were still referred to in the Indian context) usually got married between twenty-four and twenty-seven. The girls, between twenty-one and twenty-four. I was ready, even *hungry* for love. Real love, the type that would lead on to marriage. At heart, I was still quite conservative and very Indian. I did not fancy years of floating around from one *prospect* to another.

The Myers opportunity came as a bit of a jolt to my father. He had assumed that after a couple of years of working in Mumbai, I'd join him at work in Chennai. To be fair to him, I had rather hinted at that, if not actually promised. He just couldn't understand why I'd want to be an employee when I could be an employer. '*Beta*, we are Gujaratis,' he told me, 'We are entrepreneurs by nature. We have business in our blood. Even if you are employed for some time, it should only be to learn the ropes. We should be offering jobs to others, not working for someone else.'

His concern was that once I went abroad, I might permanently remain there. I *could* understand his feelings in a way, but I looked at it differently. It was important for me to do something I was passionate about. Besides, this was a wonderful break for me. My mother along with Mr Kapoor, helped convince my father. Kapoor was a Dubai-based family friend, who was both friend and adviser to the family. It made it easier for my father to accept my decision once Kapoor told him it was best to let me find my feet. He would take care of me in Dubai, he told my parents, and in any case, Dubai was less than four hours away by air, the same distance as Chennai from Bangalore by 'express' train.

The lady from HR had asked me to give Peggy a call in Dubai to confirm my acceptance and subsequently hand over the signed copy to their Mumbai office. After rehearsing once or twice, I called.

'Hi, this is Peggy Mitchell,' she said, with that pleasing and distinctive lilt in her voice that I was now able to recognize.

'Peggy, hi, this is Jai. Jack Patel from India. I am so happy to have . . .' I broke off, as she seemed to be saying something.

'. . . get back to you as soon as I can.' Beep.

Feeling rather silly, I hung up, meaning to call back later. But before I could, she returned my call. I told her how thrilled I was to have got the letter and that I had left a signed copy with the Myers' office.

'Oh, that's awesome!' she said. 'I can't wait to have you on board. I'm going to be in Mumbai next week, Jack. I'm meeting a client there. I'll call you.'

Minutes into the meeting, Peggy had crisply and clearly outlined my programme over the next few months. She seemed a very warm and friendly person. When I'd met her the previous time, my attention had been divided among four people. This time around, I had enough opportunity to observe her closely. She was tall, with rather long legs. She seemed to have a light smile all the time, even when she was seriously listening to something. She spoke rather slowly, deliberately. Later, she told me she had been advised to do that while talking to Indians, by the client whom she had met the previous day. 'We are not properly understanding the American accent,' he had apparently told her, 'so you must speak slowly slowly, madam.'

She was now dressed in casuals, which seemed to add to her charm. She had a slightly long nose, a wide mouth and nice, white teeth. She reminded me a bit of Steffi Graf, who used to be my favourite tennis player while I was at school. Peggy handed over a set of books for me to study. Myers wouldn't let me undertake any business before I passed my series three exams conducted by the NASD, the North American Securities Dealers' Association. I was to take that exam in London.

Following that, I would fly onwards to New York for a six-week training programme, where I would be joined by other recruits worldwide. I loved the sound of it all. I could visualize myself at the training centre and beyond. Jack Patel in a dark blue, pin-striped suit, shaking hands with the sultans of finance, industry bigwigs, swinging deals by the dozen and looked up to by one and all. I could almost see the headlines in big bold print: 'Jai Patel structures intricate 80-billion-dollar deal for the Fed'. 'Bill Gates transfers personal wealth portfolio to Jai 'Jack' Patel'.

When I got back home, I stood in front of the mirror and loosened my tie. I put on my 'cool' look. Jack Patel, *Financial Advisor to the World*. Of course, I would use my expertise to help out the Indian government too, I thought condescendingly. I put my phone to my ear and took a call from the Indian Prime Minister. 'Yes? *Sat Sri Akal*, Manmohan*ji*! No, I don't think so, that's not the right way to structure it. We need something more stable for the long haul. India doesn't need hot money. I'll come up with some suggestions for you tomorrow. Sorry? Sure, I'll also have a word with Montek and the others. Nahin, don't worry ji. I'll take care of that. Have a good trip, sir. *Sonia ji ko hello bol dena.*'

# 4

## BIG BEN, BIG APPLE

I collected my ticket from the office. I was going to travel business class for the first time in my life . . . Americans do things in style, I thought. They think big. No wonder they have achieved so much!

Mum, Dad and Kitty had all come to see me off. Our driver, Murugan, stopped at the Kamaraj domestic airport . . . 'Hey, Quick Gun!' I called out. '*Engay* wrongly *poray*, *thambi*? International airport, going. *Munnay po.*'

'Oh, sorry, saar,' he replied. 'I forget saar going foreign, not Indian.' Murugan and I had this unstated, unwritten pact. I'd talk to him in Tamil and he'd talk to me in English. The underlying idea was for both of us to try and improve our language skills. I don't know if it worked, because neither of us bothered to correct the other, but nevertheless, we both retained the smug satisfaction of having tried out something.

My mother had been solicitously fussing around me the last two days, anxious that I should have everything I'd need in 'all those foreign places'. Living in Chennai, we never used warm clothing, nor was it easy to find any to buy. Nevertheless, she had managed to find an old sweater of mine . . . I bunged in a half-read biography of William Shakespeare. Since the time I had seen a Shakespearean play a year back, I had suddenly become very interested in the bard and his writings. At school, my only aim had been to read just enough of his output to pass the literature exam.

Now I had begun to appreciate much of the content, especially the power and energy behind some of the quotes.

She had also kept a couple of prayer books, a picture of Lord Krishna, one of Balaji at Tirupati, some dhoklas, a pack of theplas and some other tasty traditional Gujarati snacks, freshly made. Now, all that was going to secretly travel with me to London. Business class. It was a proud moment for me to be walking left into the aircraft, while most others walked towards the right. An airhostess wished me and addressed me as 'sir'. I nodded at her, trying to look cool and not give the impression that it was my first experience in this exclusive section of the plane. What a pleasurable trip that was! No one to dig their knees into the small of your back, no crying babies, no snooty members of the crew making you feel small and unwanted. It's a different world on this side of the curtain, I thought to myself. The guy in front of me was saying something that made the airhostess giggle. I wished I could, too. But I couldn't think of anything funny and suitably appropriate to tell her. So, I stuck to looking cool.

I had a two-day stay scheduled at London before the test. I was to visit our London office. There was also a short orientation programme to attend. We were eight of us, three from London and the others from Europe and Asia.

I had been to London once before, all of us; Kitty, Mum, Dad and I. I had just completed school then and Kitty was still a whining, tell-tale, nuisance of a kid sister. I remember having been quite thrilled by the attractive pictures of buxom babes with the accompanying messages that used to be pinned inside telephone booths in central London. I had quietly pocketed a couple of them to show my friends back home and Kitty and gone and promptly reported it to my mother. Back then, we had stayed at a family friend's place at Wembley in North London which had taken away some of the fascination of being abroad. This time it promised to be different. Staying in the heart of the city, that too alone . . . boy, Kitty would be so envious!

The next morning, at the Myers' London office, we were briefed on our NY training programme. I was pleasantly surprised to bump into someone who had been at Loyola College, Chennai, with me, a year junior to me. His name was Krishnan Balasubramaniam. Most of us had called him Kitch then, short for Krishnan. Some called him Balls, an abbreviation of his surname. Myers had apparently met him over a year back. Kitch had almost given up on them when they had called him out of the blue, just a few weeks ago. He was the only other Indian in the group, one of the five who were coming in to London from other countries.

'*Dude!*' he cried, when he saw saw me. 'Are you here too? What luck, *da!*'

Apart from the two of us, there was Marco from Switzerland and Jan from Rotterdam and one guy from Poland. His name was Gregory, the Polish spelling of which was, incredibly, 'Grzegorz' . . . From the London team, there were two girls and one guy. We were given an idea about the test that we would take the following morning and about the New York programme.

We were taken out to lunch to a continental restaurant. Kitch was a vegetarian and a fussy one at that. He asked what options there were for vegetarians and they told him they could give him rice with aubergine. So he ordered that and was most disappointed with the contents of his plate. He apparently had a strong dislike for brinjal, as he had always known the vegetable, and was appalled to learn that it also went around under an alias. Kitch was what we call a Tam–Bram, a Tamilian Brahmin—known more for academic brilliance, than for entrepreneurial skills. Kitch was a bit of an exception, in that he was good at both. He had probably inherited that from his father, a mechanical engineer who was also a successful industrialist. At college, Kitch used to be the cultural secretary and the popular president of a student body called Aiesec. But he was no exception to the Tam-Bram habit of eating rice twice a day and liked ending a meal with 'curd rice'.

That evening, Jan offered to take some of us to Soho . . . 'It's a night club kind of place,' he told us. 'You'll like it.' We did and spent a good couple of fun hours there. It was glitzy and exciting.

As we sauntered down the streets gazing at the shops and the bars, a long-haired, slightly dishevelled man suddenly accosted Kitch.

'Girls?' he asked, in a rough, deep voice. 'Girls?'

Taken aback and slightly alarmed, Kitch shook his head and stepped back. 'Okay, you want men,' the man promptly concluded and attaching his arm to Kitch's, started walking purposefully towards a nearby café. Kitch was quick to extricate himself and rush back to us, but he kind of lost his colour and composure a bit, after that incident.

Next day, the test itself was rather uneventful. It was an online test, with multiple choices of answers which Kitch and I went through without much difficulty. That evening, Kitch was persuaded by Marco to join him and Jan on another night out at Soho. I, on the other hand, had had my fill of Soho and took off by myself to Hyde Park, where I sat for a long time by the lake, watching the ducks and thinking pleasant thoughts. My phone rang. 'Jai Sri Krishna, beta.' That was my father. He always began a conversation that way. It felt odd speaking to my family, sitting in a London park, so many miles away. I was excited, but I kind of missed them too.

I deciding against staying back in the room that evening and watched a show called 'Stomp', a rather unusual and interesting one in which the actors made music with just about anything you could think of—from shoes and broomsticks to chairs and man-hole covers!

On the morning after, we were on our way to New York. Six men, two women, all young, enthusiastic and ambitious. All wanting a piece of the American dream and a little bite of the Big Apple. We travelled business class, of course. I was getting to be an old hand at this now. I smirked to myself, as I swaggered into the rarefied atmosphere at the front of the plane.

We had been given instructions in London about how to direct cabs from the airport to our hotel in New York. We teamed up in pairs for the city's famous yellow cabs. Finally, there were three of us left. Kate, one of the girls from London, Jan and I. We hopped into a cab. I shut my eyes and took a deep breath, my way of paying homage to the capital of the financial world. It was my first visit to the US and the fact that I was visiting as an employee of one of the largest investment houses in the world, sent a thrill up my spine. It was November 2005.

Our hotel—it was actually a service apartment—was some forty minutes away. While Kate and Jan were busy talking about various things, I was busy looking at the sights and soaking it all in. Just roads, cars and bridges you might say, but they were the roads, cars and bridges on the haloed turf of NYC.

The service apartment block was located just down the road from the famous Grand Central Station. Just reading that name and seeing the famous Waldorf Astoria hotel adjoining it, quickened my pulse rate. And now, here I was, Jack Patel, the self-styled investment advisor to the world, almost within touching distance of one of the most famous and revered hotels in the world! The first time I had come across its name was in a high school quiz. 'Which hotel in NY has the Grand Central station in its basement?' I remembered others too; about the colour of New York cabs, the name of the lake at Hyde Park. It was like diving into a fairy tale quiz book and seeing everything come alive. I spent the rest of the day walking around in a state of 'nirvana'.

The next morning, we took the train from Grand Central itself and in a few minutes, we were outside Battery Road Station. Another moment that took one's breath away. It began to seem to me that most of my stay in New York was going to be spent either taking deep breaths or having my breath taken away. There were so many things I was in awe of. This was the 'Plaza by the Park', Battery Road—just by the sea, with the Statue of Liberty only a few hundred metres away, all queenly elegance and silent dignity. Myers York's address was Number 10, Plaza by the Park— combining the stateliness of Downing Street with the glamour of Manhattan, I thought to myself. There are many places in the world that would seem sacred to different people for different reasons. For me, Manhattan was one such place. It had something in the air that made it special, important. And it made me feel that I had found my niche and that in equal measure, it had found me. I felt I was in the thick of things. Manhattan, 'the heart beat' of the investment world. It gave me goose bumps.

We were shown into the training centre on the thirtieth floor and introduced to Helen Turner, the head of the training department. She was a smallish lady, about fifty-five, a cheerful bundle of energy. Her assistant, Megan, was a human bombshell. Tall, lissome and chiselled to perfection, she was a complete stunner. After spending a few seconds with her, I was in such a daze, that I don't quite remember what happened over the next several minutes. The next thing I knew, I was with the others on the twenty-fifth floor, having breakfast in a distracted sort of way. Shame, really, because the spread was magnificent. The dining room seemed to stretch on infinitely. I learnt later, that it catered to six hundred employees. Spread right across the length of the room were at least half a dozen counters, offering a variety of cuisines. There was no skimping or scrounging. And, what class! Even as I tucked into an omelette, I was grinning from ear to ear. I could hardly believe all this. It seemed like a dream. No prizes for guessing what I did next. I took a deep breath and said a silent prayer.

The next few weeks passed in a state of bliss. We were a young and very diverse group, which made it an especially wonderful experience. Other than the eight of us who had come from London, there were two girls from Brazil, a girl and a guy from Singapore and guys from Jamaica, Mexico and Japan. Every day, we were joined by half a dozen or so local employees who took turns to come there and talk to us and to assist the trainers.

We would be at office just after 8 a.m., fresh, eager, and looking forward to the day. It was a tough call deciding between extra minutes in bed and breakfast at the training centre. Usually, the revellers of the previous night would opt for the former and others, the latter. From the breakfast room, we'd head towards the large pantry, or kitchen as they called it, on the thirtieth floor where everyone would grab a huge cup of coffee. Kitch and I used to be

quite intimidated by the size of the coffee cups. I was amazed at
the amount of coffee some of my colleagues could down during a
session. As Kitch used to tell me in wonder, these cups were about
six times the size of the steel cups that we were used to drinking
coffee in, at restaurants back home in Chennai. Or steel 'tumblers'
as Kitch used to call them.

Lunch was always an *affaire extraordinaire*. The choice that we
had, had to be seen to be believed—from chicken biryani to pizza,
from enchiladas to chopsuey to fish and chips, it was mind-
boggling. Even Kitch, who could technically be described as a
lacto-vegetarian, found little to complain about the choice of food.

Everything was super-sized. Whether it was coffee or Coke or
fries or burgers, the portions were twice what we were used to.
How does one explain to the average American that we have been
taught almost from birth never to waste food that is put on a plate,
because 'there are thousands who go without food'? Or because
wastage is considered an affront to Annalakshmi, the Goddess of
Food and Drink. Hence, by habit, we tend to take smaller servings.
Many of the others also drink coffee 'black'. I tried it, but couldn't
stand the stuff. Kitch, from time to time, would crave for his 'filter'
coffee. Unlike me, who had spent a good portion of the last few
years outside home, Kitch had lived in Chennai all his life. It was
more difficult for him to get adjusted.

At the training centre, each morning, we would be greeted by
a small gift, neatly placed on our respective desks. Sometimes it
would be a book (Peter Lynch, Thomas Friedman, James Van
Horne, Warren Buffett's annual reports . . .), sometimes a toy of
sorts. We got a stuffed bull—representing an upward trending stock
market, a stress ball, a yoyo with the Myers logo on it, a Myers tie,
cap and jacket and stroller bag. Once we got a transparent pen that
had little cars within—floating in some sort of liquid—that would
move right across the length of the pen when you tilted it. But my
favourite was a ball that would light up inside when you bounced
it. Myers spoilt us rotten.

Every morning, we would have a two-hour session with Peggy

on the company, its work ethics, the structure, networking, product ideas and such. The sessions were interesting most of the time, but things brightened up whenever Megan came in to assist. Initially, I felt a little unnerved, even guilty. I thought I was the only one being so impacted by this gorgeous creature. But soon I realized that was far from being so ... Marco, could hardly stop talking about her during breaks. And then, Carlos, the chap from Mexico would go, 'She is so so-oo ... mmmmm ... waah!' putting the tips of his fingers to his lips and then spreading them, throwing his hand out expansively, like he was blowing a huge kiss. Not only did she look beautiful and dress exquisitely, she had this way of walking with light, almost suggestive movements that left you weak-kneed. She was completely dignified, and yet there was something provocative about her, a subtle 'come hither' look that seemed to beckon to the caveman in me and completely distracted me from Helen's monologue on dividend yields, professional ethics and interest rate swaps. She was always clad in a suit. Trousers, perfectly fitting, which to me meant just a shade on the tighter side. The jacket, again, not so tight that it caused a crease and not so loose that it hid her figure, which would have been an unforgivable crime. Occasionally, she would nonchalantly remove her jacket and drape it over a chair (she always had a matching tank-top inside) and the guys would drool en masse. She did that only if Helen was not around and I rather think she did it on purpose, knowing fully well the effect it was having on the audience. I think even the girls were not blind to her, er ... shall I say, sensuality. As Kate said, 'She's like Jennifer Aniston, isn't she? Only even better!' Once when she did her jacket act, Carlos, who had by now become sort of like the official joker of the pack, let his tongue hang out and panted like a dog, much to everyone's amusement. Kitch, who has a way with words that I, with my long-winded and hesitant manner can never hope to emulate, put it rather well. 'This Megan babe is classy and hot, da!' he said. 'Two in one. Like pongal and vadai.'

The afternoon sessions were devoted to heads of departments, senior managers and to marketing staff and money managers from various fund houses. We were very excited when a world-renowned hedge fund manager came in one day and spent more than two hours with us. On a couple of days, we had representatives from the manufacturing sector, to give us a wider perspective. Almost daily, there were games and role play. Once, we had real-life part-time actors come in and meet us, each playing a role assigned to them; as a pensioner, a young, upwardly mobile upstart, a doctor, or a businessman . . . and we were asked to spend time with them and come up with a complete solution to manage their finances and plan their investments. My work on this came in for a fair bit of praise. I also enjoyed the couple of sessions that the Head of Forex, Sally Krajicek, had taken for us. The few months that I had devoted to FX and charting at my Mumbai job came in handy. I created quite a stir with my knowledge of Bollinger bands, Head and Shoulder patterns, breakouts and the rest.

We learnt a lot. Like the fact that not all hedge funds are risky. How they can actually help to balance a portfolio. Like how a few of them were nothing but a high mathematical probability multiplied tens of times by the use of leverage, or borrowed money. If that probability turns bad, the fund goes belly up and so do thousands of investors. We discovered the best performing markets in the last twenty-five years, looked at yearly, was not the US, or the UK. It was some of the lesser known ones. We saw how a huge exposure to tech stocks just before the millennium all but finished some investors. And how a diversified portfolio at that time would have suffered minimal damage, because for every 'Cisco' that went down in price during that time, there was a 'Sysco' that moved up.

We had interesting sessions from the Head of Equity, Joe Iossifidis and the Chief Equity Advisor, a silver-tongued orator called Raj Saunders. His actual name was (or had been) Soundara Rajan, which he had shortened and 'seasoned' to American taste. He an incredible memory and the gift of the gab. He was lucid, fluent and had ready answers for any question, dividing each answer into crisp sections, with a clear conclusion to every answer.

He gave us tips to get talking the Raj Saunders' way—smooth, confident and prepared for anything. 'Believe me,' he said, 'Anyone can do this. It is practice more than anything else. Always anticipate questions and take the trouble to prepare yourself for them. I make notes every night and practise for an hour every morning at home, before I step out and meet the media.'

The Head of Technology was also an Indian, who was introduced to us as 'Linus', which was actually his real name read backwards. We hit it off pretty well and he took Kitch and me out that evening. He took us to a bar, where girls were pole dancing. Some of them come over to our table and offered to 'dance' with us for the length of a song for fifteen dollars. It turned out, it wasn't a real dance. They made us sit down on a sofa while they gyrated and shimmied around us. I had one dance each with two different girls. Kitch had *eight* dances, all with the same girl. When we teased him about liking the girl, he told us he didn't know how to tell her to stop. It would have seemed very rude, he said. Finally, it was *she* who offered to stop, perhaps unsure of whether Kitch had enough money to pay for so many dances.

On most days, we'd be back at the hotel by six. For the first few days, we formed groups and explored the city, bit by bit, avenue by avenue: the restaurants, the shops, the bars and the theatres on Broadway. All except Edwin Sin, our colleague from Singapore, who was a bit squeamish and didn't fancy anything that involved drinking, women or nudity. Funny, I thought, that a guy with the surname 'Sin' could be so prudish. One group preferred to skip the exploration and simply hit a nearby bar every night. What a waste of New York, I thought to myself.

After three weeks of rigorous exploring of everything that was good, bad and naughty in New York, I was exhausted. After that, I preferred to stay back and religiously watch *Friends* and *Who Wants to be a Millionaire* on telly . . .

I had kept a diary, making a note of the many things that happened and devoted a good half-hour to this job, daily. By the time it was time to leave NY, I had completed almost 10,000 words.

# 5

## THE CITY, THE OFFICE

The end of the training programme, came in the form of a huge celebration at a posh restaurant at a New York hotel. It was fun to see even the usually serious or demure types letting their hair down and having a blast. So there we were, hugging and kissing, all set to go back to our respective offices and take off. Someone came up with the idea that it would be fun to get all the girls to ceremoniously kiss Edwin Sin and watch him squirm. The girls too, liked the idea. Some even went back to him for seconds. One of them insisted on a lip lock. By the end of it, Edwin had gotten so used to it, it was *he* who was having all the fun while we stared enviously.

So, it was bye-bye, Big Apple. Why it is called that, I still wasn't sure after spending six weeks there. Someone had said it was a concept borrowed from the world of horse racing. Others suggested it was a term used in earlier days by jazz musicians for a major performance centre.

Kitch was going to Chennai for a few days, before going to Dubai. He needed to get a few things, he said, including equipment for making filter coffee and some other things. I suspected his visit was mostly related to food and drink. Kitch rarely made a fuss about anything else. I was going straight to Dubai. My father was in Gujarat and Kitty had gone to Mysore on a short holiday with some friends. Besides, my mum had told me they were 'seeing a boy' for Kitty, traditional Indian family style, and wanted me to be in Chennai in December.

I had been put up at a hotel not far away from the office. Along the way, I looked in wonder at some of the buildings. The architecture was a mix of the new and the very new. The traffic seemed heavy, though. Someone had told me Dubai was like Las Vegas on steroids. Well, I'd find out pretty soon. On reaching the hotel, I found that it was just adjacent to the office building with an access from one to the other . . . They were two very interesting triangular-shaped buildings called 'Emirates Towers', twin towers actually. Ironical, because during my last weekend at NY, some of us had visited ground zero and had said a silent prayer for the thousands who had died and those affected by 9/11 all over the world.

Peggy was in London and would be in Dubai the next day. I decided to call Harsh and Jaishree, my first clients! Harsh and Joi— as everyone called her—had been at IIM with me. They had subsequently got married and had lived in Dubai for a year. I had asked Peggy to meet them and she ended up getting their account for me. Harsh came from a business family and he had been sent to start an office in Dubai. What funny turns life takes. At B-school I hadn't even realized that they were, well . . . an *item*. And now, here they were, married, in Dubai and my very first clients, to boot . . . Harsh, I remembered, used to be a quiz enthusiast too. Maybe we could have some quizzing sessions together.

It was great catching up. We didn't discuss the account except for a brief mention that he would meet Peggy and me once I settled in. Joi told me what had happened when *she* had first come to Dubai. She had arrived on a visitor's visa after their wedding. Harsh had landed up at the airport with a bouquet of flowers to welcome her. Only, he had forgotten to bring the visa document with him. So there he was, flowers in hand, a bright smile and expectant look on his face, waiting at the airport for a good hour or so till he realized why Joi was not coming out. It took another couple of hours for him to return with the visa. This time, he forgot the flowers!

Peggy called me almost as soon as she landed, apologizing for not being around to receive me. Apparently, Cyrus was travelling too.

I was at the office by 10 a.m., wondering what the Dubai dress code was . . . Most people I saw around the hotel seemed to be dressed in western clothes. I had seen very few dressed in the traditional white *kandoora* or the black *abaya*.

I fell in love with the office at first sight. The reception was impressive; the walls were panelled with some dark, heavy wood, the carpets were soft and thick. Along the left side, there was an elaborate flower arrangement. To the right, there was a large colourful picture on the wall. It was rendered less conspicuous, and more impressive, by a small waterfall that cascaded like a veil in front of it. There were three magnificent meeting rooms and beyond these, the *piece de resistance*—what was referred to by the staff as the auditorium.

It was a combination of a theatre and an art gallery. There was wooden replica of Mount Rushmore, a sculpture of two clasped hands that seemed to hang in mid-air, and a crystal prism that reflected light streaming in from the window in all colours of the rainbow. Two fountains alternately squirted water at each other and then, did so in unison. It held me spellbound. There were some exquisite paintings. Towards one end of the auditorium was a large screen, with a podium to its side. Facing this were some thirty chairs and space for another twenty. There was a music system and a video-conferencing facility.

Further into the office, we had our offices and work places. There were eight rooms with glass walls. Cyrus' room, at the far end on the left, was as large as a small apartment, L-shaped, with a small rock garden in the corner with a train track in it and a red train that worked by remote control. Next to his office was that of Philippe Desbois, a millionaire Financial Advisor (FA) who was looked up to by youngsters, envied by his peers, and almost feared by his managers. Philippe had, over the years, amassed client assets of over half a billion dollars and turned in revenues of close to 4 million a year. It was said that his personal earnings added up to a million dollars each year. Then there was Peggy's room and three empty ones. On the opposite side was a large room which was shared by three people who handled operations. Just beyond, on the far right, was a room occupied by the compliance officer.

In between there were a set of cubicles, less fancy, where most FAs would sit. A set of work stations ahead were placed to seat the assistants. Between these and the reception area there was the pantry and a small library that could seat two. Alongside these was a corridor which contained the 'scoreboard', which featured every month, the names of all those who generated revenues for Myers as well as some related details.

Oh, and just one more thing. In a little nook to the left of the library, there hung a punching bag. On a ledge nearby, were placed a pair of boxing gloves, a marker pen and a sponge. This was Liberty Hall. Here, you could give vent to your frustrations by writing the source of your wrath on the bag—and then letting go for all you were worth.

You can well imagine the result of this heady concoction of luxury and comfort on the mind of a twenty-four-year-old. I was on cloud nine. I felt like a bottle of bubbly, full of fizz and ready to burst open.

I filled Peggy in with some of the details of the training programme and she briefed me on the office, the people and her plans for expansion. She told me she was looking forward to my being a part of her team. All this was doing no good at all to my ego, which had already acquired wings and was flying far higher than was good for me. It was only when I was introduced to Philippe a few minutes later that I quickly returned to earth. Philippe had that supercilious air and a tendency to simply look through you like you didn't exist.

Later, Cyrus walked in. We exchanged pleasantries and he congratulated me on completing the training programme and reiterated in his typical slow, deliberate manner what a fantastic platform Myers York offered. 'What you want to make of it is up to you. Your trainers in NY would have told you a lot of things,

Jack. But there's one more thing from me. I will give you a year to deliver. I won't interfere with your business. You will get all the support you need. There is no limit to what you can achieve and what you can earn. But if you don't show results by that time, I'm going to have to kick ass. I don't want non-performers in my office. Remember it's *your* business now, Jack.'

One by one, I met others in the office. Some were travelling. I had lunch with Cyrus and Rebecca, the compliance officer. Dinner that night was with Peggy. She referred to Kitch as 'Chris'. At this rate, I told her in mock protest, there will be no Indian names left in this world outside of India. Billions of Indians, but no Indian names. She laughed.

I was surprised to see Peggy wiping not just her hands, but even the spoons and fork with a tissue after using a spray that she carried in her handbag. As we left the restaurant, she used it again after she opened the door. I discovered later that it was some kind of sanitizer. She had this compulsive need to keep doing this and almost certainly every time she established contact with something that others tend to touch—crockery, door handles, even pens.

By the end of the first few days, while my head was reeling a bit with the suddenness of so much information, I had got a pretty good picture of almost everyone at the office.

Cyrus was a British national. As a UK-based lawyer, a few years back, he used to refer clients to Myers York, but had later, chosen to join Myers as a Financial Advisor, or 'broker', as we were also referred to. I rather liked that term. It reminded me of Michael Douglas in the movie *Wall Street* and made me feel like I was one heck of a cool guy; a tough, 'take no prisoners' kind of bloke.

After ten years as a broker, Cyrus had sought a managerial assignment. Cyrus was, by origin, a Parsee from Mumbai, who had gone to London for his university studies and had stayed on. He was, both in appearance and in manner, more British than Indian. He had that clipped way of speaking that British tend to have. His humour tended to be underplayed. He was about forty, tall, a serious-looking bachelor who wore well-cut suits and—for reasons best known to him—a bow-tie. He had bushy eyebrows and his lower lip jutted out slightly.

Rebecca Marsh was also a lawyer, in her early thirties. She had been working with a legal firm in Dubai run by a British lawyer and had switched last year. She was pleasant, slightly plump and had a friendly, almost goofy manner that contrasted a lot with Cyrus' serious approach. One wouldn't have thought of her as a lawyer or a compliance officer.

Philippe, of course, was the man who could do no wrong. He often sat with his feet up on the table, especially while on the phone. He was short, had light eyes and blonde hair cut very short and combed towards a usually creased forehead, forming a jagged V shape. I learnt that he had decided to join this office mainly for tax reasons. His share of the revenues were apparently large enough for him to base his decision of where to live, on income tax rules. His assistant Amal, wore the shortest skirts I had ever seen. People cribbed that though Amal had a lot of spare time, neither she nor Philippe liked it if anyone else asked her for help.

Rachel Broad, was the second most successful producer in the office, after the French demi-god. She was pretty, vivacious and well spoken, a girl who was conscious of her charm and saw no harm in using naturally endowed gifts to advantage. According to pantry talk, Rachel used to be a pole dancer at a strip club in London where she apparently met and mated a Jersey-based writer whom she subsequently married. Now divorced, she was said to have used her former husband's contacts to build up a good book, initially with her first employer in London. She moved to Dubai when Myers opened office here last year.

The source of much of my information was primarily three people. Each of them seemed to have taken a liking for me and appeared to be competing with each other to feed me with stories and updates.

One was Melissa, an FA from Merrill Lynch. She was a thin girl with an earnest face and bird-like, both in appearance and in behaviour. She could never stay still, always looking around and darting here and there. She couldn't tolerate silence. If someone wasn't talking, she would talk. Often, she spoke even if someone was.

The second was Janardhanan aka John. He was one of those Ops, or Operations personnel. John combined an insatiable curiosity for news and gossip with an alert brain and sharp ears. He had an uncanny ability to put two and two together. He also had this eagerness to share information. He was the one person to go to if there was some operational matter you got stuck on. The others in Ops tended to be bookish, but John—if he liked you and was in a good mood—would know of a loophole to find a way. He was efficient and thickly bespectacled, a sort of modern-day Rupert Baxter.

My third informant was Emma, Cyrus's effervescent, helpful, human dynamo administrative assistant. She was a tall, large, busty, woman, who was—paradoxical as it may sound—as efficient as she was talkative. She seemed to be everywhere all at once and not just because of her size. One minute, she'd be telling Cyrus about his next appointment, the next she'd be at the reception talking to a salesman for stationery supplies, then under Philippe's table to fix a cable and almost simultaneously, at the pantry for a quick update and a cup of camomile before disappearing to make Cyrus's flight bookings. Emma was a good two or three inches taller than I was, so that made her just an inch short of six feet. Her build, height and shoes (which added another inch) made her look almost intimidating, though she was actually quite a sweetheart. The only problem was that she sometimes talked to you from quite close, so you had to crane your neck up to establish any eye contact. If you just looked straight on ahead, it would have seemed quite rude and er . . . inappropriate, if you know what I mean. So, I generally forced myself to look right into her eyes even if that meant tilting my head upward at an awkward thirty-degree angle.

There was the man who brought our mail, made tea and did odd jobs without a murmur. His name, quite incredibly, was 'Baby Jacob'. And finally, there was the public relations (PR)-guy, as he was referred to. His name was Rustom and he handled all immigration and government related work, which usually involved documentation in Arabic. From time to time, he'd walk in, in his spotless white kandoora, greet us with a 'Hello, Habeebi! All okay? Family good?', thrust a document under our nose and say, '*Yalla!* Sign here!'

All the women called all other women 'darling'. They also addressed the men—except Philippe (who was in a different league from the rest of us) and Cyrus (whom only Emma dared to address in this manner)—as 'darling', 'honey', 'love' or 'sweetheart'. Similarly, all men referred to all women in such endearing terms. The exceptions were Philippe (who never 'wasted' a word by bothering to call or address anyone) and Baby Jacob (who referred to all women as 'madam'). It was one big, happy, affectionate family—young, footloose and fancy-free. Only three of the employees were married: Emma, John and Ahmed. Cyrus was the oldest and he was just into his forties.

# 6

## FINDING MY FEET

Kitch was terribly impressed with the office. 'It's a *killer*, da,' he told me and in a softer undertone, added, 'Some of these babes are just too good, machan! Super!' Just then, Linda—who handled the reception—passed by wearing very tight jeans and a white tank-top with one of those plastic bra-straps over her shoulder. Kitch, weakened by the sudden impact, held on to me for support.

'There seems to be no dress code for women in this office!' I said.

'That's good!' he grinned, recovering his poise.

I had taken charge of my first account. I met Harsh and Joi once at our office with Peggy and then once more at theirs. Through this office, they procured many of the goods that they imported into India. Their business in India was much bigger than I had thought. At best, I had hoped for a half-million-dollar account. It was already at that level and it looked poised to get bigger.

I had also decided on who my second client would be. My uncle Vinoobhai Patel was based in Dubai and was generally regarded as the richest guy in the family. I remember Mum telling me that if I got Vinoo *kaka*'s account, I probably wouldn't probably need any others. When my father had spoken to him about my coming to Dubai, he had been very welcoming and had promised support. He invited me to his office, saying my aunt Pramila was in India and he would call me home once she returned. So I went, carrying my stylish new satchel. I had yet to get over the practice of converting anything I bought or contemplated buying into Indian rupees. It was likewise with Kitch. When I bought the satchel, Kitch was with me. '*It's 6,000 rupees!*' he whispered into my ear. 'We can get it in Chennai for half this price.'

Anyway, there I was, satchel in hand, smile on face and all ready for account number two. In this business, if you had client money of a 100 million dollars or more, you had it made. At an average of say, 2 to 5 million a client, once you managed to rope in twenty-five to thirty clients, you were on song. Philippe, I was told, had just half a dozen accounts. But that included a corporate account for the employees' pension funds and it ran into a few 100 million dollars. That was *his* lucky break. And I had a feeling this was going to be *mine*.

'Jai Sri Krishna, Vinoo kaka,' I greeted my uncle respectfully, bending to touch his feet the traditional way.

He greeted me warmly and asked why I had not contacted him earlier. I hummed and hawed and was relieved of the task of finding an appropriate answer by the ringing of his phone. There were more calls, sometimes more than one at the same time, then a couple of visitors whom he had to see, after which he went to the loo. I started getting bored. This was taking so much time. It had been over an hour and he had hardly spent a couple of minutes with me. Vinoo kaka didn't know the value of Jack Patel's time, I thought haughtily, with all the arrogance of youth. I could have been opening million-dollar accounts somewhere else, or if not, at least getting updated with Emma's latest gossip.

He finally returned and as the ringing of the phones subsided a bit, he seemed relatively at peace. I would have preferred getting his signatures on the account-opening forms and leaving, because I was going to check out an apartment that I was hoping to be able to move into. Instead, I courteously asked about his business. It was a mistake. He started from the beginning, omitting no detail. By the time he finished, what I didn't know about building materials, its suppliers, its import, warehousing, profit margins, sales and distribution could have been written on a single bill of lading. Or, so it should have been, given the depth of information that he provided. But the truth is, after the first minute, I didn't follow a word. He had gotten far too technical. Initially, I was polite and nodded, but soon I realized I had fallen into a trap that there was no getting out of. I waited patiently for the ordeal to be over. One by one, all his employees left. Suddenly, he got up to fetch his coat, stood near the door and called me. I was slightly taken aback.

'I . . . wanted to discuss Myers York . . . I thought . . . I was hoping . . .' I stammered.

'We'll talk in the car,' he said. He started telling me about the UAE and its growth, about how, when he had first came to Dubai, there weren't even proper roads connecting Dubai to Abu Dhabi and how it would take several hours to reach Abu Dhabi, the capital. 'Now it takes less than two hours,' he said.

Again, I brought up the subject of an account with us. He waited a few seconds before replying. 'Jai, look, I don't think I will be able to open an account with you. You see, we have got two, three bankers already. How many bankers can one have? All our money is in trust and has been for more than ten years. It is difficult to change these long-term relationships, you see. It is easy to change spouses. But children and bankers, one cannot change that easily.' He laughed lightly. I was unable to join in. I found nothing funny about this frivolous, if not completely dumb, remark.

'Have you found an apartment in Dubai yet, Jai? Where are you staying?' he asked, changing the subject.

I replied, but only with difficulty and in a very distracted way. I was extremely disappointed. Somehow, I had assumed that an account from my uncle was a *given* . . . I felt a surge of anger. After almost three hours of waiting, he tells me this as if he was turning down an offer of a cup of tea, like it didn't matter at all. It mattered to *me*. This was about my career. How could he do this to me, his own nephew? It's not as if I was asking him to *lend* me money. I cursed him silently. To hell with his trust, I thought to myself. To hell with him and his building materials, its suppliers, its import, warehousing, profit margins, sales and distribution.

That night, I finalized my apartment. It was in a building called

Al Kifaf Apartments, in Karama, not far from the place where Dubai 'originated'. It had two bedrooms, was a fifteen-minute drive from work, close to several restaurants, had a small pool (not that I could swim, but it kind of added to the ambience) and more importantly, just a few minutes walk from where Kitch had got fixed up. It seemed ideal in every way. It suited both of us to be within reach of a whole lot of restaurants, almost all of which delivered food home. Equally importantly, they were reasonably priced. We weren't paid very much by way of salary. To make big money, we needed big business. Myers York believed in keeping its new recruits hungry for business, by keeping them hungry.

Peggy had given us a handful of names that she wanted us to follow up. The company had issued a series of advertisements and had got some enquiries in response. I was wondering if we should make some joint calls with Peggy initially, but she assured us that the quickest way to learn was to simply plunge into it.

I picked up the name of Kamal Lalwani from the list to start off with. It seemed to have a rich touch to it. He owned a wholesale textile shop in Bur Dubai, close to the Dubai creek, which is actually an inlet from the Arabian Gulf. Initially, the city of Dubai developed and flourished alongside the creek, with traders mushrooming on either side to collect and sell the goods brought in by boats and ships. The yester-year scenario is still beautifully preserved and the Bur Dubai souk or market area is a throwback to the times when Dubai was a small trading town, still on the brink of glory.

It wasn't easy finding a taxi.

I arrived fifteen minutes late, all set to apologize. It wasn't necessary. There was no sign of him. He came in some ten minutes later and made me wait for another ten. I was beginning to think that adherence to time was not considered a virtue in Dubai. When he did call me in, it was with the air of a man who was doing me a favour. He was about thirty, with a fat face and thin shoulders from where he bulged out in the shape of a bell. He took a cigarette from an ornamental case.

'So, what you have?' he asked abruptly.

I floundered. 'Er . . . we had got a query from you, Mr Lalwani, in response to our . . .'

'I know, I know, I know,' he said, cutting me short. 'What product you have?'

Trying to camouflage my discomfiture, I said, 'I think it will help to get a bit of background, Mr Lalwani,' I said, 'Myers York is among the world's largest investment firms. We can tailor-make ideas to suit any requirement. The relevant question is, what do you need?'

'I need money,' he replied, snapping his fingers. 'Quick, quick, quick.'

I tried to suppress a smile. He carried on. 'I'm businessman. I do deals with quick turnover. Deal done, make money, finish, come out. I did real estate Dubai Marina, Palm Island. 30 per cent, 40 per cent profit. I don't want same products, equity, mutual funds, this, that . . . no! I want new! Different, different, different.' He spoke in a staccato kind of way in fits and starts, like he was shooting bullets from his mouth. I was beginning to see the funny side of the guy. Slowly and deliberately, he blew out a long puff of smoke through pursed lips like he was trying to make a pattern.

'You ask your superior to come and see me,' he said abruptly. 'Your boss, managing director, someone.'

A minute later, I was outside, trying to hail a cab, feeling small, incompetent and used. I was beginning to wonder if this kind of thing was my scene at all. I shuddered at the thought of a life dedicated to meeting the likes of Lalwani, or my uncle, for that matter. I had a good mind to call Bill Gates and make one fervent sales pitch. If he could part with 1 per cent of his wealth, I'd not have to watch fat, nouveau riche slobs blow rings of smoke in the air, demanding to meet my boss. Or uncles who say changing wives is easier than changing bankers. Maybe I'd be better off chucking this whole sales thing and just work on charts, analysis and recommendations.

Just then my cell phone rang. It was my sister.

'Hi!' I said. 'I'm going to be there soon. Do you want anything from here? A camel? Maybe we can give it to your young man as a wedding gift,' I joked, sensing almost immediately that it didn't go well.

She seemed disturbed and hesitant in her speech. She had something to tell me, she said, about the marriage proposal. She didn't like the chap, she blurted out. She didn't feel comfortable, he seemed too eager, a little creepy, too touchy feely. He kept calling her several times a day, she didn't have anyone to confide in, her friends were confused and not in a position to advise, she has always looked up to me and since she has felt very close to me, she hoped I would understand and help her. She tried telling Dad, who didn't understand—he just brushed off her doubts. She felt like running away because she was not really consulted. How could Dad just laugh away her concerns like that No one really understands a young girl's feelings, Mum was not willing to listen because she thinks Dad will get upset. She had always been considerate to her parents, hadn't she? She loved them and wanted them to be happy but they shouldn't really force this on her, surely it wasn't right to take her for granted, didn't they care for what she felt? After all, this was about the rest of her life and in any case, she said, there was someone else.

Having packed about 10,000 words in the space of about five minutes, she asked me if I could come immediately instead of the following week.

# 7

## A QUESTION OF CULTURE

'Let's go to the Marina, Jai,' Kitty said, 'I can't talk here.'

'Are you kidding? It's Saturday evening, half of Chennai will be there! There will be no place even to stand.'

'Well, let's go to the Besant Nagar beach, then.'

'Your young man might be there,' I said, trying to keep it light. 'I believe he lives nearby.'

'*Stop it*, Jai!' she whispered, looking angry and hurt.

'Let's just go to the terrace, Kitty. No one ever comes there.'

In the middle of our terrace, there is a gazebo-like structure that has always reminded me of *Sound of Music*. There's no glass, it's just a circular sitting place, with a red-tiled roof, supported by four pillars, with benches inside. Kitty sat down on one of these. She didn't talk for some time. I could sense she was wrestling with her thoughts. I just sat quietly with my arm around her. Sometimes, silence has a more salutary effect than words. For a minute or two, she remained that way. Then she choked, put her head on my shoulder and cried. Bit by bit, she poured it all out.

'Why didn't you tell them *before* they started all this?' I asked her.

'I . . . I thought they would get terribly upset. I didn't want them to feel let down. I thought it would be better if I went through with it. I hoped it wouldn't work out . . . If not, I'd have tried to slip out of it . . . Oh, I don't know, Jai . . . it all happened so fast. I meant to tell them about Shree . . . but kept postponing it. I could never muster the nerve to tell them. You know what Dad is like.'

'Who is this Shree chap? Is he a Patel?'

'He's a Tamil Iyengar.'

'An *Iyengar*!' I exclaimed. 'Good heavens!'

She was quiet. I remained silent too. I was thinking about how my parents would take to a potential non-Gujarati son-in-law. It had never happened within the close family circle. There was a second cousin who married a Punjabi and a distant relative who married a Polish girl, but . . . besides, they were boys. Elders are much more protective of a girl. Kinnari *Iyengar*? They were definitely not going to stand up and applaud.

The problem was that people of my parents' generation didn't really socialize with non-Gujaratis, the way we did. Wherever they were, they would always manage to find some of *apna maana*s to be with.

My father's accountant was a Tamil Brahmin Iyer (like Kitch) whom my dad had known since years. My father had the utmost regard for him, both on the personal and professional front. That's probably the closest he has got to a non-Gujarati.

But marriage was different. Marriage was about *family*. In Indian tradition, girls don't just hitch up with boys. It is like families getting married. It is important for the two sets of parents to relate to each other and for the bride and groom—perhaps more so for the bride—to be able to adjust to the new family. Any non-conformist wedding invites hurt feelings, shocked whispers, slashed budgets and muted celebrations. And in this case, Kitty would have definitely crossed the *line*.

'Not even an *Iyer*!' I said, wonderingly, thinking aloud.

'What do you mean by that?' Kitty, burst out. 'What's wrong with an Iyengar?'

'Kitch says Iyers are better than Iyengars.'

'That's because *he* is an Iyer. And I don't care what Kitch says. Kitch must be an idiot if he goes around saying things like that.'

I could perceive faint beginnings of another round of tears. I remained in silent thought, grappling with the situation.

'So, now, what are you going to do?' she asked. If it is possible to wail softly, she was doing it. I could sense that she was gripped by panic. 'What are you going to do, Jai? Are you going to help me?'

'Of course, I'm going to help you.' I said quietly. 'What do you think I've come here for? Listen, this is now *my* responsibility, Kitty!' I added earnestly. 'Don't worry about anything. I'll handle this.'

She flung her arms around me and cried again. I let her, without saying a word. In front of me, the *neem* trees that grew by the side of the building swayed around in the breeze, seeming to stretch towards me, almost like they were offering a helping hand. I had no doubt I would need all the help I could get. With my tear-soaked T-shirt clinging to my left shoulder and Kitty clinging to my right, I led the way down.

I knew this was not a matter that could be handled directly by me. I had no illusions about my own capability. Even as I had promised Kitty that I would handle it, I had known what I was going to do. I was going to present the issue to Kapoor and shoot from over his shoulder.

Two days later, I was patting myself on the back. Everything had got fixed and I hadn't had to move a muscle. How Kapoor does these things, I don't know. I have met no one who is as clear in his analysis, or as convincing and persuasive in his argument. He flew down, spent half an hour with Kitty and then had requested to meet Shree. That night, he came home and spent time with my parents, after requesting us to keep out of the way. The following day, my father asked Kitty if she could invite the 'boy' for a dinner. He was there promptly. Kapoor came too and while I would not describe the evening as festive, it went off well. Shree was about my age and worked for a British real estate firm.

He made one boo-boo over dinner when he raved about the *sambar*, which was the only thing Mum had ordered from a restaurant. She felt that even those south Indians who were fond of Gujarati food generally, did not like Gujarati dal or kadi which they found too sweet. So, she had ordered south Indian sambar to go with the rest of the home-cooked meal. But that apart, I thought he put up a good show, saying and doing all the right things.

After he left, we had a long chat. The underlying tension that had been there throughout the day had reduced perceptibly. My father spoke to us at length. He spoke about things that he had never said to us before. He spoke about why Indian parents did the things they did. He spoke about Indian and western marriages, he spoke about commitment, family values, culture and adjustment. He told us about himself and Mum; about how many situations they had fought and won over together. 'Do you know how much money we had when we returned from Uganda?' he asked. 'Six hundred rupees. That is all. We had lost *everything*. For almost ten years after that, we were in debt. We borrowed money for the business, for the house, even for your schooling. Your mother never complained. Not even once. Not even when we had creditors at our door threatening to burn the factory.' He was choking a bit now. I wanted to put my arm around his shoulder, but I just sat there transfixed. 'And why?' he continued, 'Because, she and I share the same values. We are like-minded, we were brought up the same way and we came from the same community. Your mother was nineteen, when she married me, but from the very first day, she has stood by me like a rock. She has been my strength.'

Neither Kitty nor I had heard our father talk so much and so emotionally. He went on to tell us how much our happiness, Kitty's and mine, meant to him and Mum and how it was their duty to ensure our that we took the right decisions for that, even if it meant being firm. Finally, he told Kitty that Shree seemed like a nice boy, but that he would go further only after meeting his parents. Kitty went and hugged him and Mum and cried some more. It was a big day for Kitty's tears. She had turned into a human Niagara.

The subject soon changed to my work and life in Dubai. I told them about how everyone called each other 'darling' and 'sweetheart'. They enjoyed some of the gossip—Kitty especially—

and were intrigued by the punching bag. I also told them that Vinoo kaka had let me down with a thud.

'I am not *really* surprised, Jai,' Kapoor told me. 'Trusts can be notorious in this respect and transferring funds out from a trust can be tricky. Nor can we expect Vinoo to revoke a trust with a bank that has served him for so long. Besides, many people would not want details of their wealth known to close relatives. It's not unusual, Jai. You musn't hold that against him. Keep in touch. He may be able to help you some time. Meanwhile, I will get you some good contacts in Africa.'

'Listen! This Shree chap,' I asked Kitty, the next day, as I tucked into a 'mini tiffin'. A Chennai special, it has miniature versions of several of Tamil Nadu's delicacies all on one plate. For people like me, who tend to eye others' plates as much as one's own while eating, this is a good option. I don't have to worry about what I'm missing. 'What's his full name? Is it Shree Iyengar?'

'It's Shridhar,' she said. 'Shridhar Rangarajan. He doesn't use Iyengar in his name.'

'What about his parents? Are they okay with you? That's important too, y'know?'

'His mum was a bit apprehensive at first. She wasn't terribly keen on a Gujarati girl and needed some convincing.'

'Tough baby?'

'In some ways, yes.' Then, with that silly giggle which only a girl talking about her loved one can come up with, she said 'He's a bit of a mama's boy, actually!'

'Oh *no*!'

'Yes, don't tell anyone, but she still feeds him dinner sometimes while he watches TV.'

'Kitty!' I said, appalled. 'Give this man a miss!'

'I won't,' she said. 'He's a teddy bear.'

'He must be a sissy.'

'He's *not*! He's a little baby munchkin.'

I turned away, feeling slightly nauseated. This must be love, I thought. *Real* love. Even in my dumbest moment, I would not have thought of Rina as a munchkin.

# 8

## HITS AND MISSES

As I walked into office the next day, I bumped into Rebecca.

'Oh, hello, Jack!' she said. 'Some good news for you! Cyrus had asked me to arrange for a prayer room in the office, It's ready now. So, you Rustom, Aliya and Ahmed can use it.'

I started. 'Me?' I asked. 'Why me?'

'Are you . . . aren't you er . . . Islamic?'

'No, I'm a Hindu,' I said.

'Oh!' She seemed in deep thought. 'But, isn't *Ishan* a Muslim name? I thought it was.'

'Izhaan, yes, it is. Why?'

'And you are *Ishan* aren't you?' she asked. 'Jaik *Ishan*?'

It took me a couple of seconds to figure out what she was driving at. These *Westerners*! How ignorant can they be?

'Not Jaik Ishan.' I said firmly. 'Jaikishan. It's Jai—first part and Kishan, second part. *Kish* rhymes with Fish and an rhymes with run.'

'Oh, I'm sorry! I just thought . . . I knew Ishan was a Muslim name . . . I think it means their morning prayer.'

'That's *azaan*, Becks,' I told her. 'Not izhaan'

She made a self-deprecatory expression, 'Oh dear!' 'Am I making a complete ass of myself or what!'

'You might also want to check another thing' I told her. 'There may need to be a separate prayer room for women. I think that is the local requirement. I've seen it in some other offices.'

From the corner of my eye, I saw Peggy beckoning to me. 'Come in here a moment, darling.' She asked if I'd had a good trip. 'I've got good news,' she said. I hoped it wasn't the same as Rebecca's. 'The first is that Myers York has taken over KCP Securities, a medium-sized European firm that specializes in emerging market fixed income securities. That fills up a gap in our product range. I think this will be fantastic for us.'

'That's great,' I told her.

'Also, Jack, there's this guy I've been in touch with in Muscat. He's an Arab Sheikh or something. He's very nice. He wants to meet us urgently. But I'm tied up, so I'd like you to go over for a day and meet him. His name is Abdul Rashid Latif, here are his details. Just call him, honey. He will arrange to meet you.'

The next day, I reached Rashid's house at around noon. He was a small, friendly man and seemed to like Peggy a lot. He kept repeatedly referring to *Peggy madam*. He wasn't a 'sheikh' or anything, just a well-to-do businessman. He told me he was keen on opening an account with us but was just waiting for the outcome of a legal case. Soon, another car drew up outside and a man walked in. I was introduced to Abu Jaffer. 'He is very interested in investments,' Rashid told me, 'He wants to talk to you.'

After the initial greeting, Jaffer spent most of the next half hour or so talking to Rashid in Arabic. I tried to make out what the conversation was about, but couldn't really follow much. A while later, Jaffer left and Rashid gestured to me to follow him. Outside, Jaffer beckoned to me to get into his SUV.

'Mr. Jai,' he started off, 'I want to make investments. Also, I want to learn. I will learn and make investments at the same time.' Then, he added with a laugh, 'Insha allah, we will make money as well.'

Along the way, he asked me about BRIC. 'What is this new thing, this group of countries . . . Brazil something something? Is it the latest investment fad or what?'

I explained that this term referred to the four emerging countries,

Brazil, Russia, India and China, which Goldman Sachs had pointed out in a report a few years ago, had the potential as a combined force, to overtake the G6 countries—US, UK, France, Germany, Italy, Japan—before 2050.

'Of these four, which do you think is the best country to invest in?'

'I think, sir, the idea is to look at them as a package and not individually.'

Jaffer seemed to be pondering over something. 'My friend, Russia has something very good that none of these other countries have,' he said.

'Oil and gas,' I chipped in rather smartly. 'But you see, there is an overwhelming dependence on this. For most analysts, that is a negative.'

'Not oil and gas,' he said, with a disdainful wave of the hand. 'What can you do with oil and gas? It is not tall, it is not beautiful. You can't admire it.'

I remained quiet. What was this guy talking about?

'Russia has Maria Sharapova!' he exclaimed, with a chortle and then a loud laugh. 'Any country that can produce girls like that is a winner!'

We had reached what seemed like his farmhouse, on the outskirts of the city. Unlike Dubai, Muscat is a city of low-rise structures. Picturesque and clean, surrounded by the very brown and rocky 'Hajar' mountains, it presented a very unique landscape, like a hot and hilly amphitheatre.

The car stopped. Jaffer got down quickly and started walking towards a house, talking loudly and animatedly into his cell phone. I stared after him, wondering what I was expected to do. His driver turned back and looked at me enquiringly. 'Where is he going?' I asked him. 'He is going home,' he replied, simply. 'Where do you want to go?'

The truth was I didn't have a clue. It was about 1.30 p.m. Presumably, Jaffer was going in for lunch. I hadn't been invited, so I could hardly walk in. Perhaps I could have lunch somewhere and then give Rashid a call. Or should I call Peggy? What was I to tell her? That I was outside Rashid's friend's house and that I didn't know what to do? This was weird, I thought. Was this the famed Arab hospitality?

I told the driver to drive me to the nearest main road from where I could get a taxi to the city. A few minutes later, my phone rang. It was Rashid. 'What are you doing!' he exclaimed. 'Where are you?'

'I am going towards the city.' I replied, feeling rather silly. 'Er . . .can we meet later today?'

'Why you are not going to Abu Jaffer's house? He is looking all over the place for you, waiting to have lunch. Go back to his house immediately, brother.'

I turned the cab back and asked him to go back where I got on and then guided him to the farmhouse. Jaffer and the driver were waiting outside the gate. 'Where did you go?' Jaffer seemed at least as confused as I was. I struggled to find suitable words to reply to this. 'Where did you go?' he asked again, throwing his hands up in the air. 'I brought you here for *lunch*. You just disappeared!' He made a gesture with a large palm and fingers. 'Poof!' he said. 'Just like that. Khalaas. Gone!'

'*I didn't know*! I'm sorry. You didn't say anything about lunch.'

'What are you talking!' he exclaimed. 'For half an hour at Rashid's house, we were only talking about what kind of food Indians eat.'

'But that was all in Arabic!' I protested. 'And you were on the phone and got off suddenly and I didn't quite know what to do.'

He pointed skyward with both his hands as if calling upon the Almighty to judge. 'Okay, okay' he said, now looking at me with an amused smile. 'Yalla, come.' He ushered me into his dining hall, where his father and his uncle were waiting for us. I apologized to them for the delay. Jaffer told them the story in Arabic and the three of them had a hearty laugh. I felt like a bit of a jerk, though I was convinced I had been the victim. But they soon put me at ease.

It was just the four of us at lunch. There didn't seem to be any women around. I wondered if they were eating separately. The meal wasn't exactly what I was used to. But I went at it bravely. There was some kind of biryani, which they called majboos, there were samosas stuffed with spinach and cheese. There was lamb stew and Omani lobsters, highly recommended by them. For dessert, we had halwa with dates with sweetened milk and kahwa—Arabic coffee.

But for me, the real dessert came a few minutes later. 'So, how to open the account?' Jaffer asked. 'We want to do it quickly and make some investments.'

Soon, Jaffer was instructing his driver to show me the Ruwi souk and the city's famous landmarks Kantab beach and Al Bustan hotel, before dropping me at the airport. My job was done. This account could be a big one, I could sense. He had already spoken casually of transferring 'some millions'. I was ecstatic and my heart was singing songs of bliss. If business was going to be this easy, I thought, I need have no concern at all. Now, I just needed to really focus and manage this account right. I was confident of being able to handle currencies, but I was still a little raw around the edges with equities and bonds. I would need to talk to Jaffer about asset allocation—the deployment of different kinds of assets within a portfolio to create the right kind of balance in the account—he seemed far too eager to fill his portfolio with anything that caught his fancy or was the flavour of the moment.

I loved the walk in the souk—narrow, criss-crossing lanes full of exotic scents, with small shops on either side selling everything from perfumes to spices, from textiles to handicrafts. The Kantab beach and the drive there, too, was brilliant, my enjoyment enhanced by the mild drizzle that had commenced. It didn't dampen my spirits, it lifted them. Living in the Middle East, one learns to appreciate the rain.

I was still floating contentedly and it was probably this light-hearted woolly-headed feeling of happiness that rendered my senses less alert than usual and led me unwittingly into the ladies rest room at the Muscat airport. A look of complete shock was followed by a piercing scream by the lone occupant. Terrified, I beat a hasty retreat and didn't even bother to go to the gents. I rushed straight to the departure lounge where I tried to shrink and make myself invisible. It was not a comforting thought to know that I had just sauntered into the ladies room in an Islamic country. Damn those silly pictures of a man and woman on rest room doors, I thought. It made it so difficult to differentiate. They should just write GENTS and LADIES in bold letters. What was the need to draw anything?

But nothing was going to stop me from feeling happy that night. I picked up some stuff at the duty free to celebrate with and called Kitch over. We ordered pan-fried pizzas and potato wedgies. Kitch filled me in with the latest gossip from work. Linda, he had found out, used to live and work in Hong Kong. She had been a masseuse which was how she had met her British husband, before she became his wife. Love grew with the massages. 'These guys seem to have a lot of fun,' he said, thoughtfully and a little peevishly. 'Westerners half our age would have had twice as much fun. It's only we Indians, particularly us guys from Madras, who are so goody-goody. Right until we get married,' he said, looking at me, like he was expecting sympathy and consolation.

'Not me!' I said.

He stared at me like he'd seen a ghost and seemed to be expanding in size, like a balloon swelling up.

'W-wik . . . whek . . .' he said, going pink in the face and struggling to express himself. 'Who? W-w- when?'

I shrugged my shoulders. 'In Mumbai,' I said. 'And, Chennai.'

He spluttered.

'Y-you *dog*!' he said finally. 'You lucky dog!'

# 9

## THE SCOREBOARD

By now, I had met everyone at the office. Some had been away when I had joined and had returned since. There were three other advisors—Ahmed, a tall and long-haired Pakistani, who wore suits even when he sat at his desk. A nephew of a former Pakistani cricket captain, he was acknowledged to be a bit of flirt and had the knack of somehow bringing in the subject of his 'conquests' into most discussions. Then there was Aliya, a Dubai-based girl, with a flawless complexion and a lovely smile, who hated the term 'local' usually used to describe UAE nationals. Then, there was Ramzi Jarrar from Lebanon whose main claim to fame thus far in office seemed to be that he drove a flashy Chevrolet Corvette.

Rachel, Ahmed and Melissa shared an assistant, Linda, who doubled up as a receptionist. The others shared another assistant called Galiya, of whom all I knew then was that she was from Kazakhstan and had a Christian father and a Muslim mother.

With some help from John, the Ops guy, I managed to get Jaffer's account opened in less than three days—quite a miracle, I was told, given normal standards. The NY office wouldn't accept a PO Box number as an address. Jaffer's house didn't seem to have a *proper* address, one that would satisfy those guys for the purpose of filling up the forms. They didn't seem to care much for what I said about very few houses in this part of the world having residential addresses, unlike elsewhere in the world. But John, having been with Myers since several years, seemed to enjoy a special status with the guys at HO. He managed to convince them and the account went through. They still wanted a note that would help to identify the location of the farm house. After a chat with John, I sent them an email, copied to him, telling them that it was 'Farm House No. 2, Farm House Road, Behind Hajar Mountains, Muscat, Oman'. They seemed reasonably pleased with that cooked-up information.

Peggy was pleased too, though for a different reason. She thought I was the latest star on the horizon and I basked in the glory of this huge new account. I wondered if I should let her know about the mix-up on the lunch with Jaffer. It might take the sheen off my 'achievement' a bit. But I decided to, nevertheless. After all, it was Peggy's lead. So I did. She laughed in that very likeable, forthright manner of hers. 'I think you handled it pretty well,' she said, much to my surprise, since I thought I had made an ass of myself. 'It's this kind of simplicity and honesty that make the Arabs like Indians,' she said.

I hadn't thought of it like that. I had no idea whether Arabs liked Indians or not. I suppose they did, else there wouldn't be so many Indians in the Gulf. Dubai, the second largest emirate in the UAE had a population of about a million, almost half of them from India. If you lived anywhere near my apartment in Karama, you would think even that was an under-estimate. And if you walked just a few blocks away, you would come to a place they called 'Little Manila' because it was just teeming with Filipinos. The UAE was an unusual country in many senses, not least because the local population or the Emiratis, was only some 20 per cent of the total. Yet, it wasn't exactly a melting pot of cultures that you would expect under these circumstances, because each community seemed to function in isolation. But it was a very interesting city nevertheless, with myriad nationalities, rather like my office, really. We were about fifteen people, but made up of seven or eight nationalities.

I have, earlier, briefly touched upon the 'scoreboard' that was located in the passage right in the middle of the office. It was a much celebrated thing, effectively the star of the office. On the first day of each month, Emma would religiously put up three new sheets on it. One showed the list of FAs in order of total assets or client money they had and another listed them based on revenues generated. The third touched upon any special achievements during the month and also covered awards and prizes, if any. Inevitably, the corridor area used to buzz with excitement and small talk around the beginning of the month.

The excitement was generated on account of several reasons. The scoreboard basically decided one's hierarchy in the office. Not the managerial hierarchy but one that determines status, wealth and potential. The top revenue-generators could walk home with a pay packet far exceeding what the branch manager earned. Philippe was said to be earning about four times as much as Cyrus. As a broker, your earnings depended primarily on the revenues you generated, but as a manager, you were on a fixed salary, except for the annual bonus. Some of this information had been fed to us at NY. Myers as an organization had a very flat structure with minimal hierarchy and a compensation programme which was simple and transparent. There was some modest weight given to the assets held in your accounts and some for other attributes like compliance. But other than that, your earnings were almost in linear proportion to your revenues. In a sense, we were all self-sufficient, even self-obsessed islands floating on the Myers ocean. It was no accident—it was designed that way. As Cyrus told me 'The interests of the FA and that of the organization are completely aligned. There's no conflict. We're all running towards the same goal-post.' Every time Cyrus said something, he had this tendency to look at you in an expectant sort of way, like he was waiting for you to applaud.

In the first year, they fixed your minimum remuneration, but beyond that, the scoreboard determined your lifestyle. It didn't matter much what your boss thought of you, nor did your popularity among your colleagues amount to anything. No one gave a damn if you were generous to newcomers or accommodative and helpful to seniors. That was the importance of the scoreboard. In the religion of broking, the scoreboard was God.

The scoreboard also bestowed upon us certain other p
It determined whether one would have one's own ro
Philippe or whether one would merely huddle together at work
stations, sitting within striking distance of a colleague and overhearing
each other's phone calls, like the rest of us. If you generated
revenues of over a million dollars a year, you walked into a room,
no questions asked. If you didn't, even if you were at USD
710,000 for the previous calendar year (like Rachel was) you
crowded around the cubicles. The fact that there were vacant
rooms in the office was irrelevant. A room had to be *earned* and for
a broker, there was only one way of earning it.

This month, the funds that came into Jaffer's account were
enough to push my name two places up the ladder on the
scoreboard. I had been right at the bottom the previous month
both in terms of assets and revenues. I had now moved up ahead
of Kitch and Ramzi in terms of revenues and ahead of Kitch,
Ramzi *and* Aliya in terms of assets.

There was a little crowd in front of the scoreboard. We rather
made a ceremony of it, I reckon, every month. It wasn't just the
brokers concerned who were interested in where they stood. We
were all just as interested in knowing where others figured in the
list. There was a certain perverse satisfaction in knowing that others
hadn't gotten ahead, or even better, had fallen back.

The assistants too, had their strong preferences, their own likes
and dislikes among the FAs and cheered silently or sometimes, not
so silently, when their favourite FAs moved up the list. They had
a vested interest in it as well, because some brokers motivated
assistants by paying them a portion of their earnings in order to
secure their wholehearted support. It worked well.

'Boy, wouldn't I just love to be here!' Rachel said, pointing
ahead of Philippe on the scoreboard . . .

'For that, my dear,' a voice spoke from the library just behind
us, 'you will have to spend far more time outside the office, with
your clients and prospects.' It was Cyrus, who had made a habit of
dry sarcasm and had just stopped short of patenting it. He liked to

wish people good afternoon, if they walked in late in the morning.
He also specialized in wisecracks with a deadpan expression, such
as the one he just made.

'I'd like to put ants in his pants,' Rachel hissed, as soon as Cyrus
was out of hearing distance. 'Who does he think he is?'

A minute later, Rachel had disappeared, too, still smouldering
and muttering under her breath. Melissa, who I gathered, was not
a great friend of Rachel's, whispered, 'Getting up there would be
easy for her. She just has to go and do her pole dance in front of
some of Simon's clients.' Rather nasty, I thought. I quite liked
Rachel. She always seemed to have a smile and I'd never heard *her*
complain or talk ill about anyone else.

For 2005, Melissa figured at number three on the list with
revenues of just under USD 400K. The rest of us came in a heap
after that, all between practically nothing and USD 200K.

The scoreboard served one other purpose. It provided information
on various incentive plans that the firm had up its sleeve. Sometimes,
it wasn't the firm itself, but one of the third party fund managers
who liked to offer a carrot to enthuse the brokers to push their
funds. Sometimes, we were told in advance what the incentives
were. At other times, it took the form of *post facto* rewards, because
the firm did not want to encourage too much of product pushing
at the expense of what was most appropriate for the client. As I
looked at the incentive awards sheet on the board, I could see the
names of three of my colleagues staring back at me, those of
Melissa, Kitch and Ahmed. For investments of a million plus
within one in their funds, a fund manager had specially invited
them to Hong Kong for a two-day seminar.

I took the three of them down to Starbucks for a mini treat.
Emma and Rebecca were already there, sharing a walnut muffin
with their latte.

'He's quite a brick,' Emma was saying.

'Who?' asked Ahmed, quickly.

'We were talking about Baby Jacob,' she replied.

Ahmed looked at her incredulously. 'I thought you liked him.'

'I do indeed! That's why I referred to him as a brick.'

'Oh, *brick*!' Ahmed said, 'I thought you said . . .'

'I *know* what you were thinking, Mr Hormone!' Emma replied, an amused look on her face, 'And I think it's high time you started thinking of something else for a change!'

The other interesting thing that happened that month was that a brand new gym was established in the building and was offering a 25 per cent discount on the membership fee to all employees working in the building. Peggy, Rachel, Ahmed, Cyrus and I went for it. We preferred different times—Ahmed went in the evenings. Peggy and I preferred the mornings, so on most days we came in our gym clothes and changed after a shower. Peggy, of course, came armed with her sanitizer and diligently wiped every handle bar before and after use. Cyrus and Rachel went just before lunch. If you went to the bathroom just after lunch, you'd find Cyrus there facing the mirror, concentration writ large on his face, wearing his bow-tie again after his gym session.

I tried to rope Kitch in, but he wouldn't hear of it. 'Don't want any six-pack abs,' he said.

'With all that Mysore pak you have been tucking into,' I warned him, 'you might end up with six-pack flabs.'

# 10

## READY, STEADY, GO!

It was easy to understand how Peggy became successful at Myers at such a young age. She was the youngest team head in the company and she wasn't thirty yet, while most other team heads were well into their thirties. One rarely saw her flustered. She had an amazing way with people. She was pleasant, patient and yet passionate about her work. She yielded to no one in her ambition and her quest to seize an opportunity by the scruff of its neck and wring the maximum business out of it. But her approach was subtle. She didn't need to hurl four-letter words, unlike my former boss in Mumbai, nor to threaten or coerce. She had very clear thoughts and a wonderful way of persuading you to share them, adopt them. She would listen intently and earnestly to problems or suggestions. Her way of motivating others was by simply letting her own enthusiasm spill over. She never tired of work. She never switched off her phone and would seem as delighted to take a call from us at 11 p.m. as at 11 a.m. Like Rashid, I too, had become a Peggy fan.

I had briefed her on my experience with Kamal Lalwani before I left for Muscat, little realizing that she would actually take the trouble of calling him up and even meeting him. That bit about him wanting to meet a senior colleague, I had referred to more in jest than anything else. Imagine my surprise then, when she came to me one day and gave me his account number.

'His *what*!' I exclaimed in surprise.

'Oh, I happened to be in that area and I just popped in and asked to meet him,' she said. 'I told him about our strength in equities and he seemed rather keen on it. I think he will also like trading currencies, which should be right up your sleeve. Interesting chap, I thought. Rather cute. I liked him.'

'You can keep him. I didn't like him at all,' I said. 'Cute' was the last word I would have used to describe that man. I didn't even want to meet him again. I have mentioned her persuasive powers— she now put them to work. Within five minutes, I had agreed to take on the account. 'Never say no to a client, Jai, they're just part of the job. Clients are assets, clients are revenues. They are your bread and butter. You don't have to *like* them, any more than an accountant has to like debits and credits. This could be a high revenue account. Every client adds to your earnings and has the potential to bring in more clients. Clients are not family. You don't have to fall in love with them. In fact, you shouldn't. They are there to help you do your job. Treat them well. You can deal with him on your terms, but please don't let opportunities go.' She was actually doing me a favour because Peggy handled clients too, apart from the responsibilities of managing her team. It would have been easy for her to just take on the account as her own. In a financial sense, it would have benefited her more.

But that was Peggy for you. She was genuinely helpful and generous. In this cut-throat world of broking, I knew already that this was definitely not the norm. In a recent pantry talk, Melissa had told me about how Peggy's predecessor had first tagged all new accounts on to his name, pending the advisors' certification and then tried to delay the transfer, in order to allow some more income to accrue to him. Likewise, I had heard from John that he had come across several instances where a young FA would take a senior colleague along with him for a client meeting, only to end up losing the client to the senior. The FA would be told that he was too young to manage an account of such complexity and that it would be transferred back to him once the account was on track. It seldom was. Some of the star performers—Philippe was a case in point—were so powerful, the branch managers had little willingness to try and intervene in such matters.

So, I ended up with Kamal Lalwani's account after all. Peggy invited him to the office and we showed him around. This turned out to be a master-stroke. He was so impressed with our office and our technology that he got started immediately.

I hate to confess this, but I will. My first equity trade for him was a winner. But not quite in the way I had intended. We used to have regular and frequent conference calls from New York where Raj Saunders or our chief technical analyst would discuss stock picks. The ones that both of them would agree upon, would be the ones that the FAs usually favoured, as it covered the stock both from the point of view of the company's fundamentals—balance sheet strength, profit margins, future prospects, as well as the technical aspects of the company's share price movements. Then we had Ralph Kramer. Ralph was a Myers old-timer, who was widely acknowledged for his stock-picking skills. He had retired two years ago, but had been recalled by the firm a couple of months ago as a consultant. Cyrus was a huge fan of his. He had told me that Ralph's skills in his field were legendary. 'Ralph,' he told me, 'was considered a genius, a stock-picking guru at a time when the likes of you were still a sperm, perhaps not even that.' Ralph would come up with his own weekly recommendations. No one dared to ask the basis of his recommendations. You don't question forty years of experience, especially when it works.

At one such equity conference call—in March 2006—the stock of Hewlett Packard had been strongly recommended to us as a good short-term pick. Most of my colleagues seemed to like the idea. When I suggested it to Lalwani and showed him the price movements, he wanted to go for it. I suppose it was right up his sleeve, the idea of making money '*quick, quick, quick*'. So, I made an investment in it for him with a one-month perspective.

We would have a fortnightly pow-wow in the auditorium where all of us would gather and Cyrus would make some of his observations, usually a brief market update, often interspersed with some smart aleck comments and a witty remark or two. Towards the end of March, the Hewlett Packard trade was one of the subjects that came up for discussion and I was surprised to hear some of the others saying the trade had gone the wrong way. From what I had seen, the stock had actually risen a couple of dollars from when I had bought them in the first week of March, from around 33 to over 35, giving him a profit of USD 20,000. But, most others were talking of a 1-dollar fall over the period from 33.50 to 32.50. I didn't quite know what to make of it at that time. Luckily, I didn't raise the issue right there. When I came back to my desk and looked into the account, I realized that Lalwani didn't hold a single share of Hewlett Packard.

At Myers, FAs entered trades online. The system would allow each FA to do trades for his or her clients directly. You didn't need to call anyone. While entering the details, I had put in the *ticker*—the short symbol that represents a company's stock—as HP instead of HPQ. As a result, I had bought 10,000 shares of Helmerich and Payne (HP)—a company that supplies equipment for drilling and oil exploration—instead of Hewlett Packard, the one that makes computers and other hardware.

It unnerved me. What do I tell the client? That I had foolishly bought the wrong share? 'I want to complain to your superior,' he'd probably say. 'You bought wrong share? Dumb. Dumb. Dumb.' I cringed at the thought. After struggling with the situation for a few minutes, I eventually decided to tell him nothing. Instead, I just called him and told him we had a recommendation to sell HP and that I would unwind it for him at a profit of about 2 dollars a share. He agreed and that was the end of the episode. Till today, no one else knows what actually happened on the trade.

Meanwhile, I had become very close to Yashpal Kapoor. He was pleasant, well built, with a ready smile and always stylishly, even flashily dressed. Kapoor had originally come to Dubai as an employee of Standard Chartered Bank . . . Some six years ago, he had left to start his own consultancy. He had, over the years, developed some very good contacts through the bank. He assisted them in making proposals to banks, negotiated term loans and overdrafts for them. He also helped clients set up offices in and around Dubai, in the free trade zones or within the city.

I met him at his house, a four-bedroom bungalow, or villa as they call it in Dubai, in Meadows, a relatively new premium suburb in Dubai. He had bought this house about a year ago for 2.5 million dirhams or about USD 600,000. As he proudly informed me, it was now worth 25 per cent more.

Kapoor offered to introduce me to his network in and around the region. He had very close friends who were wealthy businessmen and who might be quite happy to consider Myers York for their investment needs. When I told Peggy about him, she wanted to meet with him too. A week later, Kapoor was at the office, signing what we called a 'referral agreement' whereby he would introduce accounts to us and be paid for his services.

So, there we were. Kapoor was on board. And I was all set for the ride.

# 11

## TRULY RURAL

It all seems a long time ago and very different from the present—the train ride from Chennai to Tirunelveli. It was getting decidedly uncomfortable, primarily because the two back rests which went down horizontally to make my bed were not at the same level. There was a gap of at least an inch between the two, which was kind of digging into my back. I couldn't relax. To make matters worse, the guy who had been given the berth above mine, was taking his own time getting to bed. In the meantime, he was sitting by my feet and making small talk every time I tried to close my eyes. The Tamil family on the right had long since switched off their lights, but this man obviously wasn't ready for bed yet.

'You are Malayali?' he asked me.

'Er . . . no.'

He seemed disappointed. 'I'm Malayali,' he told me with a smile and a touch of pride. I knew that already from his accent. He spoke rather like John. 'But my wife is from Palakkad,' he said, pointing towards a seat behind him. I didn't particularly care. I looked at the darkness outside. I wished he would go to his own berth.

'Ours was love marriage,' he said, pronouncing the word as 'laow'. 'From college, you know.'

I looked at him and then at his wife. She looked bigger, even older and very conservative. It was difficult to imagine the two of them in love, in college.

'Palakkad people are very *indelligent*,' he said, 'but a little bit . . .'

he paused, as if he were in deep thought. Then, lowering his voice to a whisper and with a quick glance behind him, he added, 'But a little bit different from normal people.' He winked, suppressed a laugh and then looked closely at me. 'You are Tamilian?' he asked.

'No.'

'Telugu . . .?'

'I'm a Gujarati,' I said quickly, not wanting to end up playing 'Twenty Questions' with him.

'Oh, Gujarati!' he exclaimed. After a while, he continued, 'Gujaratis are good businessmen. I know Gujarat. Ahmedabad, Baroda, Anand . . . . . . from Anand you know that man . . . Dr Kurien, who is very famous for the milk society in Gujarat? He is a Malayali.'

I nodded.

He looked furtively around and took out a bottle of whisky. He smiled and stretched it towards me. 'You want hot drink?' he asked.

This time I shook my head.

'During recession, this is all we have,' he said, shaking the bottle. 'All these bangers have gone and simbly put us in trouble.'

I blinked. '*Bangers?*'

'All those foreign bangers, you know,' he said, creasing his forehead and waving a spacious hand. 'Sub-prime and liquidity crunch and credit cards and this and that. All bloody bakwas. Making a fool of us. I work for one foreign company. They were supposed to start a huge project in Kerala. Now, it is cancelled. Because of all this humbug, you know.'

I remained silent, trying to think of something to change the subject. I hoped he wouldn't ask me about my work.

'So, what work you are doing?' he asked.

'I . . . er, we have farms.'

'That is the best,' he announced. 'That way, at least we will always have something to eat. You give me rice, I give you potato, everyone is happy. Something is being produced. Not just taken away, like with these bloody *bangers*.'

I turned over and pretended to be asleep.

Somewhere down the line, the pretence must have changed to reality. When I woke up some time later, the Malayali gentleman was fast asleep on the bunk above mine with one hand hanging down limply. There were faint traces of sunlight creeping into the train and signs of early morning activity in the train.

Every part of my body was aching; my back, my sides and my neck especially. I stretched myself and observed that the couple opposite had woken up. The man had got back into his trousers, the lady was reading *Kumudam*.

A few minutes later, sharp cries of of '*Chaia, chaia! Kaafi, kaafi!*' cut through the air and almost at once, one could sense that several bodies were getting up simultaneously.

Shortly after that, I was in an old Ambassador car, giving the driver the address of the man Kitch's dad had put me on to. There were miles of green paddy fields on one side of the road. On the other side was the river Tamirabarani, the life blood of the region. Both sides of the road were punctuated at regular intervals by trees. From time to time, forcing the driver to keep slowing down, there were small groups of monkeys who would keep crossing the road and climbing up the tree on the other side.

Occasionally, we would zip past a miniature temple, which looked more like a small igloo in size and shape, except that it had red and white stripes painted on it at the bottom. Every time we crossed one, the driver would take his eyes off the road, both his hands off the steering wheel, turn towards the temple, close his eyes and pat his cheeks with religious fervour. And every time he did that, my heart would skip a beat and I would stick a nervous hand towards the steering wheel.

Finally, we reached the village where this guy lived. His sons apparently lived in New Jersey and he had decided to wind up in India and stay with them. He had requested Kitch's dad to find a suitable buyer. A couple of kids started running behind the car and soon, they were joined by a few of their friends. The driver, a trifle unsure of the directions, stopped the car to enquire about the way to the 'agraharam' an area inhabited predominantly by Brahmins. Even as one of the kids started directing him, another—obviously the more entrepreneurial type—quickly negotiated a car ride in return for directions. The driver agreed, not realizing that the kid was representing the whole team. Before I knew what was happening seven kids had crowded in at the back of the car. Feeling like quite a spectacle we drove further down to our destination: the residence of Mr Krishnaswamy, the potential seller.

The road was narrow and dusty. On both sides, there were identical stone-walled row houses with heavy wooden doors. The verandas were all interconnected, so you didn't even have to step onto the street to visit your neighbours.

Mr Krishnaswamy's house, like all the others, was all wood and stone. It had a narrow entrance, but plenty of space within. The flooring was of red oxide. There was a large wooden swing on one side and an old-fashioned sofa on the other. A brightly coloured woven mat was laid out on the floor. Several old framed photographs adorned the whitewashed walls. I could smell coffee. I realized I was starving.

'Welcome, welcome, Mr Jai,' he greeted me, quickly wearing a white kurta over his vest. 'Balu told me you would be coming today. Geetha!' he called out loudly, presumably to his wife.

We exchanged pleasantries.

'Er . . . are you a Brahmin?' Mr Krishnaswamy asked me, less than a minute into the conversation.

'I er . . . actually we are . . . no, er . . . not Brahmins, not quite,' I concluded lamely. I was beginning to feel a little persecuted. I was also hesitant because I was unsure if this had anything to do with the prospect for the deal going through.

'Muslim?'

'No, no. Not Muslim.'

'Not Christian?'

'Hindu,' I told him. 'We are Patels. Gujaratis.'

He seemed relieved. 'We have nothing against any religion,' he said, softly. 'But the community here is very sensitive. Both Hindus and Muslims live in this village in amity. But they live separately and they respect each other's customs and privacy. My land is in an area that belongs to Hindus, almost entirely Brahmins. Once, some property was sold to someone from another community and they started a butcher shop there. There was a mini riot which lasted for weeks. I hope you understand.'

I nodded intelligently. In a sudden and unusual burst of inspiration, I blurted out, 'My wife is a vegetarian.'

That seemed to please him. 'That is good!' he said. Meanwhile, a few of the neighbours walked over uninvited and joined us. I was introduced to them as, 'a friend of Kitcha, Madras Balu's son'. I sensed they were probably assessing me, sizing me up.

'Geetha' walked in with coffee, *murukku* and some kind of *ladoo*. 'I'm just bringing *idli*s and *bajji*,' she announced, smiling at me. I was beginning to like this woman already!

Half an hour later, I was in the fields, mesmerized as a couple of peacocks proudly strutted their stuff alongside a small pond right at the centre of Mr Krishnaswamy's 150-acre land. I was introduced to his cow. 'Her name is Lakshmi,' he said, patting the top of her head. 'She has just given birth to a calf last week.'

A cool wind was blowing. In the distance, the paddy crops were swaying like a musical fountain. A small boy ran across alongside a cycle tyre which, from time to time, he hit with a stick to keep it rolling. A couple of farm workers walked past. On their heads was a rolled up piece of cloth and perched on it a curved metal plate containing what appeared to be—going by the stench—some kind of manure. A bird plunged into the pond briefly and flew away. Unseen creatures chirped. Leaves rustled. A peaceful world. This one was soothing. Comforting. I remembered one of my clients saying something about keeping close to nature. I realized now what he meant. This was another world altogether, very unlike the one I had seen in the last four years. But let me tell you more about *that* story.

# 12

## MORE ABOUT OFFICE

'His Nibs wants to see you,' Emma told me, as I was sipping green tea for a change and trying to like it. 'Mr Bow-tie himself.'

'One thing I never figured out,' mumbled Rachel. 'Why on earth doesn't he wear a regular tie like everyone else?'

'Maybe he just wants to be different,' suggested Linda.

Emma shrugged her shoulders. 'I think it comes from his having been a lawyer. Lawyers used to wear bow-ties quite a lot in the UK. Maybe it's just a habit.'

I walked into Cyrus' room. He motioned me towards the sofa next to his rock garden. I sat down and gazed at it intently, following the movement of the little train in and out of a tunnel, up a hill, behind a plant, under a rock and back again into the tunnel. Cyrus meanwhile was 'approving' a few emails. All emails sent by the staff came to Cyrus for approval. If they were sent out to a single receiver, then the message got sent out immediately and was received by him for *post facto* approval. If it was sent out to multiple receivers, Cyrus had to approve it first before the email got sent. I am not sure if this was an internal requirement or NASD regulatory guidelines. I suspect it probably was more to do with the latter.

When he was done, he decided to light his pipe. He always had two pipes on his table. He had told me earlier that he used them to smoke different flavours. He sprinkled some tobacco in one of them and pushed it in with his finger, taking his time doing it.

Then he put some more, poked at it and twirled it. Adding some more, he pushed it in a bit, tapped the bowl of the pipe all around, put the pipe in his mouth and drew at it. 'It's all in the packing,' he said, turning towards me and pointing to the bowl of the pipe. 'It can't be too tight and it can't be too loose.' He then went on to light it again in a rather ceremonial kind of way, as I watched, half-fascinated, half-irritated. Having got all these preliminaries out of the way, he looked more relaxed and held up a trade slip that lay on his table. It was a small document that Ops produced for every trade that emanated from the office. It contained all details of the trade, the FA who did it and the commission charged to the client.

'I must confess,' he said, waving the slip and looking straight into my eyes, 'that I found this somewhat intriguing.' I looked at it. It was the one showing I had sold off HP for Lalwani. A small shiver went down my back. Damn! Was I the bad kid who had got found out? Was I going to be a laughing stock in the office? But what the heck, I was the only one who made money on that recommendation in March!

'I looked at the commission column,' he said, in that typical mock-serious way of his. 'And, I was . . .' (here he paused for effect) '. . . startled,' he concluded. 'Why would anyone do a trade free of commission?'

He cocked his head and raised his eyebrows simultaneously and stayed that way, obviously waiting for a clarification. I took my time replying. The truth was that I hadn't had the heart to charge Lalwani because notwithstanding the profit he had made, I had made a mistake and I had sort of felt morally obliged to waive the commission. But I didn't want to let Cyrus in on that. He straightened his head, but his eyebrows were still raised.

'He's a new client, Cyrus,' I said. 'I just wanted to help him make some more money.' He seemed to be expecting something more. 'I wanted to excite him a bit,' I added, 'so he'd do more business with us.'

'No self-respecting broker waives a charge,' he told me, slowly and deliberately. 'We are in the *business* of doing trades for our clients, Jack. We deserve to be paid for every trade. Every single trade. Trade is work. We should learn to value the work we do,' he said. 'That work has to be paid for.' He looked at me expectantly. There didn't seem to be much to say. I nodded and prepared to leave. 'Oh,' he said, handing over a sheaf of papers, 'if you would be kind enough to hand these over to her. The belly button.'

I looked towards where he had pointed. Galiya was walking towards her desk. It was to her that he had referred. I was a little shocked, but then, that was Cyrus for you. He said pretty much what he wanted to. Sometimes, it was funny, at other times not. You didn't expect your branch manager to refer to one of his staff in this manner, but to be fair to him, I must say it wasn't a bad description of Galiya Shvedova. In a physical sense, Galiya practically revolved around her belly button. You might say, so does everyone, the navel being positioned where it is, but in her case, it was different. For one thing, it was always visible and very clearly at that. Nothing covered it. No clothing even came near it. If she wore a jacket, it was unbuttoned. Her shirt or top always ended a few inches above it and her trousers always began a couple of inches below it. Often, she took the trouble to *enhance* it—not that it was needed—by embellishing it. Sometimes, she stuck a shiny thingy on her midriff. Sometimes, a ring clung to it.

Today, it was different. It had assumed all the glory of the sun. She had painted (or maybe it was a tattoo) lines resembling the rays of the sun, all around her navel. 'Look here!' it seemed to be shouting out. 'Look at me!' I handed over the papers to her and walked over to my desk.

Melissa was looking at me with a smirk on her face. 'You didn't have to stare at it like that!' she said.

'I wasn't staring,' I mumbled, probably quite untruthfully, shuffling my feet uncomfortably—as much as it is possible to shuffle one's feet while sitting down. 'I just sort of . . . er, looked at it briefly since it had just been drawn to my attention.'

Then I got busy looking for some more interesting equity ideas. I had already carried out quite a few currency trades for Harsh and made profits on seven trades while registering a negative on two of them through stop losses. Overall, he was up about USD 35,000 since we started. I was now quite confident about getting him started on equities as well.

I suppose no successful trader can function without a stroke of luck. You can devour company balance sheets, you can talk all you want to the chief financial officer and the investor relations people, but if the planets are in the wrong place, you still won't make money. My planets and stars were obviously in the perfect place, because I did a whole series of trades for Lalwani and even for Abu Jaffer after that and had both of them eating out of my hand within a few days.

Money really does talk, I realized. The same man who had kept me waiting, blew smoke patterns into my face and asked to see my superior, was now dutifully calling me every day—shortly after the US markets opened—to wish me good evening and to hang on to my lightest word.

I went over to the pantry to have my cup of tea. Around this time of the day, Baby Jacob made refreshing ginger tea. This routine had started with John, who had first tapped into Jacob's tea-making skills. I discovered that I rather liked it and so did Ahmed and Usha. So, it became a regular thing and Baby Jacob had a small fan following for his tea. Kitch hated tea. He was a devout coffee drinker.

'What, man, JP?' John asked me, in his strong Keralite accent, his teeth gleaming underneath his carefully coiffeured moustache. 'Melissa is saying you and Cyrus are staring at Galiya's belly button.' Everyone burst into laughter, Baby Jacob loudest of all, as I blushed and looked into my tea, marvelling at Melissa's almost instantaneous communication network.

That weekend, we had an office party at a nearby emirate. It was at a beach hotel. The idea was to celebrate the fact that the office had touched the billion-dollar mark in terms of assets. (Of which, of course, some 620 million was Philippe's). Also, possibly because this might be our last chance this season to party outdoors. Summer was creeping in and the next four or five months in Dubai, I was told, would be like a furnace, with temperatures going up to 50 degrees C. Already, I had stopped switching on the hot water geyser at home. I had started using the cold water tap for hot water, since the water in the building's water tank would get heated up. The hot water tap, I used for cold water.

The evening began on a serious note with Cyrus making his customary, almost mandatory speech. It was unusual to see him not wearing his suit and his trademark bow-tie. He was wearing a pair of jeans, a white shirt and a light brown jacket with similarly coloured suede shoes. Peggy had brought her boyfriend along, a nice, friendly guy called Richard, whom I'd met at the office on Valentine's Day, when he had turned up in the evening with a huge bouquet of flowers.

I don't think Cyrus liked Philippe very much. He passed lightly over his business and much to Kitch and my embarrassment, made a pointed mention of our fledgling efforts as being 'most promising'. John, already on his third drink, drew me aside and said, 'He is so much like a Britisher, you know! Talking, looking, everything. Just like coconut. Brown outside, white inside.'

It was amazing to see how relaxed even the more serious people could get after office hours. The talking got louder, looser and slightly more slurred after some time. I guess beverages work differently on different people. I tend to turn sober and quiet. Others turn energetic, aggressive or even belligerent. Soon, the jackets and shawls came off. Some of the girls were wearing . . . well, let me not get into those details. There was very little of it anyway. A belly dancer had been arranged to perform exclusively for us. As the Arabic music started playing, she swayed, moved and wiggled in tune with it. It was incredible, the control she displayed over different muscles in her body—pectoral, abdomen, hip. She could wiggle a part of herself while keeping the rest of her body absolutely still. It was like watching a yogi at work. She seemed almost like an ensemble of beautiful body parts. Towards the end of the performance, when she invited us to dance along with her, Rachel put up a rather nice show. Then Galiya did her bit as did Linda and Amal. I was surprised that so many of them could dance rather well. Finally Ahmed and Ramzi took over and soon it became less exotic. Shortly after that, the dancer called it a day and left with all of us cheering her wildly.

In the middle of this, I got a call from my mother. I had been getting updates from Kitty, but this was the official, final one I guess. Parents on both sides had agreed. The wedding had been fixed for early August.

A very satisfying ending to a pleasant evening.

# 13

## C IS FOR SUNNY

Life at Myers was never one long party. There were highs. And then something would come by and pull you down. But the latter was becoming relatively infrequent.

I met Dinesh Parpia, again referred to me by Peggy. 'The man is loaded,' she told me, 'let's see you go grab him.' She was right. He was loaded. He started by demonstrating it right away, showing me his bank statements and copies of deposit receipts with several Indian banks. With each of these, he'd delve into its history—how they begged him to open the account, how well they take care of him and how they give him 'free gifts'. After some time, I got tired of nodding my head and pretending to be interested.

He said he wanted an alternative to deposits. 'What is 2, 3 or 4 per cent?' he asked, 'It doesn't even cover inflation.' I liked that line. It is always a good cue to sell investments. But it was easier said than done though, because he found a problem with every suggestion. He didn't want equities because they were too volatile. He didn't want bonds because interest rates could go up and that would bring down bond prices. He didn't want money market because interest rates could go down and that would bring down his yield. He didn't like gold because it had just crashed sharply from over 700 an ounce to below 600. He didn't want real estate because it had moved up sharply. He concluded by saying 'Let us wait and see.' He also asked me if my company could give him any 'free gifts'.It was not one of my better mornings.

I had scarcely reached office when Peggy, ever smiling, breezed across enthusiastically waving a piece of paper. 'Honey, would you like to meet this guy?'

I think she deduced from my face that I would rather not. 'Don't let a bad meeting get you down, sweetheart,' she said. It was almost as if she could read my mind. 'Don't forget, clients are assets.'

'They are also *asses*,' I said petulantly, but taking the paper from her all the same. It read 'Bharat Saxena' and it had his contact number. 'He's a senior executive with a bank and has been in the Gulf for a long time. He sounded very nice over the phone. Go for it, Jack, and let's see that charming smile of yours.'

I knew I was being childish and immature in expecting every meeting to bring in business. Kitch, I knew, had met twice the number of prospects I had over the last three months and what's more, had done it without a complaint. So, I got down to it. Saxena was a youngish looking fellow, must surely be older than he looked, I thought. He worked with a local UAE-based bank and seemed to know quite a bit about Myers York, so I could do away with the boring introduction sequence.

He said that he had about USD 400K to spare immediately and that he would be comfortable topping it up to a million. We started off speaking in English, but towards the latter stages of the meeting he switched over to Hindi and so did I. He seemed to be a rather jovial sort of guy. He had to take a couple of phone calls in between which were packed with humour and wisecracks that spilled on to our conversation as well. He told me about how his forays into equity usually ended in disaster as his 'speculative quick buys' invariably ended as 'long-term investments' because the price tanked as soon as he bought them. But he had made a pile on Dubai's real estate. Rather unusually, he spoke as willingly, openly and happily about both the losses and the profits he had made. Most investors, I have found, tend to either hide their losses while discussing it with others. If at all it comes up, it does with a sense of either anger, or grievance.

I told him about our equity ideas, about our technical charts, about Raj's fundamental analysis and about Ralph. He listened in all seriousness and then smiled. 'It all sounds good, but we also need *this*,' he said, drawing an imaginary line across his forehead.

I liked the fellow. He was upfront, communicative and ready to take quick decisions. Even better, if he could accept sharp falls in share prices as *kismet*, what more could an advisor ask for! I was buoyant once more.

Later that week, Kapoor and I were set for our first trip together. He had spoken to one of his closest friends, a Sikh whose family lived in Kuwait, which was just an hour's flight from Dubai.

I suppose I must have subconsciously expected Kuwait to be like Muscat, because I was a bit disappointed. It didn't have the charm of Muscat, nor did it have the new and glossy feel of Dubai. It was just a regular, Middle Eastern city state, its more recent history shaped firstly by the discovery of oil and subsequent to that by the invasion by Iraq. In the evening, we drove around the city for an hour or two, seeing the 'sights', the most prominent of which was a unique and high structure, which the driver told me was a water tank with a restaurant on it. I couldn't quite figure that out, but I let it pass.

Later, we left for Satwinder Singh Bali's house for dinner. It was quite obvious that Kapoor knew the family very well. They were all over him, the man, the wife, the kids. No one called Mr Singh by his real name. He was 'Sunny' to one and all, his wife Parminder Kaur, was 'Pammi'. There were a couple of other families too and the first half-hour or so was spent in excited Punjabi chatter, exuberant handshakes, enthusiastic hugs, thumping of backs and peals of loud laughter. It was rather a long time to spend standing silently on one side, waiting for an introduction. Finally it came and for a very brief while, I was the centre of attraction. It lasted only a minute or two, though. 'Oye, brother, will you have some beer sheer?' Mr Singh asked me, 'or will you prefer some lassi vassi?' I settled for the latter. It would be a shame to come to a Punjabi house and not have their lassi. 'Pammi ji!' he shouted, his voice comfortably carrying through two or three rooms. 'Manjit, oye!' he shouted, '*Ik glass lassi laavin*! Patiala peg!'

Soon they were back to talking in Punjabi—of which I could follow little—recalling jokes of the past, trading gossip about common friends and asking about their whereabouts. Meanwhile, I sat with a fixed, dazed smile on my face, licking my lassi-coated lips from time to time.

Only once, when the topic of discussion had switched to cricket, I could faintly make out what they were saying. I tried to join in the discussion, but my voice was drowned in a roar of other excited remarks. I shut up and slipped into a cocoon of self-pity. I wished I had asked for beer instead. That way, I could have gone on for some time. How much lassi can one drink?

Soon we were all seated at a huge dining table, the biggest I have ever seen. It could seat about twenty, I think, and we were about sixteen, including the kids. I managed to sit towards one end along with the kids. I had no wish to be at the centre of any unintelligible cacophony. Two hours of it had made be tired and bored. They didn't seem to mind. Sunny had started some story and had the rest of the group in splits. I focused on the food and made small talk with the kids. My hosts had three children. There were another couple of kids from the other families.

The eldest Singh kid, a plump, pleasant-faced girl, was apparently interested in quizzing. I asked her if she would like me to test her with some quiz questions. The children got excited and a couple of them even clapped. I heaved a sigh of relief. Finally, I was on familiar territory.

I started throwing a few at her. I needed to pitch it just right, always the trickiest part of being a quiz-master. I searched my memory for questions that could suit eight to twelve-year-old kids. 'Who lives in 10 Downing Street in London?' Two of them got that right. Ha! 'Which vitamin is commonly produced in the body by sunlight?' Hmmm. Not sure. Multiple suggestions were C, A and B in that order. Not so good. 'Who is the President of India?' Chorus of A.P.J. Abdul Kalam! Excitement in the air!

But now, I had a problem. The kids were all keyed up for the next one, but unfortunately for me, so were the adults. I realized that, suddenly, the attention of the entire group was focused on our little game. The only time I had felt more conspicuous was at the Muscat airport when I rushed out of the ladies' restroom and felt the eyes of the entire airport on me. I'm the sort of chap who can carry himself off pretty well in a small group of say up to three or four, but get intimidated by a large group. Nevertheless, I carried on bravely, speaking a little softer now in the hope that those at the other end of the table wouldn't hear too well and consequently lose interest. 'Er . . . what do the initials A.P.J. stand for?' No one knew, none of the sixteen. I mumbled the answer to the kids. I smiled and started eating with some vigour as if to convey that the quiz was over. Mild chattering started again at the table.

'Okay, everyone, *silence*!' roared Sunny Singh from the head of the table. 'Next question!' Everyone looked expectantly at me. I hastily swallowed a piece of butter chicken. There was no way I could back out now, so I valiantly ploughed ahead. 'Hmm . . . er, what is the capital of Australia?' I asked.

The younger kids looked at each other and then at the twelve-year-old, who pretended to think deeply. 'Okay!' shouted Mr Singh again, now obviously considering himself a central figure in this whole thing. 'Okay, everybody, I give *clue*! Clue number one!' he screamed, excitedly. 'It starts with S!'

I stared at him appalled. S! What on earth did he think the capital was? Everyone was looking eagerly at the kids. I was in a quandary. How was I supposed to get out of this spot, now?

'Er . . . Sunny ji, it starts with C,' I told him.

'C?' he asked, incredulously. 'Not S? Okay, children. Don't know answer? I give clue number two. C-I,' he announced. 'Capital is starting with C-I!'

I closed my eyes and said a silent prayer. I wished I had concentrated on the delicious food, instead of getting into this tangle.

Kapoor stepped in, possibly with the intention of putting me out of my misery. 'Jai bhai, I think it begins with S,' he said confidently. 'S-I-D-N-E-Y.'

I stared at him in horror. 'That city is actually spelt S-Y-D-N-E-Y, Kapoor saheb,' I proffered. 'But that is not the capital. The capital city is *Canberra*.'

There was silence, a disbelieving hush. 'Kan bera?' said Mr Singh 'Oye, I never heard of it, *ji*. How can it be capital?' Most people seemed to agree with him. I think only Kapoor was willing to give me the benefit of doubt. There was some murmuring. One of the ladies said in Punjabi, 'It is definitely Sydney.' Someone else said, 'Or it may be Melbourne.' I pretended not to hear, as I—grim-faced and red-eared—chomped on my rice and rajma. Not that it mattered because shortly before we left, the elder girl brought out a book with a list of all capital cities and announced loudly that I was right.

More importantly, Sunny and Pammi Singh thanked me for coming over and signed the account-opening forms. Another biggie, I knew. Kapoor must have done a good bit of preliminary on the guy, I thought. Else, why would he sign the forms without even asking me a word about the company or about our capabilities? I was feeling good. Very good. It was worth it, I thought. The time, the trip, the quiz, everything.

Mr Singh had the last word, though. 'I'm giving you account. But remember,' he said raising his index finger in mock seriousness, 'Capital of Australia is Sydney, not that *Kandoora*.'

# 14

## KITCH ROCKS THE FAR EAST

The following week, I told Peggy and Rebecca about the encounter with the Singhs over lunch. I had taken them out for a Gujarati buffet lunch at Bur Dubai, at a restaurant called Rangoli. Peggy rolled with laughter. Indians, she concluded, lead much more interesting lives than others do.

Rebecca had a question. 'Why didn't you understand what they spoke? Was it not Indian?' she asked.

'It was,' I replied, 'It was Punjabi.'

'Isn't that Indian?' she wanted to know. So, I proceeded to give her a lesson on India and how there were fourteen major Indian languages, several hundred dialects and how little some of them had in common.

They loved the lunch. 'So *much* flavour,' Peggy said, 'and fortunately, *not* spicy.' I knew she was referring to an earlier occasion, where I had made her taste *pani puri* done my style. By the time she had popped the second one into her mouth, there were definitely tears in her eyes and I could almost see smoke coming out of her ears. She didn't want to spit it out, she didn't dare swallow it and she just stood there, pink and watery, wringing her hands helplessly. Finally, I made her swallow it and then eat up some yoghurt to cool it down.

Back in office, I was at my desk checking out my earnings in the previous week. We had a very up-to-date system. You could check on a daily basis what revenues you had generated the previous day and what your personal earnings were likely to be. This being my first year, there were added incentives that had been promised for bringing in assets. Meanwhile, Melissa walked up and slid into her seat. She looked a little different. Then I realized she had straightened and blow-dried her hair. I didn't think it suited her. She had also worn a rather colourful outfit, which was unusual for her. I knew she'd have something to say because she and the others had just got back after their Hong Kong trip.

'You look very pretty,' I lied. She seemed to be expecting a compliment and I didn't want to disappoint her.

'Thank you!' she said, even before I had finished my sentence, using that high-pitched voice that girls use when they have received the compliment they feel is due and feel shy about it.I refrained on purpose from asking her about the trip. I wondered how long it would be before some gossip would come my way. It took all of about twenty seconds.

'Looks like the stud's not turned up yet,' she remarked, tilting her head towards Ahmed's desk. 'Perhaps he is resting, after all the action.'

'Ahmed?' I enquired, curiously. It was all the cue she needed.

She tightened her lips and nodded, looking smug. 'Our man had arranged with the representative of the fund manager for entertainment at Macau and I don't mean just a massage and gambling. Can you believe it?' She seemed shocked yet pleased, in a way. 'He was boasting to us that he always carried a condom in his wallet. That man is something else,' she said, with a slight shudder.

'What about Kitch?' I asked, my own appetite for information now nicely whetted. 'What did he do?'

'Poor Kitch completely lost it,' she said. 'He came to my room mewing pitifully, in a state of paranoia. If I hadn't taken charge, he'd have turned into a nervous wreck. He's quite a baby. Here he is,' she added, lowering her voice to a whisper, 'the big chief himself—I'm surprised he's not beating his chest. Watch his swagger!'

As Ahmed came in, he took a detour towards me. '*Yaar*, your friend Kitch' he said, 'Just two days with me and I have turned him into a real man.' He walked away, with a proud smirk.

I stared at Melissa, hungry for more information, but she started making some client calls, leaving me hanging in the middle of nowhere. I wanted specifics, not just hints. I called Kitch only to find out that he was feeling the after-effects of travelling and had decided to stay at home. I promptly landed up at his place that evening to put the pieces together and get the full picture.

Apparently, the so-called seminar itself in Hong Kong was just a two-hour presentation. After that, they arranged for all the participants, about sixty of them, to be ferried to Macau, a nearby island formerly owned by the Portuguese and now a part of China.

Once there, the 'programme' basically involved a couple of bar sessions, various forms of gambling, a spa session with massage and beauty treatment and a cabaret of sorts. For the more enterprising men, the hosts had arranged for an evening out at a less formal place for a few drinks and a slightly rowdy late evening out, which Kitch had apparently chickened out of. But Ahmed had apparently asked one of the host's representatives to send a lady to Kitch's room and had told him to expect a knock on his door.

'I thought he was only joking, machan! He actually *sent* someone. The man is mad.' When Kitch looked through the peephole and saw a young lady at the scheduled time, he promptly called Ahmed, who laughed and told him to open the door. Kitch, unsure of what to do, took another look through the glass, just as the young lady, in a moment of whimsical fancy pouted and thrust her bright red lips forward towards the peephole. To an already nervous Kitch, it appeared like a pair of giant lips distending from her face and threatening to engulf him.

He retreated, palpitating, and remained in the far corner of the room, trying not to breathe. A few minutes later, after ensuring that the coast was clear, he went and took refuge in Melissa's room. ('mewing pitifully', as Melissa put it.)

'But weren't you telling me the other day that we guys don't have half the fun that westerners do?' I asked, not able to resist rubbing it in a bit.

'Not like this, *da*,' he said. 'Not a stranger, I want someone I know, like . . .' he trailed off.

'Like who?' I asked, trying to keep it casual. He just shrugged his shoulders.

Later that week, I had been invited to Harsh and Joi's house for dinner. I'd been called over at 8 p.m. so of course, I went at 9.30, fashionably late, Dubai style. We had realized that in Dubai if you are punctual for your dinner appointment, chances are that you will meet your hostess in a house coat and the house in the process of being cleaned.

So I went by 9.30 and the others were just beginning to come in. There were three or four families, including some family friends, who also happened to be business associates. It turned out to be a rather big evening for bank bashing. The American guest told the group how his bank in America had no issues when he remitted money from his business account from Saudi Arabia to the USA, but would not allow him to have funds transferred from the US to Saudi, unless he visited his US branch in person. The Dutch businessman complained that when he drew dollar cash from his dollar account in Dubai, he was debited with 'charges in lieu of commission'. Someone else referred to banks as money-making machines. Another guy spoke about how awful the phone banking system was, another about how his bank sent him a New Year diary in June. They were referring to retail banking for the most part and not private banking, but nevertheless I squirmed in my sofa for a goodish part of the evening, tried to switch off and think about the next week's programme.

Kapoor and I would be making a visit to Kenya—my first trip to the African continent. He was going to introduce me to Dilip Kochar, whom he had known for over ten years. I was happy to get away from the summer heat of Dubai. It was now way above 40 degrees C. It smote you like a blow as you stepped out of your air-conditioned offices and seared through you in a most unforgiving way. This wasn't the hottest yet, I was told. In August, the temperatures would kiss 50 degrees. In contrast, Kenya, being in the southern hemisphere, would be experiencing winter, something I really looked forward to. Kapoor had asked me to bring along some warm clothing, so I had carefully packed that. Not that torn, old sweater of mine, I was now the owner of two new ones that I had picked up in NY ...

Just a day before the Kenya trip came some good news for me. I had finally obtained my UAE driving licence. It was my fourth attempt. For my first try some five months ago, I had turned up for the test in jeans and a T-shirt. When I flunked it, I had received unsolicited advice from several friends, well-wishers and acquaintances. Taking some of that tactical wisdom, I went to take my second, fully suited. I was told the inspectors treat you with more respect and kindness if you are well dressed. Obviously, it didn't work for me. For the third attempt, I experimented with an in-between approach—just a tie, no jacket—with the same result. For the fourth, I had reverted to my jeans and T-shirt.

Buoyed by my 'Sunny' success (USD 7,29,970 had landed in his account a few days ago), I decided to buy a Lexus. While in India, I always had a fascination for a Merc, but when I test drove this one, I decided on an impulse to buy it. So, Lexus it was, that weekend. I happened to tell my client Saxena about my getting the licence and he asked me to let him know before buying the vehicle. He said he knew senior people in almost all the car agencies and could get me a good price. He did just that and even arranged for a 'free' first year insurance. He seemed a very helpful sort of guy. My first 'outing' in the car was to Saxena's house that night. He had called me home for dinner, where he had arranged a musical night. The next morning, still beaming with pride over my new car, I drove some of our colleagues over to Planet Hollywood near Wafi's for brunch.

# 15

## JAMBO!

At the Dubai duty free, I picked up a ticket at the millionaire promotion stall. This was a raffle draw in which one out of every 5,000 ticket owners, tickets at USD 280 each, gets a million dollars. Who knows, I thought to myself, this could well be my lucky phase. Only a few days ago, Sunny Singh had sent in another USD 5 million into his account, sending ripples through the office. Jack Patel was making his presence felt, I could kind of sense it. Coming on top of Abu Jaffer's account just a month or two ago, it definitely set my name apart as a man who would bear watching.

'Choose one,' the lady said, pushing a box of some twenty tickets in front of me. I picked up the very first one. Then I changed my mind, put it back, substituting it with one from somewhere in the middle.

'This one,' I said confidently, carefully filling in my contact details and handing it over.

Dubai, I was beginning to realize, was like Mumbai in many ways. It was a city of dreams. People came here from all over the world, with little except hope in their hearts. Every year, there were more coming in. Dubai's population was growing at a rate of over 10 per cent a year and so was its economy, primarily on the strength of construction, trade and tourism.

With the golden-coloured millionaire ticket safely tucked away in my new stylish tote bag, I boarded the flight. To the land of the wild, I told myself. The continent of bushes, hunters and animals.

In my hand, I held a book of Shakespearean quotes. After all, a 'bard' in hand is worth two in the bush. Kapoor told me he had picked up some gifts for the prospects' families. If you keep prospects' wives happy, he told me, business can never be far away.

We landed at Nairobi's Jomo Kenyatta airport.

*Jambo*! We were greeted by the airport staff as we stepped out. *Karibuni Kenya*! Jambo was Swahili for 'Hello' and I was hear it several times thereafter.

I passed through the airport, looking with interest at the duty free shops selling curios, books, nuts, chocolates and small wooden sculptures—giraffes, rhinos, elephants, tribal warriors. There were large colourful advertising hoardings with lovely pictures of wildlife. I was beginning to get excited. There was something different about this place. Most people around seemed to be Africans, but there seemed to be quite a few from the Indian subcontinent. There were several westerners as well, some of them wearing khaki and military green shorts and shirt, with rucksacks on their backs and cameras slung over their shoulders. I also saw a large group of Japanese tourists.

'These *gora*s (whites) are crazy about wildlife,' Kapoor told me. 'They hold their cameras and run all over the place taking pictures. It is so silly!' I wondered why he found it silly, but decided to let it pass.

Outside the airport, we looked closely at the placards being waved. But none of those names were ours. 'It is better to wait,' Kapoor told me. 'One has to be extra careful with security in Africa. I take only known drivers. But where on *earth* is this fellow?'

Five minutes later, a tall man walked lazily across, grinning from ear to ear. 'Ah, Mr Kapoor!' he said. 'How are you?'

'Daniel, where were you?' Kapoor asked, frowning instead, 'We have been waiting ten minutes!'

'Ah!' said the man, with the confidence, 'I went to have tea.'

'This is the way it is here,' Kapoor told me, in a loud complaining voice. 'Everything is very relaxed.' Daniel grinned again. He seemed to be one of those jolly, unruffled types.

We had barely got out of the airport area when I saw fields of green on both sides. I inhaled deeply. The windows were raised, so I may have just imagined the fresh, uncontaminated oxygen that seemed to fill my lungs. Suddenly, in front of us, I saw a whole herd of elephants. *Out there in the wild*. Just minutes from the airport. What a country, I thought. This was the way to live! They were elephants, only they were made of tin. Later during the trip, I found there was a Kenya-based sculptor who worked on steel and iron scrap. The government had commissioned him to 'beautify' the city with elephant sculptures at some of the city's roundabouts. Pretty soon, caught in a traffic jam with buildings all around me, hawkers displaying their wares and a beggar or two pounding the window, I realized Nairobi was just like any other city. The weather, however, was cool and pleasant, in complete contrast to the sizzling Dubai heat.

We stayed at a hotel right in the city centre, overlooking a large park. It was a little difficult getting used to the idea of so many people around you who looked very different from what one is used to. Hair, skin colour, facial features, language, even the English accent. It was quite fascinating in a sense. I was pleasantly surprised to find that a lot of people did speak English, if not very fluently. Kapoor had told me to be careful with my belongings. There were also warnings here and there that I found a little disconcerting. I found myself walking with my hands rather close to my pockets.

We relaxed for a couple of hours at the hotel and then set off to meet Kochar at his office. On the way, Kapoor told me that he was an extremely nice and helpful person. But, he added, he had become, over the years, a bit of an alcoholic, much to his family's chagrin. They had been planning to send him to a rehabilitation centre in London. Kapoor wasn't sure if that had already been done.

From what we observed a minute or two later, it had either not been done or it hadn't been successful. Even as we entered Kochar's office, the first thing I saw was a smart little hip-flask on his desk. I recalled a quote from the book that I had read on the flight. 'Drunk several times a day if not many days entirely drunk.'

He looked sober enough. He was dressed in a safari suit, displaying a hairy chest and all. Behind him was a large calendar which carried a picture of a tall and lissome Bollywood starlet. She was wearing a pout and little else. Her right index finger was on her lower lip and her left thumb tucked into her bikini at the waist. Dilip Kochar himself was quite the opposite. He was a short, bulging man. He was partly bald, which he had tried—with limited success—to hide, by brushing hair from the back of his head down to his forehead. On his chubby fingers, he sported several rings, on his wrist a copper bangle and on his face a large smile, which he retained almost all the time.

'What is this!' Kapoor rebuked him, in his typical forthright way. 'Still not stopped this habit?' Kochar switched instantly from smiles to seriousness. 'Completely under control, Kapoor saheb,' he said with almost exaggerated seriousness. 'Completely under control.' He looked at me beseechingly, as if seeking support. He pointed to the flask and said 'Only for time pass, you understand? Just for time pass.'

He was an entertaining, even amusing, talker and had me grinning frequently. He would keep poking fun of everything and everyone, including himself. He told me he was fed up with his existing bank and was eager to change. My ears perked up. Some banks he said, were incompetent, others were expensive. His bank, he said, was both. He said they specialized in recruiting people who were slow on the uptake and who were socialists. They believed that the customer's wealth was like their own and liberally helped themselves under the pretext of various charges.

The long and short of it was that he enthusiastically signed the forms and also thrust into my hands a copy of a recent statement from his bank. He insisted on first taking us out for 'bitings' and then home for dinner. This was the first of many times that I have come across the word 'biting', commonly used among Indians in East Africa as a synonym for snacks. '*Biting*' is both a noun and a verb, out here. As we sat at our tables in an Indian restaurant contemplating what kind of biting we should be biting into, Kochar complained to me, tongue in cheek, that Kapoor pretended to be a teetotaler only when he was with him. Otherwise, he claimed, he drank like a fish, even worse than him. Kapoor, refusing to be drawn into any debate, maintained his stoic calm and continued to sip his passionfruit juice with quiet dignity.

Our prospect for the next day was Dr Chimanbhai Patel, a very cultured, soft-spoken and polished gentleman, an accomplished and very well-to-do doctor, who had worked in the UK for over three decades and had recently started a charitable hospital just off Nairobi, in memory of his late father. He was in his early fifties, small-built, almost frail, but his eyes still shone with the enthusiasm of a five-year-old. Impeccably dressed in a sparkling white shirt buttoned at the wrist and in light grey trousers with a knife-like crease, he fussed over us like a mother, offering first water and then juice, which he insisted on making himself. A refreshing new concoction he said it was—the juice of sweet melon mixed with mint and lemon with just a dash of tabasco sauce. He seemed an eminently likeable man, in complete contrast to his son, whom we also met.

Hitesh Patel, the son, was rude, arrogant and was dressed in jeans that threatened to slip off at any moment. He wore a shiny steel chain around his neck, a tattoo on his arm and two rings on his left ear—one on the lobe and one higher up. His face sported a look that clearly conveyed boredom or perhaps his contempt for us. As his father introduced him to me he extended a limp, distracted hand. As if that was too much effort, he waved Kapoor's hand away. Having condescended to spend a minute or two with us, he left abruptly, leaving his father to apologize for him. Hitesh was apparently twenty, a college dropout, who spent most of his time hanging out with like-minded friends. Dr Patel told us that he had aspired for his son to be a doctor, but he had showed no inclination at all. 'He is a good boy,' he told us, without much conviction, 'but today's youngsters are different.' As an afterthought, he added, 'Perhaps he has got into bad company.' He seemed to be soliloquizing. His eyes suddenly clouded over, as he looked up at Kapoor. Then, he said very softly, in a voice packed with pain, 'How I wish my son was like Jai bhai here. I would give up all my awards and citations if only it could help Hitesh settle down in life.' I felt sorry for the doctor. I wished I could comfort him somehow, but didn't know how.

'It is just a passing phase, Doctor saheb,' Kapoor told him. Kapoor never seemed to be at a loss for words and they always seemed to carry conviction. 'Hitesh carries your genes and Ushaben's. He can't go wrong. Don't worry about it.'

Two successes—two new accounts in two days and I could have asked for nothing more. Left to myself, I would have stayed back an additional day or two and possibly checked out the Masai Mara. It was that time of the year when a large-scale migration of animals takes place from Kenya into the Serengeti region in Tanzania. But Kapoor, I discovered, was not an animal lover unless you presented it in the form of a kebab or a steak. He quickly curbed my enthusiasm. 'There's nothing in it,' he opined. 'If you have seen one buffalo, you have seen them all,' he said. 'What is the point in watching buffalos moving here and there, whether it is in Kenya or anywhere else? I have seen enough buffalos on our farms in Punjab. All this is just media hype,' he ridiculed. 'Everybody falls for it, especially these silly, camera-toting goras. Nowadays, people are more concerned about animals than humans.'

So, I dumped all thoughts of four-legged creatures and focused on two-legged ones on the flight back to Dubai. I thought of Melissa, Kitch and Ahmed. Of Peggy. Of Cyrus, Rachel and John. Of Ramzi and his Porsche car. Kitch called me that morning to tell me that he had got his licence and had bought a Toyota Camry. Ramzi had apparently mocked Kitch on his selection of a car. 'You have to think like a private banker, to become one,' he had apparently told Kitch. 'I have acquired more assets in six months than he has in over a year,' Kitch told me, still brimming with anger. 'I'll show that bugger who is a private banker and who is not!'

Meanwhile, Kochar's account got opened. The process was distinctly and unusually smooth. It was obvious that the bigger the FA, the more amenable the Ops and compliance team were. It was really a measure of strength. If the FA was new or had minimal assets, he could get bullied by the back-office. If the FA was a star or one in the making, he could turn the heat on.

While completing Kochar's documentation, I had realized that in all the time I had spent with him, I hadn't even found out what his business was. I called Kapoor to check. 'Oh, he makes Moto Moto,' he said.

'He makes *what?*'

'Moto Moto,' he replied. 'Chips, you know. "Moto" means "hot" in Swahili. He is the largest manufacturer of ready-to-fry potato chips in Kenya. The brand name is Moto Moto. Didn't you notice he had many chips packets on his table?' I had, but I had assumed, not unreasonably, that those went with that little flask that he had placed there.

So as part of the account documentation, I wrote a little story built around Kapoor's information. Back-office liked stories. They loved websites even better, but if that was not available, stories with figures and interesting titbits were the next best thing. KYC or 'Know Your Customer' documentation had been growing in importance since 9/11. Recently, an account of Kitch's had got rejected. It happened to be that of the son of the President of a small West African country. Kitch had asked the client to fill up a page which included 'Source of Income'. In that form, the young man had written, 'My father rules the country.' Both Ops and the compliance team dropped it like a *moto* potato! Subsequently, it got cleared after Kitch managed to establish that the son operated some businesses independently of his father and got the son to re-do the form.

I thought also of Kitty and her wedding, which was due in the next couple of weeks. I had been in regular touch with her and my mum over the last few weeks and all arrangements had been made. I was looking to forward to the occasion. So far, all marriages I had attended had just been an occasion to have fun, an excuse for unbridled merrymaking. But this would be different. It was Kitty's wedding. My parents were as apprehensive as they were excited. I felt a sense of responsibility.

I remembered my high school time, when a friend and I had once, on a whim, attended the wedding dinner of some perfect strangers. The groom's side had thought we were invitees of the bride and vice versa. It was one of the more memorable dinners of those days and, I think, one of my first experiences in eating off a plantain leaf, Madras style.

# 16

## KITTY TIES THE KNOT

The following week was a hectic one for me. There was plenty of spare cash in my clients' portfolios now. More money had come in from Harsh, Jaffer, Lalwani and Sunny. Jaffer's uncle had also opened an account a couple of weeks earlier and had funded it with a couple of million. Saxena and Dr Chimanbhai had sent in USD 0.5 million each. Kochar was in the process of transferring his entire holdings of cash and securities from his bank.

The number of trades I was doing was increasing now—there were at least nine to ten trades a day, often more—and I was on the phone quite a lot, sometimes right until midnight, Dubai time, which is when the US markets closed. Occasionally, if I got lucky with my currency positions, the number of trades used to be many more. On one particular day, when I was trading on the Euro for Harsh, Lalwani and Jaffer, I was able to get in and out of that currency four times, making each time, a profit of thousands of dollars. Twenty-four trades just on one currency for these three and there were another fifteen trades that day. That night I went to bed feeling like a king. *Jack Patel, Financial Advisor to the World*! The financial universe was like putty in my hands. I felt I could achieve anything.

The June scoreboard saw me move just a little further up on the list. Up one spot. I still had my off days, like when I met this weasel-like creature in Mushrif Bazaar in Deira, Dubai. He listened to my marketing spiel—by now nicely polished and perfected, *à la*

Saunders—in a distracted kind of way and when I was done, he told me he preferred to deal with girls. If we had any relationship managers who were girls, he told me, he wouldn't mind meeting them. I left, fuming. Kitch, too, had had his share of unpleasant or unhappy experiences, but I found he had more patience than I did. I was possibly a better communicator of financial information, but I think he had the better temperament for this business. He kept his balance and didn't test the highs and the lows on a daily basis.

Meanwhile, I left for Chennai a little ahead of schedule. My mother was getting a bit nervous and Kitty wanted me to be around for a few days before the festivities. Any marriage in India, apart from being an event of joy, also inevitably involves several other emotions. Parents worry about meeting expectations of their *samdhi*s, about marriage expenses or about how their daughter will be treated by her in-laws. About whether their son will still remain devoted to them after his marriage. Or will the bride prove to be the 'evil one' and take their precious son away from them? About how much to spend, about where and when to have the function. About horoscopes, priests, auspicious dates, hours and minutes. These important aspects apart, there were a hundred minor details to be looked into.

The fact that our families belonged to different cultures and communities complicated matters a bit. We followed different rituals and customs. The food we served was different. The clothes worn were different. Each of these issues had been thrashed out over the last few weeks between the two families.

My parents had been lucky in managing to find venues reasonably close to one another and all within a twenty-minute drive from home. That made commuting easy. The wedding itself was at Raghavendra Kalyana Mantapam, which was a twenty-minute drive from home. The sangeet function, which is an evening of music and dance, was at the banquet hall of the Chola Sheraton, which is within easy walking distance from home. Some of our guests stayed here and some were put up at Hotel Maris and Woodlands, both nearby.

After some preliminary religious ceremonies, we had the mehndi (henna) function. Halfway through this ceremony, I was very pleasantly surprised to see a lehnga-choli-clad Peggy and Rachel suddenly make their appearance, giggling and laughing at the expression on my face. I was not expecting them at all! They hadn't given me any indication at all when I had invited them and had managed to keep their visit a secret. Suddenly, the two of them moved apart and Kitch showed up from behind them, wearing a maroon and grey churidar kurta. I was thrilled to bits to see them there.

Two days before the actual wedding ceremonies were the relatively lightweight events, ones that the youngsters from both families particularly looked forward to. The most important among these was the sangeet, a function of music and dance, one that is generally arranged by the younger lot. Among Gujaratis, usually, this would consist of the graceful and colourful garba by the women, followed by the dandiya raas, a dance where men and women, move around in an elliptical pattern, while simultaneously dancing lightly and twirling the colourful sticks that they hold in their hands. The music carries a rhythmic beat and the participants dance to it, tapping their sticks against those of the dancers next to them.

Most of us Gujaratis have grown up on a healthy diet of the dandiya raas and it comes very naturally to us. As a result, we sometimes make the mistake of assuming that everyone would find it as simple as it looks. We forced Shree, his sister and a few other members of his family into joining us. While his sister put up a pretty good show, the others ended up tying themselves into knots and stopping the flow of the dance. It came as a bit of a shock when we saw some of them clumsily tread the floor and we made no effort to stop them when they withdrew after a minute or two. Poor Shree himself, who had apparently never danced before—in any kind or form—sort of froze after attempting a couple of movements. He could either move or tap, he just couldn't do both and the subsequent dancers ended up tripping and falling over him as he remained rooted to the spot.

Kitch—who himself is a total non-starter at any type of dance—and I stared in wonder. 'The poor chap is as bad as I am,' said Kitch. 'He's got two left feet.'

'And they're both wooden,' I added in a quiet undertone. 'Poor Kitty'.

Kitch empathized completely with Shree. 'There will be no dancing at my wedding!' he declared.

Rachel and Peggy on the other hand, were completely at ease. Rachel, of course, I would have expected to be. I had seen her dance before at Myers' get-togethers. But Peggy was the surprise package. All rhythm and grace, she danced like a pro, as if she'd been doing it all her life. She looked gorgeous—tall and resplendent in her red and gold attire. I stared in wonder at her as she waltzed past, staring at her smiling face, her flowing hair, her slender waist and long legs. In her formal clothes, I had never realized Peggy looked this sexy.

Suddenly, a voice spoke. 'C'mon, Jack! That's your *boss!*'

It was my inner voice, I turned my head away in deference to it.

Red, green, cream, orange ... the place seemed aglow with colour. A rather attractive, light-eyed lady caught my attention. From certain angles, she seemed to be all cleavage. I wasn't exactly staring at her, but the cleavage seemed to be thrusting itself on my retina. She was probably in her thirties and her dance was calculated to attract eyeballs. I wondered who she was.

Again I heard a voice. 'That is Sushmaben! I know the family.' I started violently. This time, though, it wasn't my inner voice. It was the voice of Kapoor. 'They were in Kenya earlier,' he continued. 'Now, they've moved to Tanzania. I have told her husband Kirit Desai that we will meet them next month.'

Later, I met with both Kirit and Sushma Desai. The lady had a rather husky voice that didn't seem to go with her feminine features and it was disconcerting initially. She was very friendly and pleasant to talk to and made a point of stressing their invitation. Her husband was a male version of Melissa, but not as interesting, or likeable. Bird-like face, two front teeth sticking out like a beak, he was full of nervous energy, but limited in thought and action to just one thing. Making money. He could speak of nothing else. 'What's new?' he asked us. 'Any new investment opportunity?' In the first five minutes that he spent with me, he used the word 'opportunity' about four times and the word 'money' about twice that.

Shree, I must say, made up for his dancing (or the lack of it) with his singing. The dandiya dance programme was followed by a stage-show of sorts, where various members of the family took turns to perform to the tune of several Bollywood hit songs. Though I say so myself, I must report that I put up a rather good show along with my cousins, Sonal and Jaymin. We danced to the tune of *Beedi jalai le*, a foot-stomping number and the current rage. Kitty had been planning to do this one herself, but Dad put his foot down. He didn't want the bride dancing on the stage to any suggestive lyrics. So, Sonal took her place and did a neat job. Earlier, Sonal had paired up with Kitty to do the *Dola re* song from the film *Devdas*. They received a standing ovation for this one. Following these and the subsequent medley put together by some other cousins and close friends, young Shree took the mike and sang two songs for Kitty.

He was quite awesome and held the audience spellbound. I didn't realize till then what a good voice he had. I looked at Kitty while he was in full flow and was in time to capture on video a nauseatingly sweet look of pride on her face—which could be a great tool for blackmail, for all times to come.

For our family, who had organized the wedding, it hadn't been easy, deciding on what ceremonies to have, considering that we were dealing with two different communities. Finally, we had agreed to have a mixed—Gujarati, Iyengar—style wedding.

It wasn't without problems though, some of them quite comical. Shree's mother wanted his clothes to be traditional Iyengar, which is basically a silk véshti, worn in a traditional style and an angavastram, which is draped over the shoulder. It is in contrast to what a Gujarati groom would have worn—a sherwani and churidar.

The typical Gujarati groom would, on the evening of the wedding day, come to the mantap, astride a horse, in a ceremony called varghodo, one in a continuing and somewhat exhausting series of ceremonies over three days. We had to leave out or rather modify this one, because it surely wouldn't do for the groom to ride a horse wearing a véshti. One wouldn't want the groom to be arrested for indecent exposure in public. Besides, the idea of riding a horse seemed to send a chill down Shree's spine. Actually, it's not really a *ride*, it's just a few minutes of remaining astride the animal, as the horse keeper slowly leads the horse to the entrance. But to listen to the prospective groom talk about it, you'd think he was being pushed into suddenly competing in the Derby, without any training or proper attire. So we switched to a convertible car instead and Shree sat in it, wearing a Western suit and a look of embarrassment. In front of him, a band clad in red and yellow, belted out Hindi and Tamil film hits. The varghodo turned into a vargaado as someone put it.

In the ultimate analysis, the whole affair turned out to be a mish-mash of differing cultures, keeping parents and elders from both sides a little apprehensive and constantly on their toes, but it was good fun for the other more dispassionate observers, family members and guests.

For lunch and dinner, we had one version of the meal prepared without onion and garlic and served on a separate table, because on both sides of the family, there were elders who preferred their food this way. That apart, what was primarily a Gujarati meal was interspersed and made more interesting by a few Iyengar items like a sweet called ashada varusal, which is made of rice, milk and jaggery. From time to time guests were offered tea, coffee, tender coconut water and almond-flavoured milk. At lunch, an elderly gentleman possibly from Shree's family came and plonked himself between Peggy and me, on the chair meant for Rachel. I smiled politely at him, but it kind of backfired, because using that as an excuse, he started talking non-stop and collared the conversation for the next ten minutes discussing politics in Tamil Nadu.

Towards the end of the meal, when he found out I lived in Dubai, he became all excited.

'Then you must be knowing my daughter!' he said enthusiastically.

'Er . . . just been there a year,' I mumbled.

'But she's very well known in Dubai. Hema! Hema Ramanujam is her name.'

I shook my head. He seemed disappointed, but persevered. 'But,' he said protestingly, raising his voice as I tried to edge away, 'you must have come across her. She used to be the secretary of the Tamil Ladies' Association. She is a *chartered accountant!*'

I pretended not to hear and beat a hasty retreat to a few feet away where Rachel was just eating her dessert with relish.

'You know what all this means, sweetheart?' asked Rachel, as we both tucked into a second helping. 'It means more visits to the gym. Lots more.'

I nodded.

I was looking at Peggy. She was listening to the elderly gentleman, looking rather helpless. 'She is a very smart girl,' he was telling her. 'You *must* meet her. If you don't mind, can you take a small packet for her? It is just some sambar powder. You know sambar? That brown liquid which they poured on our rice. It is made from dal. You know dal? In English, it is called lentil . . .'

# 17

## KITCH'S AFRICAN FORAY

I advanced my flight back to Dubai by a day, so I could travel along with Kitch, Peggy and Rachel. The girls were chatting so much and with such great excitement, that I could hardly get a word in. Just as well, because I kept getting calls one after another. Nowadays, I was doing currency and equity trades full swing for Jaffer, Harsh, Sunny and Lalwani. With the way the markets were moving, I was keeping quite busy taking positions, adding to them and closing them whenever I got a chance. I had also started investing in several mutual funds at Peggy's suggestion. She had convinced me that not all clients would be suited to individual equities and currencies. Besides, it would be easier for me to take on more clients and add to my assets, if I had investments in instruments like funds where I did not have to spend too much of my own time and where there wasn't too much attention required on a day-to-day basis . . .

On the flight, I sat with Rachel and Peggy sat next to Kitch. Having switched off my cell phone, I could focus completely on the chatter. Rachel told me about how she and Peggy had, in between functions—taken an auto-rickshaw ride which they thought would be the last ride of their lives, as it weaved in and out of the city traffic. The auto-rickshaw driver had apparently observed them pointing at a tender coconut stall and had suddenly taken a U-turn in the middle of a busy one-way street to buy them coconut water. What's more, he had refused to take money from them for it.

'This, my gift,' he had apparently told them. 'Welcome to Chennai, madams!'

She spoke a lot about herself. She *had* been a dancer at a club for a short time, while at college, to help with her pocket money. After completing her graduation, she had worked with a bank in Jersey, Channel Islands. That, she said was when she met her husband, who was one of her customers at the bank. We spoke a lot and there was a good deal of laughter and leg pulling. By the time the plane crossed Muscat, we were holding hands, much to my surprise. Hey, what's this, I found myself thinking. Is she a very good friend? Or is this something more? Maybe we had just had one too many. Or perhaps this was just the pleasant after-glow of Kitty's wedding. Anyway, I was too tired to think very deeply about it. But it did remind me of something that Kochar had told us. He told us that right from his youth, he had always 'wanted a white woman'. For many years, he said, the idea had fascinated him, *possessed* him. But he seemed to have erred in his communication to God about his desire, he said, because instead of giving him a white woman, God had given him an Indian wife with a British passport!

Talking of British, I opened an account of a Brit the following week—Stuart Wilson, an oil and gas consultant who had been introduced to me by my uncle, Vinoo kaka. He had been recently posted to Abu Dhabi and had come here following a stint in Russia and Kazakhstan. Stuart was a widower, in his late fifties, a tall, weather-beaten, soft-spoken gentleman. His wife had died three years ago. He had two children, a son in Australia and a daughter in the US. I met Stuart at Vinoo kaka's house where I had been invited for dinner. There were a few others, too. Like Suresh Shah, who was wearing what I initially took to be a brightly coloured napkin, but subsequently discovered was a tie. It was large and diamond-shaped and ended some six inches above his navel. It was a polka-dotted tie too—red dots on a shiny yellow and orange background, which had additional comic ramifications.

Vinoo kaka, whose brand of humour was rather unique, told the group at large that the Patels were very different from the Shah community. The former group, he told me, liked show and pomp. If a Patel had a million dollars, he told me, he would act like he had five. An average Shah, if he had a million, would behave like he had a quarter.

'Don't go by appearances or lifestyles, while looking for potential clients', he advised, pointing at the Shahs. Mr Shah grinned.

Stuart couldn't help shoving his oar in. 'That tie itself must be worth a quarter million,' he chided, 'I've never seen anything like it!'.

I got a call from Sunny Singh that week. We were now in touch quite regularly. He had so far remitted USD 12 million. I had set up a credit limit for him. The borrowing in the account was USD 3 million. The total NAV or Net Asset Value was USD 16 million, which means we had added a cool 4 million over the last four months! A good portion of this increase came from his holdings of State Bank of India shares listed in London and the Infosys ADR listed in New York. Both these had risen over 30 per cent just in the last few months. I had also bought into mutual funds and ETFs (Exchange Traded Funds) that gave him access to Indian markets as well as BRIC (Brazil, Russia, India and China) funds which had risen about 10 per cent or so. Holdings of Citigroup shares had also risen about 5 per cent during the period. I had also taken exposure to oil in the expectation that oil prices would rise over the next few months from the current levels of about USD 65. So, all in all, I had him practically eating out of my hands.

'Oye, Jack bhai!' he boomed. 'Arre, tell me yaar, what is the capital of UK?' That Canberra incident had apparently rather tickled him considerably and he kept making references to it in different ways.

'Southall,' I said, after a moment's hesitation.

'Correct!' he replied, 'Changa! Good answer! I will send another 2 million this week. Oye, Jack brother, my wife is asking you to come here this weekend. She will make special dinner for you along with your favourite rabri dessert.'

Kitch, in the meantime, buoyed by the success of his first African foray (The West African President's son's account) had plunged headlong into a misadventure. An uncle of his had invited him to Zambia but had completely forgotten that Kitch held an Indian passport, which meant that visas had to be applied for prior to arrival, like at Dubai.

The poor chap landed up with bag and baggage and was made to stand in a corner. He called up his uncle to try and arrange something, but the officer in charge was AWOL, apparently having decided to accompany some friends to a nearby resort. No one else at the airport was empowered to issue a temporary visa and it took some four hours to have someone sent to the resort to get a written okay from the officer. In the meantime, the airport staff tired of nursing Kitch—possibly he was a restraining influence on their regular gossip—decided to hand him over to the cops. There was a police station attached to the airport and Kitch was shunted off there. He told me that he had his hand luggage, passport, wallet and cell phone taken off him and locked securely and somewhat ceremoniously in a large safe.

He was then asked to sign a register, where a policeman had referred to his passport and laboriously written his full name 'Bremadesam Balasubramaniam Krishnan'. 'What is this book?' Kitch had asked. 'Ah, this,' the policeman had replied reassuringly, 'is our criminal record.' Kitch had jumped and balked, whined and pleaded, but there was no choice. He had to sign. For the next two hours, he sat there under the watchful eyes of half a dozen cops, one of them a large, squint-eyed chap looking particularly menacing. Another one had a squint to boot also. Kitch told me later that he had never been more scared in his life. I could empathize with him completely. To find yourself in a strange country where not everyone spoke English, in a cop coop, without a phone, wallet and passport, having just signed the criminal record register, can be unnerving to say the least. Kitch says he couldn't help imagining the worst possible outcome and it was only several minutes later that he managed to get a grip on himself and started praying fervently. The saving grace, Kitch told me, was that two of the cops were women. Under the circumstances, that was a major source of comfort for him. He kept inching closer and closer to them and away from the grim-faced others. By the time the ordeal finally reached its end—with his uncle rushing in with a member of the airport staff, waving the piece of paper containing the officer's sanction to issue the visa—Kitch, a pale shadow of the optimistic go-getter that he had been only four hours back, had practically turned into a whimpering puppy huddled nervously between the two policewomen.

In the end, Kitch left the country with a large Patel account, with some help from me over the phone. He had realized that they would feel more comfortable dealing with someone who could speak Gujarati and so had requested me to talk to them and make them feel comfortable. I was happy to do that and soon the account was in place. Kitch insisted on the two of us and Peggy celebrating at his apartment with a bottle of champagne followed by ordering food from Kitch's favourite south Indian restaurant in Dubai. Peggy pushed off after dinner and the two of us watched a DVD of Kitch's all-time favourite film *Michael Madana Kama Rajan*. For the first time in my life I spent an evening being entertained by a jailbird, the ink from whose pen was probably still fresh on the criminal record register in Zambia.

The weather being so pleasant this time of the year, I had asked my parents to visit me in Dubai. It was a great feeling being able to welcome them into my apartment and give them a feel for my work and what I had achieved.

I told them about my successes, about what plans I had for myself and my intention to see my name on top of the scoreboard. Mum blessed me and asked me to seek God's blessings and remain humble at all times. Dad told me not to get carried away and to keep my feet firmly on the ground. I must confess I was just a shade disappointed. They were not half as euphoric as I thought they would be. Worse, they cautioned me! 'Always remember, Jai,' my father told me, '*Aapna be haath pahoda thai atla antare rokaan karvu.*' (Handle only that which is comfortably within reach of your two hands). I smiled a wry smile. This, I told myself, was probably what the generation gap was all about. The world had changed, but not everyone recognized it. Definitely not my father.

'*Havey duniya bahu naani thai gayi che,* Dad,' I responded. '*Mara be haath ma duniya samai jashe*' (The world has become very small now, Dad. It can easily fit in my grasp).

# 18

## MINA!

I had just got my visa for another Kenya trip. Kapoor said there was a family of Patels he had lost touch with, whom he had recently managed to contact and renew ties with. They were keen on meeting us. He seemed to think this prospect was important, so we put this ahead of our planned visit to Tanzania to meet the Desais.

Returning to office after having secured my visa, I was just about to take the lift to my office when Peggy and Ahmed walked in. I had been about to reach for my comb, but quickly put it back. It is my habit to lightly brush or comb my hair whenever I find myself alone in a lift with a mirror. But I never do it if there is anyone else in there with me. It seems just a little girlish, somehow. I turned away from the mirror, just as Peggy turned towards it and proceeded to do some magic with her hair, her hands and an elastic band. One moment she had a certain hairstyle and just a few of seconds later, a completely different one. All it took was two twists and a turn.

I pressed the button that had the number '20' embossed on it. Peggy herself never pressed the lift button unless she was the only one in the lift or the only one going to her floor. When she *had* to, she'd pull out a tissue from her handbag, cover her finger with it and then press it.

The lift had the names of offices printed next to each button. That Myers York commanded a lot of respect was obvious by the way people would look at us when we pressed the button for our floor. Some would look admiringly at us, some enviously. A few others would make small talk. It was not unusual to have a perfect stranger say, 'So, you work for Myers York . . . er, tell me, where do you see the markets six months from now?' We had different ways of responding to it. Peggy would smile enigmatically. I'd point to the heavens. Melissa would come up with a snappy street view. Kitch would shrug his shoulders and say 'I wish I knew, boss.' Ahmed had once invited one such guy to the office, hoping he could be a potential client. Much to his disappointment, the chap turned out to be a poor but passionate insurance salesman.

Back in the office, Ahmed announced in the pantry, 'Jack is going back to Kenya, I think he really likes black women.' As I smiled, he gave me a thumbs-up sign conveying the Ahmed stamp of approval and said, 'Way to go, man.' He got support from a rather unexpected quarter. John. 'Black women are ravishing,' he said suddenly, almost causing Melissa to spill her drink. We all looked eagerly at John, hoping for further details to emanate from him, following this confident sounding statement, but there were none. He seemed to have gone into a shell.

Talking of black women, I met several of them on the flight. Unable to get my regular Emirates flight, I had got a ticket on Kenya Airways. They were elegant, clad in red uniforms, were attentive and smiling—the airhostesses of 'The Pride of Kenya'. I read in the 'in-flight' magazine about a drink called Amarula, made from the fruit of a local tree. It claimed that elephants love the fruit of this tree called *marula* and tend to get tipsy after doing so. I decided to try it. What better way of being one with nature, I thought. It tasted like a liqueur, sweetish and creamy, rather like Bailey's, I thought.

Kapoor was to meet me in Kenya, he was coming to Nairobi directly from Uganda, where he was visiting someone.

There were five others in business class. There was a British couple behind me, both immersed in their books. To my left was a Kenyan with a professor-like appearance, who was going through some presentation material on agriculture and scribbling notes on a pad. There was another large man, wearing a bright, printed and embroidered Kenyan dress like a gaudy version of the Indian kurta. In front of me was a young lady. She was pretty, wore jeans, a V-necked short, white, tight shirt and pink thongs that I could see every time she either stood up, stretched, took her luggage out from the rack above, or put it back. Which seemed to be happening most of the time, making me blush and look away. Like an officer and a gentleman. It reminded me of Linda at office, who has made it a habit of displaying her underwear, either by wearing a strappy top that didn't cover her brassiere or—like this girl in front of me—by wearing her jeans very low. Funny how fashion changes, I thought. Something that used to be a no-no a few years ago, now had become very acceptable.

A few hours later, Kapoor and I were in the car to meet Ashok and Saroj Patel. 'He has promised me,' Kapoor told me on our way. 'This account is pukka, and it will be a big one, too. They don't look wealthy, they don't behave wealthy, but they have the money. I think they are from Nadiad in Gujarat,' he said, wrinkling his forehead, trying to recollect.

'Achcha!' I exclaimed. 'Then they are practically my neighbours! Nadiad is quite close to Bhadran, our village.'

'Chalo, that's good. These little things help. Their investments are now handled by their younger daughter, Minaben. She's a chartered accountant from London, I think . . . that girl. They have two girls, Miraben and Minaben. I think there's a boy too, the youngest of the three. I have brought a gift for Sarojben. Like I always say, Jai bhai, always keep the wives happy. Everything else will follow automatically.' I guess there is a certain type of wisdom that only experience can unravel.

On the way, I noticed people walking briskly on either side of the road. I was told many factory workers walked miles to and from their work places. I remembered having read somewhere that one of the reasons why Kenya produces so many great athletes— apart from natural ability—is that so many children who live in the countryside have to walk and even run long distances to reach school on time. So as young adults, they make light of running a few tens of kilometres.

The Patels' house was plain, almost drab. We first met Mr and Mrs Patel, a somewhat dowdy but nice couple, simply dressed. Vinoo kaka's theory on the Patels was obviously not always right! Some basic *Kem chos* and the usual exchange of Gujarati greetings followed. After some preliminary talk, we went in for tea. Their elder daughter Mira had already laid the table for tea. There were samosas and other eats were in five glass jars, each with a lid shaped like Disney characters. I expressed wonder at the variety of eats that had been laid out. 'Just some snakes for biting, Jai bhai,' Sarojben replied. 'Snakes for biting'. I made a mental note to tell Kitch about this.

A rather sullen-looking lad, joined us at the table with no visible or audible sign of invitation, almost as if he had smelled the snacks. He was Bakulesh, their son. Mira then walked in, dressed in a maroon and black salwar kameez, looking nice and somehow vaguely familiar. She seemed to think so too. She paused for a second as she looked at me and then said, 'I think you were on my flight.'

Good Lord! I thought. It was the thong girl! How different she looked now in her Indian clothes and in these surroundings.

There were more surprises in store. I noticed that Mr Patel had only three fingers on his right hand. Sarojben saw me looking at it and proceeded to explain. 'They shot him,' she said simply. There had apparently been a robbery at their home a few years back and when he tried to leave the room, he had been shot at. I nearly congealed. It took me several minutes to get over the shock of this little bit of information. I marvelled at the way residents of crime-ridden countries dealt with the situation in such a matter-of-fact manner. She might have been describing a cold in the head, the way she put it. I remained silent, Kapoor made sympathetic noises and the conversation soon switched to other topics.

'Our gardener will join us soon. She is busy watering the plants,' Sarojben said and the others laughed. It turned out that he was referring to their second daughter, for whom gardening was a passion. She had been out in the garden since lunch. 'At least three hours every day, she is just wasting time in garden, Kapoor sahib,' Mrs Patel complained. She was obviously no great friend of the plant kingdom.

Based on a couple of stray remarks during tea, it seemed that they had already decided to start a relationship with us at Myers, based on Kapoor's recommendation.

A little later, as I was washing my hands in the basin towards the back of the house, the 'gardener' walked in through the back door and I imploded. It was like one of those stories of spontaneous combustion that you read about in Ripley's *Believe it or not*. If this was the gardener, then these must be the original gardens of Eden.

'Minaben', to say the least, was a stunner. An extremely attractive, twenty something girl, with a terrific figure and dressed to show it. Clearly, she was still dressed for the garden and not for us; a very short pair of shorts and a tank-top, with traces of mud on one knee, some grass stuck on her forearm and slightly wind-blown hair.

There was a bead or two of sweat on her forehead. As she swept her hair back with her wrist, some of the mud on her hand got stuck on her hair. She smiled. She looked like a dirty little goddess. How these two lovely girls came to be mixed up with this otherwise ordinary-looking family, I had no clue. Nor did I care. I was just happy they were.

She smiled again and stretching out her hand, said, 'You must be Jai.' I stared at her, transfixed. I could hear what she was saying and in a vague sort of way, I even understood it. But to respond to it required alertness and composure, which at that moment, I did not seem to possess. The moment I had set my eyes on her, my heart had stopped beating. When it started working again a few seconds later, it seemed to be singing.

She excused herself, saying she would be with us in a few minutes after a wash. I walked back in a dazed manner back to the living room. I found it difficult to listen to the others talking about mundane things like the falling value of the Kenyan shilling or the rising share prices in the country. Absolutely meaningless. I mean, I had just experienced love at first sight. Nothing else mattered.

Mina came in, looking like a dew-drop and prettier than ever, in a pink shirt and jeans. If I could get the job of a gardening assistant in this house, I thought, I'd leave everything else and grab the offer. Three hours a day with this girl, under shady trees in that cosy nook. Lazing on the grass and . . . discussing documentation. *Documentation*? I came out of my reverie. Mina was inviting me to go with her to another room to discuss the documentation for the account.

I nodded quickly and alertly as if to make up for my earlier woolly-headedness and as we passed through a corridor with a mirror in it. I showed enough presence of mind to pause briefly, take a quick look at the mirror and brush my hair with my fingers.

We sat down in what looked like a study. While Mina spoke freely in a nice, warm and friendly way, I was still tongue-tied. Normally, I am a guy who can hold my own with girls quite well, but at that time, my brain seemed to have got substituted with cotton candy.

She did most of the talking. I am a bit cagey about the exact details, as I wasn't paying attention. I was, instead, wondering if there had ever been a girl who had affected me as this girl had done. I was thinking how I could come to Kenya more often. I was telling myself that Mina was too ordinary a name for her. I was . . . in the midst of all this though, I could sense that she was asking me something about W8 BEN forms. Nonsense, of course. No such thing existed. All that existed was romance. Pretty pink. Green grass. Red roses . . . Jai . . . *Jai*!

I blinked. Mina was calling out my name. I think I must have switched off briefly.

'Is it okay for all of us to sign off on a single W8 BEN form?' she asked.

That damn form again. 'No,' I said. 'Separate forms. I will need to get you some more forms. We must meet again tomorrow morning. Tomorrow. We *must* meet again,' I repeated firmly.

'Okay,' she said. 'You seem somewhat distrait . . .'

'I *am* distrait,' I said, spotting an opportunity and pouncing on it like a leopard. 'Clients have no right to look so pretty. It is distracting and we lose our focus.' I smiled and established eye contact. She giggled a bit and looked coy.

I was quite pleased with myself. That had accomplished several things, I thought. It had explained my earlier behaviour to an extent. It had paid her a compliment. It had also told her how I felt about her. The earlier the better, I thought.

'Tomorrow morning, I think you are meeting Kochar uncle,' she said. I had heard Kapoor mention that.

'Well,' I said, the regular Jack Patel slowly creeping back. 'He will have to wait. He can have a drink or two in the meantime. He can drink some drinks and bite some bitings.'

She laughed a musical, silvery laugh. I joined in. In fact, I seemed to be just about getting my usual form back when Kapoor looked in to see if we were ready to leave.

Back in the car, Kapoor asked me if everything went well and if Mina was generally aware about banking and investment matters. I didn't even bother to reply. I had no interest in banking and investment matters.

'You never told me!' I exclaimed, almost as a protest.

'Told you what?'

'About the daughters. Mina especially!'

'I did tell you. I told you, remember, that she was a chartered accountant from London and that she handles the—'

'I don't mean that! I mean about her and what she's like and . . .' I only managed to embarrass myself trying to finish the sentence. Kapoor teased me about it no end that day. 'Have some patience, Jai bhai. Let us open an account for them first, before you start trying to abduct their daughter. Ashok bhai's immediate need is a banker, not a son-in-law!' he chided.

But I was barely listening. I was thinking of gardeners.

# 19

## THE 'HAVEN OF PEACE'

A couple of weeks later, Kapoor and I were headed for Tanzania. The country's Serengeti National Park notwithstanding, I had no expectations from the trip in terms of its wildlife. For one thing, I had realized from my Kenyan experience that most cities the world over were probably alike. Secondly, travelling with Kapoor, I was unlikely to get much of a chance of having a pop at the local fauna. This suspicion was confirmed pretty early on in our Tanzanian innings.

From the Julius Nyerere airport at Dar es Salaam—which I was told means 'haven of peace'—we headed straight to a newly refurbished hotel, known locally as 'The Kili' and named after Tanzania's world-famous, snow-capped peak, which thousands of mountain lovers try and conquer year after year.

A personal friend of mine who happens to live in the city, dropped by and took us out for a drive, initially through Indira Gandhi Street, India Street and what he called Temple Street, where there were several Indian temples—I must have counted at least four of them. It was interesting to find so much of India in the Tanzanian capital city. Later, he drove us to Oyster Bay and then down the beach road. No one actually went down to the beach, possibly there was too much seaweed or maybe it was not clean enough, but there were several cars were parked by the side of the road. Apparently, the normal practice was to stop by, get a whiff of sea breeze, get a snack or two and leave. We did the same and dug into some corn on the cob, sprinkled generously with salt and chilli powder, following it up with *mogo* (tapioca) chips—a local specialty—and tender coconut water.

There was less than an hour to go for dinner at Kirit Desai's house and we were feeling pretty stuffed. Maybe it was just as well, though, because on the way, Kapoor told me about what a kanjoos Kirit was. The last time Kapoor had met him in Dar es Salaam—or Dar, as it was known locally—was to help him with a deal, which turned out extremely profitable to him. Most of his clients gave him a share in profits, but Desai only offered to take him out for dinner and even there, ended up ordering next to nothing. Since it was Desai's invitation, Kapoor couldn't possibly place orders by himself and had to contend with the little that came his way. There was no soup because Desai said that would spoil their appetite, there was no dessert because he claimed we all needed to watch our calories these days. Unfortunately, there was very little of the main course too, with Kirit advising Kapoor that since one should never waste food, it was better to order less than more.

Well, they couldn't possibly spring a mean trick like that on us at home I thought, as we drove back towards the hotel, from where Desai was to pick us up. He called a little while later and said his driver would reach the hotel in less than five minutes. Sure enough, a driver did.

We peered inside. 'Mr Patel?' the driver enquired, looking at both of us in turn.

'Yes, yes,' we said, clambering in. We drove along for a good ten minutes.

'So, how is Tanzania?' Kapoor asked the driver.

'It is nice,' he said and laughed. 'Nice, but little hot, now.'

'How long to Mr Desai's house?'

'Mister who?'

'Mr Kirit Desai. How long to reach Mr Desai's house?' Kapoor asked, a little loudly and with a trace of irritation. He was always impatient with slowness of response.

'Who is Mr Desai?'

Kapoor and I exchanged glances. 'Are you not Kirit Desai's driver?' Kapoor asked him.

'No,' he said simply.

'Then why did you pick us up?' I asked in some alarm. The last thing I wanted was to be 'car-jacked'.

'My boss Tony asked me to pick up Mr Patel. You said you are Mr Patel.'

Just then, Kapoor's phone rang. It was Desai wanting to know where we were. His driver had been waiting at the hotel for the past fifteen minutes. Half an hour later, we made it to his house, looking sheepish.

Sushma Desai was there at the door, looking slimmer and prettier than at Kitty's wedding. Kirit came in a moment or two later, complete with his trademark toothy half smile and wearing a shirt far too tight for him, revealing some of his skinny torso in between buttons. Theirs was a joint family. Kirit's brother, whom they called Motey (meaning 'elder' in Gujarati) and his wife joined us. Rather to my surprise, his wife addressed him as 'Motey', too, like everyone else.

'So, what's new? Anything new?' Kirit asked us quickly, like a bookie in a hurry to grab some sensitive information before placing his bets. He kept asking us this at regular intervals. 'What's new? Any new opportunities? Nothing new?' It's very difficult to think of anything new when people keep asking you for it. 'Cotton prices have shot up,' he told Kapoor with a gleam in his eye. 'Luckily, I had imported in bulk last month. We are minting money.'

Meanwhile, having caught me looking at a painting on the wall, his brother told me about his trip to France in 2005 and how he was one of the last few visitors allowed to take pictures at the Louvre. 'The next week, they banned photography at the museum,' he told me proudly, almost as if he had been responsible for the move. He disappeared for a while and much to my dismay, came back into the room with three albums of pictures, most of them, it seemed, of paintings at the Louvre and a couple of other museums in France. Politely, we went through them and asked a question or two.

'What's this one?' Kapoor asked.

They didn't know. I pointed to another one. 'This looks interesting,' I said. 'Yes, yes, very interesting, it was all very interesting and unique,' Motey told us.

Some ten minutes later, towards the end of the third album, Kapoor pointed to a picture of a young woman looking at a sleeping baby partly covered by a mosquito net. 'Who is this?' he asked, as if to round off our series of questions.

'Ah, that one . . . er . . . that is Mono Lisa,' he replied, confidently.

'*No!*' I burst out, more in shock than any real enthusiasm to refute him. 'That's er . . . *not* the Mona Lisa,' I mumbled as a follow-through, conscious of suddenly being the focus of several pairs of eyes, some of them appalled that I had the gall to dispute his claim.

He seemed to take offence. 'Arre bhai, I have been there,' he said, irritably. 'Have you?'

'Er no . . .' I said, 'but . . .'

'Then, what are you talking? I have *been* there,' he repeated. He seemed to think that settled the issue. 'Beautiful museum. You must see it. Very unique. Unique and interesting!'

I let it pass.

Meanwhile, Kirit bhai seemed distraught after taking a phone call. 'In August, we had agreed to deliver copper to one Mombasa cable company,' he complained to Kapoor. 'Now, they want copper at those old prices. How can we give? Prices are now higher. Those guys are just *minting* money,' he said, angry sparks flying out of his eyes.

Dinner was served. There was a small pizza, a little Chinese food that looked like leftovers, four chappatis, carrots, half a bowl of rice and a loaf of bread. There were two types of pickles, half a bottle of Coke, a full bottle of Mirinda and a small jug with buttermilk. It seemed to me that they had ordered a pizza, a loaf of bread and a bottle of Mirinda and had added to that by cleaning out the refrigerator.

I initially thought I'd have some pizza and Coke, but Kapoor had already taken the Coke and there wasn't enough for two. I don't like pizza with orange, so I ditched the pizza altogether. Motey's wife announced loudly that she and Motey ate only chappatis at night. So, I skipped the chappatis as well and had toast with pickle, followed by a carrot and buttermilk. As Motey would have described it, it was a unique and interesting dinner.

It was not just the stuff on our plates that was unique and interesting. During dinner, Sushma sat down next to me and discreetly placed her hand on my right thigh. It remained there for almost the entire length of dinner, despite my attempts to move my leg away. I have never been more unsettled in my life, not even when Mina had walked into my life last month.

Worse was to follow. After dinner, Sushma offered to show me the house and the garden. I hesitated. For two weeks or so, I've been all for gardens, as you know, but something told me this garden was best avoided. Kapoor, confound him, loudly said, 'Go, Jai bhai, you will like it. Sushmaben is very good at interior designing and gardening.' With all others also looking expectantly at me, I had little choice.

I was taken straight to the dimly lit garden. She sat a good couple of feet away, which helped me regain my composure somewhat. Both the house and the garden were undoubtedly beautifully done.

She asked me questions about myself and I reciprocated. The first time I got disconcerted during this conversation was when she referred to her husband as 'budda', which means 'old man', in Hindi. From then on, things started looking distinctly dicey. She asked me if I would like to be her friend. As I hesitated, she offered the incentive of a large family account. I muttered something about thinking it over. For some time, there was no conversation. I suggested we return to the house and we started walking. As I was about to open the door, I was jerked back. She had flung her dupatta over me and across my chest and tugged. As I turned and faced her, in a state of shock, she whispered, 'I want you to decide *now*, Jai. Now.'

'N-no,' I stammered, shaking my head.

She pulled away her dupatta. Her eyes flashed angrily. 'Get lost,' she said. 'Get *lost!*' She slammed the door shut behind me as I walked into the house. She remained in the garden, I assume, fuming.

I stumbled inside. I didn't want to go straight into the living room, as I felt sure I'd give it away. I was sweating all over, my lips were dry and I was feeling hot and uncomfortable. I headed to the washroom and sat on the edge of the bathtub for a minute or two. I rinsed my mouth, splashed some cold water on my face. Then I went to the living room, trying to look normal and relaxed. This can't be real, I told myself. It's like a weird dream.

On the way back to hotel, I told Kapoor, 'I don't want this account . . .'

He was shocked. 'But, he has agreed!' he said. 'It will be a big account, we have to take it. Why don't you want it?'

I struggled to find the right words. Struggling with words seemed to be the norm in my life. I was getting into far too many tricky situations for my taste. 'I . . . that lady, Sushma is not . . . I mean . . . she was, well, sort of . . . she was trying to get too friendly and I am not comfortable. Uncle, I *don't* want this account,' I said, finishing the sentence in a rush.

He remained silent for a few seconds. Then, he said, 'Jai, I think you have just misunderstood something she may have said. They are actually nice people. *He* is a bit kanjoos, of course, but otherwise they are good people, both of them. It will be okay. Trust me.'

I didn't reply. I had nothing to say. I closed my eyes. My head was swimming. There was a throbbing near my temples so severe that I felt the whole world would feel it . . .

# 20

## A NEW YEAR

The year 2006 was nearing its end and it was a relief to think of the holidays ahead. I had hardly taken any leave in my first full year at Myers—just eight days in all, six days while in Chennai and two days in Dubai, nursing a viral fever.

I had become busier than ever and was on a high. I was likely to end the year with revenues close to USD 800K. I had moved well up the list on the scorecard. Only Philippe and Rachel were ahead of me now; Rachel just marginally so. I was followed by Melissa, Kitch, Ramzi, Aliya, Ahmed and two newcomers, Charulata Chandgadkar and Harry Bauffeurhaugham (pronounced Boffam). The name 'Charulata', I found out from her, meant 'leaf of a vine' in Sanskrit. She told me it was also the title of a very famous Bengali film of the 1960s. I'm not sure exactly what characteristics the name is meant to describe, but if a vine leaf is supposed is supposed to be slim, long and graceful, then the name fitted her perfectly. With a name like this, I happily told myself, at least it will remain Indian. No one can turn a name like Charulata Chandgadkar into anything even remotely western. She had a Bengali mother and a Maharashtrian father. She was said to have contacts with several Indian industrialists and film stars.

Harry was the Oxford-educated son of a British naval officer and typically British in many ways. Many of his actions and speech were understated. He had a wry sense of humour, but unlike say Cyrus, he came across as more open and honest. He also came in with a 50-million-dollar book, from just half a dozen clients. Saudi Arabia apparently, was his segment of focus. He was a fitness enthusiast and had joined the gym in our building on the very first day. He was tall and slim with an athletic look about him and Melissa was quick to dub him 'Hot Bod' for his initials HB.

In terms of assets, Aliya had shot up and had overtaken even Melissa. She had acquired a USD 20-million account from someone, said to be a relative of hers.

I felt very good about myself and the business. What a great thing it is, I thought, to be fortunate enough to be working in a line that you were passionate about. And one that gives you the freedom to run it almost like an enterprise of your own. Of course, occasionally, that freedom tends to get misused in the industry. But you could consider that among the minor negatives that the system invites. I was not beyond misusing it either. I went to Kenya again, ostensibly to meet Kochar, Mina's dad and two other potential clients. I met only one of them, Mina's dad, and that too only briefly across the dining table. I went just to meet Mina. It was a wonderful three days. Kapoor did tell me that he had given them a damn good spiel about me. Perhaps it was that or maybe it was simply that we hit it off. They were all very nice to me and Mina and I got to spend a lot of time together. We spent a whole afternoon at a place called Village Market, where we weaved in and out of shops selling local handicrafts and sipped passionfruit juices, had a vegetarian lunch (she had turned vegetarian a few years ago, while she was in London) and watched the movie *Dhoom 2*, she for the first time and I for the second. I had seen it just a week back in Dubai and had rather liked it. We found we had similar tastes. Both of us liked really Hrithik Roshan in the movie. She felt that Aishwarya Rai didn't come across too well. 'She doesn't look hot when she tries to look cool,' she complained. I thought she had looked—to borrow John's word—'ravishing', especially in the kissing scene, but cleverly didn't tell her so. We loved Hrithik's dance steps for the title song and I told her—quite needlessly perhaps—how I had won an inter-collegiate dance competition at

Chennai, dancing to Hrithik's *Aye mere dil* song in his debut film
a few years back. She said she loved dancing and insisted that I try
out the steps from this new song. I made a mental note to rehearse
them at home so I could impress her the next time I met her. I
could shake a pretty good leg and anything that I could potentially
impress her with would be useful. We met for several hours every
day and at the end of this trip, I was sure that this was a girl I really
liked. She promised to come to Dubai in early 2007.

Meanwhile, Sudhir Shah's account had got opened and funded.
The clients who were already in, were happy and looking for ways
to increase the asset size. Some brought in funds from elsewhere,
like Saxena, others like Sunny borrowed from us against their own
investments to take advantage of the growing investment values
combined with the low borrowing cost. The markets had been
kind to everyone in the last year or two. Equities, commodities,
real estate, bonds, were all looking up. The one speck of grey that
showed up in the horizon was some negative report about sub-
prime lending in the US, but that we had been told, was a passing
cloud and would disappear in 2007.

Abu Jaffer's account was up 27 per cent for the year. He,
however, wanted to start trading options rather than just take the
fund and equity route as he had been doing. He was a good student
and an eager learner, much of which he tended to camouflage in
humour. He grilled me a good bit about options.

'If I like a stock and am bullish on it, I can buy a call option,
right? But how is it different from just buying the shares? Why not
simply buy the shares?'

I explained that for a given sum, his exposure would be much
higher using the option. He also runs the risk of losing the entire
amount if his expectations on the share price are belied on expiry,
unlike in the case of buying the underlying shares, where it is only
a question of a fluctuation in the value of the shares held. There
is no definitive closure, you can simply continue to hold and ride
out the tide, should the prices go down.

'If it is the other way, if I feel a stock is likely to go down, what
options can I trade?' he asked.

'You can sell a call,' I told him. That way you get a premium and if you are right about the price, the option will not get exercised. Alternatively, you can buy a put. You will have to pay a premium, but you get the right to sell at a strike price that you can choose. If the share price goes down at expiry, you have the right to sell it at the higher strike price. So, you get to keep the difference in the two prices, less the premium that you have paid.'

'Or I can just short sell,' he said, 'if I am confident about the price going down.'

'Yes, like in *Casino Royale*,' I said.

'What? That James Bond film?'

'Yes, there's a guy in the movie who sells stocks and tries to ensure that their prices fall. I won't give you more details, else it will be taking the suspense away.'

'My friend, I don't want to see a Bond film for information about short selling shares. I will come to you for that. From James Bond, I just want action, gadgets and bikinis. Khalaas!'

Made sense, I thought.

Meanwhile Sunny Singh dropped by with his family—Pammi, elder son Bunty (Balwinder) and younger Monty (Maninder) on a short winter vacation. The daughter had gone on a school trip . . . On one of those evenings, the rest of the family were packed off to the *Wild Wadi*, a water park right next to their hotel. He stayed back and we had a long chat. He told me the story of his working life. He had started off his career as a *thin* (he kept emphasizing on that) sixteen-year-old, in Ambala, Punjab. During the day, he cleaned tables and cleared plates at a restaurant. At night, he cleaned the kitchen of a dhaba, a roadside eatery, after its close, for additional income. He slept between 2 a.m. and 7 a.m. At that time, the fire in his belly served to fuel his sole ambition: to become a truck driver. A year later, he had got a job in a garage, not as a driver, but as car-cleaner-cum-odd-job man. In that latter capacity, he had to fill car batteries with distilled water and also keep a diary of all the cars that came for servicing, the dates, names of the owners and their addresses. Occasionally, when his boss wasn't around, he'd drive some of the cars.

At nineteen, he had landed in Kuwait, this time as a garage mechanic . . . Just over three decades later, he had a thriving auto spares business in Kuwait and planned to start one in Dubai. He owned two restaurants in India—in Ambala and in Chandigarh. He had a fleet of trucks in Punjab, all of them with the words 'Singh is King' written on them at the back. 'I'm very happy, Jai,' he told me in Hindi, sipping his beer contentedly, 'thanks to the grace of the Wahe Guru and the blessings of my elders. I have money and more importantly, respect and credibility. *Goodwill shoodwill to bahut hai apne paas.*'

For New Year celebrations, I joined Harsh and Joi. They were going with a group of friends into the desert, a not uncommon evening out for people in the emirates. *Dune bashing*—where you ride the sand dunes—has always been one of UAE's favourite pastimes. So, there we were, on the evening of thirty-first December, going up and down the dunes. Desert driving is usually in the hands of experienced drivers who learn special techniques to deal with the terrain. It is not uncommon to see the odd amateur adventurer stuck helplessly in the middle of nowhere, shouting into his cell phone, desperately trying to give directions to the police. After all, how exactly does one give directions when one is surrounded by desert sand on all sides?

It was only my first venture into the desert, though I had lived in Dubai for over a year now. I had a thoroughly enjoyable evening. We had an exquisite view of the sunset, and I took dozens of pictures of it with my newly acquired digital camera. Following that, there were games, shisha (I didn't know till that day that you could smoke it in so many different flavours, including strawberry!). Dinner was followed by a belly dance. We were at a camp, beautifully lit up with lanterns. It had actually been a long time since I had spent so much time together with Harsh and Joi. As Joi said, the great thing was that, being where we were, we couldn't access the mobile network and were completely uninterrupted for a change by our cell phones and the Blackberry.

I couldn't help thinking of Mina. The twilight, the sunset, the camp fire, the colourful tents, the camels and the lanterns had made me feel mushy and I was filled with a dull sort of ache. I had been hoping she could join me to usher in the New Year (notice how conscientious I was about keeping in regular touch with my clients?) but she couldn't make it and promised me she'd come and meet me in Dubai end of January.

In the meantime, Cyrus had decided that we needed to celebrate our 2006 achievements. Prompted by a strong recommendation from Melissa and Kitch, he decided to take the entire staff to Hongkong and Macau for a three-day off-site. Ahmed grumbled a bit, because Macau gave visas on landing to both Indian as well as British passport-holders, but he held a Pakistani one, which required a bit of work to be done in advance. But it was the first off-site of our Dubai office and it was an exciting week for all of us.

In Hongkong, we met, all together, for just a little over an hour at one of the large conference rooms at the hotel. Cyrus made a little presentation and also gave us a few dos and don'ts for the next couple of days. After that, we were pretty much on our own except that we would travel together to Macau and back and also have dinner together on the second night there. At Hongkong, I along with Kitch, Aliya, Ashraf, Rachel and Charu visited the Disney Park. In the evening, Ahmed, Ramzi, Kitch and I headed off to Wan Chai for a drink or two. On the way, Ahmed told us that the topless bars at Wan Chai were a little different in that the clients also had to be topless.

'I'm not going to take off my shirt,' Kitch whispered to me.

'C'mon, Kitch, relax,' I said, 'he's just pulling our leg.'

It was an interesting proposition though at the bar. The beer cost us some 40 HKD a pint, probably about six times times what it would cost at a shop. But what's thrown in is some pole dancing and a 'companion'. The companion keeps swigging Chinese tea which is also priced at 40 HKD. Naturally, you can't possibly refuse your companion 'tea'. So, effectively, the cost of your beer is doubled. Make it triple if you include a mini plate of peanuts! Every time you order something, they immediately write a bill and slap it in front of you, so you don't dispute it later, when your memory may not be as sharp. We spent about an hour at the bar and headed back.

Kitch has a weakness for things like chips and peanuts and can't stop eating them once he starts. He ended up paying 400 HKD just on peanuts. On the way back, he told me, 'But it was all worth it, da.'

'Why?' I asked, curious. 'Because,' he replied, with a smirk, 'that girl told me I was very sexy.'

'Mine did, too!' I told him.

'What!' he exclaimed, shocked.

'That's what they all say,' said Ahmed, the pro. 'They're trained to say these things. It's part of their job. Don't get carried away, Kitch.'

Kitch could hardly hide his disappointment. He looked like a deflated balloon. 'It's a con job!' he mumbled. 'A bloody con job!'

It wasn't the only 'con job' that Kitch encountered that day. He had his usual problems with the general absence of vegetarian food and was rather horrified to find pieces of meat in his innocent order of tomato soup that night. He was really upset and turned so ashen that I decided to skip dinner at the hotel and accompanied him to an Indian vegetarian restaurant—Woodlands, I think it was—that we had been told was just round the corner. We had a *thali*, a typical Indian vegetarian meal served on a steel plate, complete with dal, vegetables, chapatti, rice and yoghurt. On the way, he spoke feelingly of joining 'some vegetarian society' and propagating the cause of vegetarianism worldwide. He spoke of Amitabh Bachchan, of Linda McCartney and of Aishwarya Rai. I told him if he ever became a celebrity, he could be among the contenders for 'sexiest vegetarian alive'. After all, I joked, he was the only FA with a moustache.

At Macau, we were taken to a place called Hackett Skywalk Tower, where the rabbits among us walked along a ledge a few hundred metres above the ground. The more adventurous ones did a bungee jump. Harry went first, followed by Galiya. Amal changed her mind after getting her ankles tied up and beat a quick retreat. Ramzi and John then lined up. The rest of us poltroons decided to go down so we could get to see the view from there as well. We missed Ramzi, but were in time to see John dive down. As we clapped and screamed, we saw John get on to his feet and totter dazedly with his hands stretched in front of him. Even as we rushed towards him to help, I heard Peggy asking an onlooker about medical help. But as we discovered a few seconds later, John was fine both in body and in spirit. It was just that they had forced him to remove his glasses before jumping. Without his glasses, John said, he 'couldn't see a damn thing, you know'. Relieved, we laughed merrily as we trooped up again to collect his glasses.

We were put up at a huge hotel called 'The Venetian'. So big that you could easily get lost in it. I did, on more than one occasion. In fact, by the time I began to get the hang of the place, we were almost done with our stay. Most of the ground floor was dedicated to rows and rows of glitzy slot machines. And dozens of tables where you could play blackjack or roulette. Each table had a uniformed employee who would initiate you into the game. I tried my hand at roulette and got the hang of it after some ten minutes or so. They would spin a wheel and you had to place bets on a silvery ball settling on one of the numbers that were inscribed on it. You could place multiple bets on numbers. Or, you could play it safe and diffuse or spread out your bets. You could place a bet on an odd or even number, or a black or red colour. I started with HKD 1000, telling myself I would go no further. Close to an hour later, I found I had made HKD 3400, after being down to 300 at one time. I decided to quit while the going was good. Besides, the whole place was getting rather smoky. It was only on the next day that I realized there was a separate non-smoking area. There was still hundreds of people sitting and playing, completely absorbed. I was told some of them start off in the morning and keep going all day. I wondered where Kitch was. I hadn't seen him for a while.

The next morning, I met him over breakfast at the food court. He was with Emma, Jo, Linda, John and Rachel.

'Yo, darlings!' I said, 'Hey, Kitch, where were you yesterday?' I asked him.

'I was with Galiya for some time,' he replied. 'She wanted to pick up a couple of things. Then, I took a nap. I was feeling tired after the flight and the late night.'

'So, who lost how much last night?' Rachel asked.

It turned out that I was the biggest winner among this little crowd. The only other known winner from office was apparently Galiya, who had started with 200 dollars and had finished with four times that amount. 'But she lost twenty times that at the boutique,' Kitch quipped.

'Rachel and I are going to the spa this afternoon,' said Emma. 'Don't you guys want to come along? It's good. We were there yesterday. You must come. Remember, Cyrus said one spa session a day is on Myers. Largesse doesn't come easily to the man, so we need to take advantage when it does.'

Kitch looked a shade embarrassed. 'Oh, I don't know,' he mumbled, 'these spas and things.'

'How do you mean?' Emma asked him.

'I mean, its like . . . you know, I'm told the place is rather relaxed in the shower area. I'd be very uncomfortable if people walk around in their er . . . birthday suits.'

'Kitch!' Rachel exclaimed 'You aren't living in the stone age, y'know! Besides, it's not quite like you think. It's all very professionally done. In any case, they have separate areas for men and women. So, it's quite all right. Come with us.'

Kitch squirmed. It's always good to have someone like Kitch around you who will say or ask the things you wanted to ask. That way you get the answers you want without the strain or embarrassment of asking the questions.

'I don't want to. Er . . . it's an Indian thing!' he said, looking at me pleadingly, for some support.

'An Indian thing,' he repeated, 'We are against nudity!' Everyone burst out laughing, a red-faced Kitch included. He looked like an embarrassed tomato.

'Stuff and nonsense!' Emma said. It was the first time I had come across that expression outside of books. 'Stuff and nonsense! You didn't get to over a billion being fully dressed, sitting cross-legged and levitating. Against nudity, Kitch? What about Khajuraho? And Kama Sutra! Get real, man!'

'Yeah' added Rachel, enjoying Kitch's discomfiture, as he squirmed in his chair. 'Cut the crap, sweetie, and get real!'

'I'll go if Jai does,' Kitch said, neatly deflecting the spotlight on to me.

'Oh, it's probably just for a minute or two in the shower, Kitch,' I said, 'Let's give it a shot!'

The others didn't stop at that. 'I used to be here at Macau as a masseuse for two years,' said Linda. 'At one of the smaller places. Maybe I should talk to my former colleagues here to take extra care of Kitch.'

'Good idea!' added Rachel, needlessly. 'Ask them to give him a very special one. Very very special!' she said, making her voice meaningfully husky.

Meanwhile, Ahmed walked across in a black sleeveless shirt and tight jeans. 'John has asked me to co-ordinate for tonight,' he said. 'Do you like Chinese?'

Rach, Linda, Emma and I nodded. Jo and Kitch voted against. Ahmed looked at John. 'Chinese *food*, I don't like,' he announced. 'If you are talking about girls, I can try.'

# 21

## LOVE TAKES CENTRE–STAGE

'Linda, where do we buy all these plants from?' I was busy trying to think of schemes to make Mina's visit to Dubai a hit. She was to come in two days. She did have some work relating to her family's business, but I was hoping that the bulk of her time in Dubai would be spent with me. I had already wrestled with several ideas and imagined them in vivid—occasionally lapsing into titillating—details. Helicopter ride, with her shutting her eyes and holding my hand tightly. A desert drive, with her clinging to my shoulder. I even thought of getting a T-shirt with the words 'My life is behind me' inscribed on the front and 'Mina' at the back. As an alternative, I considered one that would simply say 'Me, na?'

Then, I had this brainwave. I would write a poem. What an idea! I got right down to it. I have never had too much trouble stringing words together in the form of prose, but I didn't realize till that day how very difficult it is to write poetry. My mind seemed to go blank. Somehow, I couldn't think beyond the 'moon'. So, I started with that. I wrote:

*You look like the moon,*
*When I look at you, I swoon.*

What an awful start, I thought. Puerile. This is the kind of thing I would have probably written if I had been asked to write a poem fifteen years back. This is the difficulty with Indians, I told myself. We are so overwhelmed with academics and stuff that romance and poetry rather takes a back seat. Maybe twenty-six was way too late for this kind of thing. I gave it another go.

*It was some hours past twilight*
*We were bathed in moonlight.*

I decided to transpose some of the words and make it sound more poetic.

*T'was some hours past twilight*
*Bathed we were in moonlight.*

Hmmm . . . that was better, I thought. But, only just. A few minutes later, I had made some progress.                              \

*T'was some hours past twilight*
*Swathed in serene moonlight*
*Two souls, young, restless, free*
*Lay there under the tree.*

Lay there under a tree? So juvenile. I needed to improve on this. Substantially.

I worked on it some more.

*Two souls, young, restless, free*
*Entwined in poetry.*

Ha! This sounded better, I thought. More whimsical. 'Entwined in poetry'. I liked it. But what did it mean? *Entwined in poetry.* Or should it be *Engrossed*? No, that didn't sound romantic. Besides, poems should remain slightly vague, I decided. It should leave something to the reader's imagination, provide fodder for fanciful thought.

But I couldn't convince myself. It seemed too unsophisticated. An idea struck me. Why should it rhyme? Rhyme wasn't fashionable. I would write something 'modern'. Stark. Angry. Rebellious. So I wrote:

*I stand alone*
*Fuming silently*

*Raging*
*Like the waves*
*That thunder against the rocks*
*My heart is*
*Pounding*
*Like the raindrops*
*That beat relentlessly*
*Against my windowpane*
*I am nothing but*
*An empty space*
*A hollow, meaningless*
*Vacuum*
*Wanting to be filled*
*By you*
*But you are far away*
*Doing your own thing*
*Smiling, laughing*
*Like I don't exist*
*Do you not know?*
*Or don't you care?*
*I seethe, I writhe*
*I clench my fists*
*Do not mistake*
*My silence*
*For indifference*
*Nor weakness*
*Know this!*
*And let the whole world know*
*I love you*
*And I want you*
*It's a race,*
*A struggle*
*Even a battle, maybe*
*But I will fight*
*I will conquer*

*I will win*
*If I have to spill*
*Every drop*
*Of my blood.*

I read it again. It wasn't bad, I felt, for a first attempt. Rather
pleased with the effort, I put it away meaning to work on it . . .
But when I read it the next day, it sounded so silly that I put it
away, blushing. Finally, I gave up on all these ideas as being too
corny and decided to keep it simple.

I bought some pots and plants and fixed up them in the balcony
of my apartment and in one or two corners of the living room at
home and my room at office. I spruced up the place and fixed a
painting on the wall. This trip of hers would have to be something
to remember. I decided to take her to the Burj Al Arab, Dubai's
rather spectacular sail-shaped wonder.

The entire visit went like a breeze from start to finish. You
know how it is. Sometimes, you put heart and soul into something
but goof up terribly. At other times, things fall into place almost
effortlessly. This was one of the latter cases. I fancied she liked me
as much as I liked her. On the first day, we had dinner at Kapoor's
place. He had invited an uncle and aunt of hers, who lived in
Dubai and another family, who were Kapoor's neighbours. Elders,
all of them, which was just as well, because that gave me plenty of
time to chat with her. The second day, we spent a couple of hours
at the office, where I showed off a bit and introduced her to Kitch
and Peggy and to Baby Jacob's special masala chai. I showed her
our meeting rooms and the auditorium . . . We then spent an hour
or so in the meeting room—there was one with a Bloomberg
screen on it—and went through the account. We decided to avoid
trading and invest in a whole range of mutual funds. I also
recommended to her a few of what are known as 'alternative
investments', which are very unlike the traditional equity or bond
investments in their approach. We zeroed in on a few—from Man,
GAM, Permal, Fairfield Sentry and a couple of private equity
investments. That evening, I took her home, where she insisted

that I keep my promise and do those 'Hrithik' steps from *Dhoom2* which both of us had liked so much. I started off tentatively, but quickly came into my own and put up a rather decent show. She tried out a few steps with me. I could see she was good too. We decided we would go out dancing the next time we met.

We left soon thereafter for the Burj Al Arab, what was and still is referred to as Dubai's first and only 'seven star' hotel. I had never visited the place before and I must confess being slightly overwhelmed, what with the pressure of needing to make a success of the evening and that of trying to look cool at this hip place and not like an awestruck visitor. We went to the Skyview bar. Located on the twentieth floor, it presented a magnificent view of the sea and the Dubai coast. Some of the wines listed there cost over 1,000 dollars each. I think I even saw a single drink which cost more than 3,000. It had cognac and a few other things in it 'sprinkled with gold dust'. I ordered a relatively modestly priced mocktail each, with a snack or two, taking care to avoid any kind of miscommunication with the waiter. I didn't want to get mistakenly billed for more than my credit card limit at the bank! The hotel is one of the most interesting in the world and has many things that set it apart. Among other things, which other hotel can boast of a helipad—high up in the sky—where Roger Federer and Andre Agassi have played exhibition tennis!

We spent about an hour there and then after a brief exploratory look at the hotel, its aquarium, its fountain and a couple of other restaurants, we left and headed towards Khazana, an Indian restaurant that served signature dishes of Sanjeev Kapoor. As Mina spoke smilingly to the saree-clad lady who was taking our order, I gazed at her admiringly. Mina, I mean, not the saree-clad one. I don't know if the word *smitten* describes it strongly enough, but I knew that night how much she meant to me.

That entire night, I spent in a trance. I don't know if I slept at all. I kept re-living every moment of the last two days. What she had said, how she had said it, what I had said and how I could have said it better. Very briefly, I even contemplated giving poetry another shot, but just as quickly, I discarded the idea. No poetry could ever describe the feeling, the sensation that I was going through.

That evening I switched off my phone for the first time in over a year. I woke up next morning to find fourteen missed calls. On a normal day, it would have been both a source of pride and of concern. That day, it just irritated me. I wanted to just continue to float in a world unfettered by trades, deals and profits. At 10.30 that morning, there was a meeting scheduled with Lalwani. He had wanted to introduce Peggy and me to a friend of his. I couldn't have wished for anything worse to follow so soon after a wonderful two days. It was nauseating to sit there and watch that slob spewing smoke and talking about money like it was the only thing in the world. Peggy had suggested to him that he could introduce just me, but the guy would have none of it. At the meeting, it was obvious that he was trying to impress the other by projecting Peggy as a great personal friend of his. I felt sick. But there's a silver lining in every cloud. Money talk over, he switched to small talk.

'Yesterday, I saw your colleague. He was going for dinner.'

I looked at him sleepily, trying to keep my eyes open. 'That south Indian boy. He was with that foreign girl in your office. Walking down this road, holding her hand, doing koochie-koo and all. Are they married?'

There's this thing about sleep. It can actually be turned off and on like a light bulb. It only needs the right switch. In this case, I jumped like a bomb had exploded under my seat.

'Kitch!' I spluttered. 'Which girl? Whose hand?' I almost shouted, even as Peggy gently kicked my ankles, to sober me down. But I'd have none of it. I needed to get to the bottom of this.

Lalwani was no good at describing anyone. All he could do was keep repeating the term 'that foreign girl' and gesticulating rather crudely in an attempt to convey some meaning. But there weren't too many women in office, so on our way back, Peggy and I narrowed the mystery woman down to three. Emma was too big to fit into the description, such as it was. Likewise, possibly we could rule out Rebecca. Usha and Linda were married, so it couldn't have been them. Hopefully, we could trust Kitch on that. A new lady had joined, but she was much older and was the serious sort. That left Joanna, Melissa, Galiya and Rachel. Could it be Melissa, I wondered? Thinking about it, they did seem to have become rather close, after their first trip to Macau.

'That guy had no business discussing personal stuff about any of our colleagues,' said Peggy, frowning, as we were returning. 'You should have discouraged him.'

'But, it was Kitch!' I protested. 'Can't have him running amok on the streets of Dubai. How come he has told us nothing about it? We need to know!'

Kitch was at his desk, making a cup of 'filter coffee'. He made his own coffee with a small steel, compartmentalized cylinder. He would buy a specific brand of coffee-chicory mix from Chennai. This, he mixed with hot water in the top compartment of the contraption. It produced a dark decoction in the lower compartment, which he then mixed with hot milk and sugar.

'Did you see the *Gulf News* today?' I asked.

'No,' he said, looking up only briefly. '*Khaleej Times*.' He went back to the task on hand. He was very particular about his coffee. Everything had to be just right.

'Oh, then you'd have missed it.'

'What?'

'The picture of you and a girl walking on the streets of Bur Dubai holding hands and worse!'

He nearly dropped his coffee. I now had his undivided attention. He stared at me wild-eyed, like an animal just before it gets captured.

'What!'

I nodded my head.

'How can they do that?' he shouted. 'They can't do that! It's ridiculous!'

'There is no escaping the paparazzi,' I told him, shaking my head slowly, 'If you're a celebrity, you have to pay the price.'

He rushed off. Some twenty minutes later, he was back with a
frown on his face. 'Was it in today's paper?' he asked.

'Which?'

'The photo, dammit! Was it in today's paper? I can't find it.'

I smiled sadly. 'Gone!' I said, spreading my arms theatrically. I
was enjoying myself. 'Such is fame,' I advised him, solemnly.
'Fleeting, fickle fame. Here today, gone tomorrow.' Then,
remembering a line from Shakespeare, I added, 'Like a circle in the
water, which never ceaseth to enlarge itself, till by broad spreading,
it disperses to naught.'

Kitch glared at me. 'What's wrong with you?' he barked. I
remained silent, staring at him fixedly. I was loving this.

'Was it just a photo?' he asked, 'Or was there a write-up?'

'Now, you're behaving like Paris Hilton,' I told him. 'You are
falling into the trap of . . . hey! what are you doing, you idiot?'

'I'm going to pour this hot steaming coffee right down here!' he
said, holding his mug with his right hand and pointing with his left
at my crotch. 'Unless you stop being a bloody smart aleck.'

'Okay, okay!' I said, hurriedly.

There was a mad gleam in Kitch's eye. The fellow probably
meant every word of what he said. 'I was just kidding, there's no
picture, though there could easily have been. My client Lalwani
told me he had seen you and this girl walking down his road. He
asked Peggy and me if the two of you were married. You shouldn't
be pawing women on the streets of an Islamic state,' I told him.
He remained quiet, looking thoughtful.

'Listen!' he said. Then he relapsed into silence for a while he
went back to his chair and sat down. 'Listen, Jai!' he began again,
'Been wanting to tell you for some time, but somehow I never did.
I wasn't sure about it initially and was very confused. Then, I
thought I'd mention it after my parents agree. After that, things
moved very fast and I thought it would be fun to keep it a secret
till the invitation got printed. Sorry, Jai, I just thought it would be
jolly to keep it under wraps a bit and then spring a surprise. The
wedding date is 24 September. They tried August, but halls were

not available. Our priest was also booked for several weddings that month.'

'Who?' I shouted, unable to control my excitement and curiosity.

'The priest.'

'Who, idiot?'

'What do you mean, who?'

'Who's the *girl*, you *ass*? *Who's the girl*?'

'Oh, I thought you knew that,' he said. 'Didn't Lalwani tell you that?'

'No, he didn't. For the last time, Kitch,' I said, menacingly, between clenched teeth, 'Who-is-the-girl?'

'Er . . . it's Galiya, Jai,' he said.

'*Galiya!*'

'Jai!' he said fervently, 'I will need all your help and support.'

'You have some nerve, dude,' I said, 'Not a word to me and now you want my support!'

He grinned sheepishly. 'Honestly, da, I didn't quite know what was happening. Suddenly, we became serious. I desperately tried to call you just before we left for Chennai on New Year's Eve, but you were at that desert camp and I couldn't get through to you.'

'But Kitch . . . your parents . . . Tamil Brahmins and all . . . are they okay? With Miss Borat?'

'Her mother is French,' he said, a little stiffly. Though, why that should make a difference to anyone other than a Frenchman, I didn't know. 'She had come with me to Chennai for New Year's,' he continued. 'She was dressed in a beautiful salwar kameez when she came to Chennai last month. My mother was bowled over by her. She felt she looked like a north Indian princess,' he said, smirking horribly.

'Oh, please, Kitch!' I begged, 'You look like a parent whose two-year-old has just recited her first nursery rhyme in front of an audience. Take that obscene look off your face and let me offer you my congratulations!'

# 22

## SARAH'S GRANDSON

I had become an old hand at travelling in Africa. I was back in Kenya less than two weeks after Mina's Dubai trip. It wasn't just to meet her, nor only to increase my travel miles to get a Frequent Flier Gold Card, though incidentally, that did happen. Of course, I badly wanted to meet Mina again. But she had also put me on to someone she knew who was looking for a friendly banker who would travel to Kenya regularly. He lived in a place called Luanda, near Kisumu, Kenya's third largest city after Nairobi and Mombasa. I had been advised it wasn't very safe to drive down from Nairobi and that it would be best to take a flight down to Kisumu and drive down from there . . . The guy I was supposed to be meeting had made several millions in real estate over the last decade or two in Europe and had recently come back to the place of his birth. He was of Indian origin and was married to a Kenyan. He owned a three star hotel in Kisumu, a couple of lodges, several acres of agricultural land and had recently set up a charitable trust to promote AIDS awareness and control its spread in the region.

At the destination, I was greeted by a driver arranged for by my host, Madanbhai Dodhia. Well, not 'greeted' exactly. When the first lot of visitors had found their hosts and left, there was just this one guy left. He looked suspiciously at me and I looked back hopefully at him. I decided to make the first move.

'Mr Dodhia sent you?' I asked.

'Madan!' he said, shortly. Ah! They were on first name terms, I thought. I asked him *his* name and he said something I couldn't quite catch. I got into the car and tried to chat. But he was one of those strong, silent types and only mumbled briefly in response to my queries, so I clammed up. After a few minutes of driving, he slowed down near a sign board where a couple of families were having their picture taken. 'Here, equator,' he said. 'Going like this,' he added, moving his hand in a broad sweep.

I remembered now. The equator does pass through Kenya, Somalia and other African countries. Funny to think that one day, someone thought of an imaginary line across the globe and then, for decades or even centuries after that, there are photographic points along that line where tourists clamour to get pictures of themselves taken. We were on our way again. Having warmed up with the equatorial line point, my friend the driver became chatty. Relatively, that is. 'There, sanctuary!' he said, pointing.

'A wildlife sanctuary, wow!' I exclaimed. I had come on this trip by myself, without Mr Kapoor to dissuade me. Perhaps I could find an hour or two to check this out. 'Is it a big one?'

'No,' he replied, quickly deflating my enthusiasm. 'Small.'

Further down, he pointed again. 'That side, Hippo Point.'

'Oh! Er . . . many hippos there?' I asked, and then immediately felt silly, for asking such a question.

'No,' he said, again, making me feel sillier still. The conversation wasn't quite what you'd describe as 'sparkling'.

Further down, he pointed. 'There, left. *Kit Mikayi*. Wife crying rock,' he said cryptically. 'First wife.'

I had no clue what he meant and didn't think I'd get much further by probing. I decided to just enjoy the sights. It was picturesque, quaint. Even from the flight, the view had been lovely.

My friend wasn't done. 'Here turn,' he said pointing to a road. 'Turn left go right, Obama house,' he said.

'What's that?'

'Obama house. President.'

'Oh, your President has a house here?'

'Not my President,' he said. 'America.'

I remained quiet again. The pressure of the conversation was beginning to get to me. He continued, however. He was obviously made of sterner stuff than I was. 'Obama,' he said. 'American President, maybe.'

'Bush,' I corrected him. 'The American President's name is George Bush.'

'Not today. Tomorrow, maybe. Obama.'

I shook my head and closed my eyes. What a nutcase. A few minutes later, I was at the farm house having lunch with Madan bhai. A soft-spoken, pleasant, bald and round-faced man in his fifties, he wore a shapeless, much-worn pair of blue jeans and a white, loose kurta that revealed most of his chest, grey hair and all.

'Flight, car, driver, everything okay, Jaikishan bhai?' he enquired.

'Yes, fine, thank you very much, sir,' I replied. 'The driver was nice, a bit funny, though. He was telling me about an American President in Kenya,' I added, with a light chortle.

'Yes, he is right. Obama.'

I started violently. Either I had gone completely crazy or everyone in this town was a little weak in the head.

'That's what he said!'

'US Senator Barack Obama's father was from Kenya. He grew up just a few miles from here. Now his son may be the nominee of the Democratic party for the 2009 American elections.'

'Surely not?' I said, wrinkling my forehead in an attempt to jog my memory. 'That's Hillary Clinton, I think, Madan bhai?'

'Also, Obama. We hear he has filed his nomination as well. Senator Obama was here last year. A school in Kogelo has been named after him. His father is no more, but his father's mother, Sarah Obama still lives here, just behind the school.'

I pondered over this. 'Is this Obama guy black?' I asked. He nodded.

'Wow!' I said, expelling a huge breath. 'That will be a big change in America. If it happens.'

'If!' laughed Madan bhai. 'A very big if. They will not let that happen, the Americans. But we are hoping.'

After lunch, I went through the routine of my introduction and sales spiel. Myers York. Among the largest American financial institutions. Billions of dollars in assets. Profits of over 7 billion last year. Presence in over fifty countries. Products . . . Account opening form, W8 BEN, KYC . . .

I met Madan bhai's wife, a lovely Kenyan lady with bright eyes, a dazzling smile and rough brown hair that made me want to wash and comb it. She wore a dress with bright floral patterns. She was plump with very noticeable hips that seemed to jut out almost perpendicular to her back. She spoke with a very distinctive accent. As I left, she gave me a basketful of mangoes to take to Dubai. It was only after much protest from me that she reluctantly let me go without it and that too, only after I told her that the basket would be confiscated at the Dubai airport and that I could get into trouble with the authorities. 'It is all nonsense,' she said 'Give some mangoes to the Arabs as well. Kenyan mangoes are the best in the world. They will love them.'

Soon, I was back in the car. This time though, I was looking at the driver with renewed respect. His name, I had found out from Madan bhai, was Susai.

'So, Susai, er . . . this man Barack Obama, is he well known here?'

'Everybody know. His father. Good man, die accident.'

'What was *his* name?'

'Same same name,' he said. 'Barack Obama, Barack Obama. Father, son.'

'Luo tribe, Obama,' the driver continued, after a pause. 'Luo tribe, many name start O. Obama, Odinga, Okumu, Orengo. Luo, Luo, Luo, Luo,' he finished triumphantly, 'all Luo!'

As we were nearing the airport, he filled me in with another bit of information. 'No circumcise,' he said.

'Sorry?' I asked, unsure if I had heard him correctly.

'Luo tribe. No circumcise,' he repeated, pointing at his zipper and shaking his right hand vigorously to make sure he was conveying the right meaning.

Not knowing quite how to respond to that, I remained passive and imagined a big black man standing in the nude in front of the White House, foreskin intact.

You never know what life has in store for you, I thought. I met with Myers, expecting a job in Mumbai. And here I was, living in Dubai and getting business from a small town in Kenya, where I hear about a local son hoping to contest the American presidential elections . . .

When I narrated the story to Mina, back in Nairobi, she was in splits. 'You needn't feel so bad about it,' she said. 'It's not as if everyone has heard of him. It's probably only the residents in that province and a section of the rest of the Kenyan population who know of him.'

I wanted to go out with her for an early dinner, but her mother had arranged dinner at home. A feast, it seemed to me. The problem with dinners in many houses out here I found, was that there was plenty to eat (Kirit Desai being an exception) although the hosts themselves barely nibbled at the stuff, being quite health conscious. Mina herself was not only a vegetarian, she ate very little even of the veggie stuff. She hardly ate anything other than fruits, salad, soup, wholemeal sandwiches and porridge made from maize or corn. Worse, she would go on a diet of juice and herbal tea every three months, to 'give the digestive system a break', she said. Why it needs a break was beyond my comprehension. It seemed to function perfectly well doing its daily thing. This veggie and diet bit was the only blot I could foresee, gazing into the future of our relationship. It wouldn't be easy being romantic if my tummy was rumbling and my nerves were rapidly communicating pangs of hunger to the brain.

Before I left, I also called on Kapoor's relatives, Rakesh and Pratibha, whom we would meet and join for a meal each time we came here. They were always extremely hospitable and friendly—their whole family—and always made me feel very welcome. This time, since I had already had dinner, they insisted on feeding me an ice cream and gave me packets of Kenyan chivda to take back with me to Dubai.

'How much weight you are carrying, Jake bhai?' Pratibhaben asked me.

Kapoor had once told them I was called 'Jack' at work. Since then, she always called me that. Only, she pronounced it as '*Jake*'. 'Oh, I have just one suitcase,' I told her. 'About ten kilos.'

She seemed genuinely shocked. 'Can I give you something to take to Dubai?' she asked. 'Chivdo, macadamia nuts, avocado, sweets, . . . anything. I can pake it nicely for you. You can take so many things for your office, your friends. You are allowed forty kilos.Why are you wasting thirty kilos?'

I bid a hasty goodbye and headed off, before she could thrust any avocado into my hands.

Mina was waiting outside to drop me at the airport. On the way, we were stopped by a cop. He asked for the registration and the driver's licence. Then, he examined the tyres and the seatbelt and told us that the car was not in very good working condition. I stared at the cop, puzzled. Even a car mechanic wouldn't look at a car so closely, I thought.

'I'm just doing my duty, sir,' he told me. Mina said something to the driver who got out and spoke briefly to the cop. Then both of them then got into the car and the driver mumbled something. Mina parted with some of her wealth, the driver passed it on and the cop got off, smiling. Once outside, he saluted smartly.

It certainly pays to do your duty. But, sometimes, it pays more!

# 23

## BREAKING THE GLASS 'WALL'

Following five consecutive months of over a 1,00,000 dollars of revenue a month, I was firmly on track to becoming a million-dollar producer for the office. In the first six months of 2007, I had done USD 690,000, which included USD 200,000 from currency trading, 80,000 from bonds, 65,000 from structured notes, 170,000 from equities, 120,000 from mutual funds and hedge funds. The balance was from interest on borrowings against securities in some of the accounts. I had four accounts of over 10 million—both the Jaffer accounts, Sunny Singh and Madan Dodhia. In addition, there were four that had built up to over 5 million Dilip Kochar, Mina's family, Lalwani and Sudhir Shah. Then there were several that were in the million-plus category; Harsh, Saxena, Dr Chiman and some others. Only Philippe and Rachel had higher AUM (Assets Under Management) than I did. And in terms of revenues, I was now even ahead of Rachel.

In recognition of this, I had—just that morning—been given the room next to Peggy's. It was a special concession that Peggy had wrangled for me based on revenues of USD 1 million, not in a calendar year as was normally the norm, but over twelve consecutive months. Another dream of mine had just got realized. From being seated bang in the middle of the office, I got to move into my own room. I was also told I would get a new assistant whom I would initially have to share with Kitch and Rachel. The workload was getting far too much for Galiya and Amal to comfortably cope with.

There was no ceremony about it. Cyrus told me about my room on the morning of 1 March. He and Peggy had agreed on this while discussing the end of February figures the previous night. Less than an hour later, I was on the other side of the glass, the one that separates the men from the boys. Everything was in place and neatly arranged, with help from Baby Jacob and Emma. I sat in my swivel chair and turned around. *Jack Patel, Financial Advisor to the World*! I wondered if I should put my feet up on the table like Philippe often did, but decided against it. It didn't seem respectful. I swivelled around again and put them up on the ledge behind me as I gazed out through the glass and looked at the road down below. There were hundreds of what looked like miniature cars, zipping across and changing lanes, the odd car weaving in and out, pushing through wherever it found space, like in a video game. If I moved to my left, I could see—through a gap between two buildings—the Burj Khalifa; potentially the tallest building in the world. They had already completed over a hundred levels of the building and it was scheduled to be ready for occupation in a year or two. In front of me, right below, I could see a whole lot of greenery and a parking lot almost shrouded by the cluster of trees around it. To my right, the DIFC—Dubai International Financial Centre—with some buildings complete and others in various stages of completion. In Dubai, it is said, buildings don't get constructed, they drop down from the sky; such was the pace of construction. Further down in front, I could see the stables of the ruler's horses and to the left, one of his palaces. And beyond that, a large patch of sand, which seemed to accentuate the greenery. More than oil or anything physical, I thought, this country had been fortunate in having leaders with vision and commitment. Nothing else could have turned what was once just a hopeful desert into one of the fastest developing countries in the world.

It was a great feeling. There are a few things that tell you that you have 'arrived' in life. Like when you get into the university of your choice. When you buy your own car. And your own room. I had experienced all these, but this was a 'new high'. I was tingling all over, but trying to remain calm. Peggy had told me I was in line to become the fastest million-dollar producer that Myers had ever seen.

It had been a fabulous few months. My driving licence, my car, Mina, my first monthly 1,00,000-dollar revenue, my room—each of these was a fresh, renewed dose of adrenalin that spurred me on to new heights. My relationships with my clients were getting stronger and I was being treated with respect that I was unaccustomed to. I lapped it up, I revelled in it.

Myers, too, was sparing nothing in an effort to show our clients our appreciation for their business. In March, earlier that year, we had acquired a corporate box at the Dubai Open Tennis Tournament, where we had invited several of our clients. We had about sixty or seventy guests, including about a dozen of mine. The women's tournament is always held prior to the men's here perhaps owing to the limited number of courts at the stadium. The clients came at different times during the tournament. Sunny Singh came towards the end of the tournament. Jaffer planned to stay the length of the women's tournament to see Maria Sharapova play all her matches. Unfortunately for him, she pulled out of the tournament owing to a hamstring injury. Sunny Singh was disappointed that Sania Mirza couldn't take part in the tournament that year. But he thoroughly enjoyed himself and his excited squeals and grunts could be heard so loudly from the stands that one almost didn't miss Sharapova.

One client—a very jobless one—stayed the entire length of the tournament, swaggering around and acting like he owned the place. In addition to his other idiosyncrasies, he now sported a little tuft of beard under his lower lip. On one side of his head, he had had a 'H' shape shaved off from his hair to form the initial letter of his name. It was Hitesh, Dr Chimanbhai's son. Dr Chiman had called me and asked me almost apologetically if his son could accept our hospitality on his behalf. I couldn't very well say no, much as I'd have liked to.

The women's tournament was won by Justine Henin-Hardenne.

Roger Federer lifted the men's cup. The much awaited clash between Federer and Rafael Nadal didn't take place this year, as Nadal got knocked out of the tournament by Mikhail Youzhny. The newspapers carried plenty of pictures each day from the previous day's play. It included pictures of the players in action as well as those of the spectators. There was one of Sunny Singh doing a celebratory dance of sorts, with his wife watching in amusement, with her palm under her chin. I excitedly went through the pictures every morning in the papers and on the net. I wondered who did the selection when it came to publishing pictures of women tennis players. One rarely sees pictures that do not show their undergarments. Is it deliberately chosen by the editor, or is it impossible not to take a picture that is not that revealing, given the costume that is worn nowadays?

Since we were expecting many clients to be in Dubai around that time, we had also arranged guest speakers from New York. Raj Saunders was there. He had replaced Joe as Head of Equity since Joe had left Myers a couple of months ago to join Merrill Lynch. There was another guy too, called Dan Streep. Dan had joined us in February. He was a brilliant speaker. He was at least as effective as Raj, possibly even better, because he was good-looking and had blue, hypnotic eyes. When he held you in his gaze, you felt convinced that whatever he was saying was true. Later on, when you sat and thought about it, your conviction might get watered down a bit, but at that time, you couldn't dispute anything he would say. He knew his presentation inside out and never needed to look behind at the screen. He knew exactly what was there and what was coming up next. He just focused on holding us spellbound and did a neat job of it. Raj spoke well and powerfully about Citigroup and how, despite the difficulties it had been facing in the last few months, it was a prime candidate to bounce back. Citi, of which I already had a bit of exposure in Sunny's account, had dropped to below 50 from its high of 56.41 in December 2006, one of the few stocks I held which had actually gone down during that period. 'At the end of the day,' Raj announced, with his customary flamboyance, 'Citi is a universal name like none other. Its reach, its diversity and its brand are unique and impossible to replicate in our lifetime. Citi, at below 50 is a great opportunity. Do your clients a favour. Ask them to buy this.'

Dan, on the other hand, spoke at a more macro level. He spoke about the sub-prime business in the US and how a certain recklessness in mortgage lending had caused a problem that threatened to turn into a crisis. It could affect the US economy, he said, and could bring about a correction. The Dow Jones had crossed 13,000. 'Don't be surprised,' he told us, 'if it takes a 10 per cent drop from here. Position your accounts accordingly. Be proactive. That is what will distinguish you from the rest of them. Anyone can execute a trade. You need to give them sound advice. *That* is what will help you claim your clients' respect. If *they* win, *you* win.'

Talking of winning, over the last year, two of the biggest winners in most of my clients' portfolios, had been shares of Indian companies. State Bank of India and Infosys. These companies were diametrically opposite in many ways. SBI was the country's largest bank, a somewhat slow-moving financial institution, still partly owned by the Indian government and one with tremendous reach and clout throughout the country. In a sense, SBI was representative of the country itself between 1947 and 2000, like a big lumbering elephant; strong but not supple, big but bogged down by bureaucracy. Infosys, one of the country's best-known software companies, symbolized youth, flexibility and agility. It ushered in qualities which were not usually associated with Indian companies in the western world. Confidence, perhaps even audacity, quality, transparency and the ability to think out of the box. Infosys not only harnessed the country's pool of young talent, but managed to catch the attention of the rest of the world like no Indian company had done before. It published its annual statements according to American GAAP standards and had become the first Indian company to be listed on the Nasdaq.

In 2006, the single largest equity holding in some of my clients' accounts had been Infosys. I had bought most of these between USD 34 and 39. The accounts of Sunny Singh, Harsh, Saxena, Lalwani, Jaffer and others, all had this. In February 2007, it almost touched 60. It had since come off a bit, but it was well above the purchase levels. In many cases, I had taken profit and was considering buying it again or alternatively, buying notes linked to its equity. This year, my biggest performer was SBI. I had bought a lot of this scrip last year at prices between 37 and 50. This year, I bought it again in February and March at average price of 58. Now, just a few weeks later—in July 2007—it was close to 100.

Like I said, it had been a great quarter and now getting my own room was like the icing on the cake. It is pretty much one of the key goals in an FA's life in the broking world. And the competition is fierce. You get your first account, then your first dollar revenue to remove the blank against your name of that list on the scoreboard. Next, you look to getting your name off the last line on the list. Then, you work towards a series of small goals—assets of USD 25 million, maybe, then 50 million. Revenues of USD 500,000 then a million. And then the room. Beyond that, there are not too many goals to aim for except building your assets further, strengthening the depth of your relationships with your clients and delivering the returns they want. And I, Jack Patel, had done all this well within two years of joining the business. No one else had. Was it luck, or was it plain, simple genius?

I decided to go over and get a cup of tea. I decided I should make it a point to try and take every opportunity to step out of the room. I didn't want to be like Philippe, who kept very aloof and practically lived in his room.

I walked into the pantry, hoping I wasn't wearing my look of pride too visibly on my face. Ahmed was there. So were Melissa, John and Ramzi.

'Ah! There he is!' said Melissa. 'The big man himself!'

'Jack, the giant killer,' said John, grinning.

'Jack the Ripper!' added Ramzi, meaninglessly and quite

unnecessarily. 'He's come to mingle with the masses.'

I felt uneasy and unsure of myself. Maybe I should start talking something 'normal' before they continued in this vein, I thought. But I couldn't think of anything to say. So I just smiled and poured out my tea.

'The man with a room,' said Ahmed. 'The room with a view!'

I wished I had stayed in my room. The one with the view. I wished I could think of something clever to say. I was feeling a little angry inside. Why couldn't they just share my happiness instead of making these uncalled for comments? Or was I needlessly feeling that way? I shrugged my shoulders. 'Aw, c'mon guys,' I said, weakly.

'Okay, hold it, hold it,' butted in Ramzi, raising his palm. 'Don't give us any Indian philosophy spiel now, man. What's the big deal? The room means nothing to you, it's just another day, the only thing you care about is the welfare of clients . . . *yeah?*'

I looked at him, slightly shocked. I could sense the tautness of my muscles as they stiffened in anger. I couldn't help feeling what he was saying was partly true. That didn't make me like it, though. I didn't respond. I didn't want to dampen my day. So I just drank my tea and simply went with the flow of conversation when Melissa changed the subject. But I was still thinking of how nice it would be if I could empty my cup of scalding tea over Ramzi.

# 24

## BACK TO 'DAR'

Much against my wishes, Kapoor dragged me down to Dar again. Apparently, Kirit Desai had kept telling him that he would be ready with cash soon and didn't want to keep it idle, 'while others were minting money'. I didn't really want his account. But I suspect Kapoor still didn't entirely believe my story about Sushma. So we made a compromise. He assured me we wouldn't visit their home this time and would just meet Kiritbhai in the office. Prior to this, Kapoor had fixed up a meeting with another friend of his at a town called Arusha. We were to fly down there Monday morning and take the evening flight back.

We reached Dar on Sunday afternoon; Kapoor, myself and Kapoor's luggage. My luggage didn't make it, for reasons best known to the airline. I was told to come back in a couple of hours, so I did. I was informed that the luggage hadn't yet arrived, Our best bet, they said was to come again the same time next day. Being Sunday, all the shops were closed. There was nowhere to pick up even basic stuff from. I politely declined Kapoor's offer to lend me some of his clothes. They would have been far too big, in any case. So, he called a friend of his, who said he knew of a market that was open on Sundays. He brought his car and off we went in search of some clothing that would see me through the night and at least until the next evening. We inched along a narrow stretch of road, packed with hand carts on both sides, stacked with various items of clothing—cotton shirts, shorts, underwear and vests. Yonder, a couple of stalls which had trousers—in all colours of the rainbow—hanging from hooks. Violet, red, yellow . . . they were all there. In fact, only four colours were not to be seen— black, grey, blue and brown.

'First, we will buy you some underwear,' the friend told me and signalled to one of the hawkers. Immediately, the car was surrounded by about half a dozen underwear sellers each thrusting samples through the open windows and making a vigorous sales pitch in Swahili. One of them thrust an underwear right in front of my face and tugged repeatedly at the elastic in a bid to demonstrate its sterling qualities. Suddenly, a rather perturbing thought came to my mind. 'Er . . . this isn't second-hand clothing, is it?' I asked the friend, nervously. 'No' he replied confidently. 'Second-hand clothing is at the other end of the road.' Since the other end of the road was only some 30 metres away, I don't know if that made me feel better or worse. I decided to pass the opportunity to buy one of the trousers. Finally, armed with a pair of shorts, a T-shirt and a couple of underwear, we drove back to our hotel. Live and learn, I thought to myself. Every day, there was something new. And when I joined Myers York, I thought all I'd be doing was sitting in front of a computer and deciding on investments.

At the entrance to the hotel was a pond of sorts with a few small nondescript fish swimming around. As I walked through, I saw a small group of Japanese tourists rushing around chattering excitedly and trying to capture the fish on film. Kapoor, who had gone on ahead, turned around on hearing the commotion. 'Any problem?' he asked. I shook my head. 'There are some fish in there. They're taking pictures.' Kapoor's face turned grim as he stormed towards the reception. 'The world has gone mad!' he growled, as I joined him, grinning. 'People have completely lost their minds, Jai bhai!'

The next morning, we had to leave early. I wore the same clothes that I wore on my flight along with my brand new underwear. At least, I hoped they were new. I didn't entirely share Kapoor's friend's sunny confidence in this matter. I hadn't washed them since they wouldn't have got dry this soon. I wore them rather gingerly after wrapping myself in the relevant places with a page from the newspaper. It made a rustling sound every time I took a step. It wasn't exactly comfortable and I realized after we had got into the taxi that I could have used some soft tissues from the bathroom instead.

My main motivation to go to Arusha was not so much business— I was close to USD 100 million in assets now and didn't need to push myself beyond a point—as a chance to view Mount Kilimanjaro. In fact, the airport nearest to Arusha is called Kilimanjaro International airport. I was thrilled to have a terrific view of the mountain from the flight ; the snow-capped Kilimanjaro, the highest peak in Africa and Mount Meru, another mountain not far away from it. In fact, it was quite close to Arusha town. Or rather, Arusha *city*. When asked how I liked Arusha, I told our prospect that I found it was a nice, pleasant town. I thought it would please him. Instead, he admonished me for berating the place. Arusha, he said proudly, had officially become a '*city*' the previous year. No business transpired for us because the gentleman turned out to be a US green card holder and intended to settle down permanently with his two daughters in Chicago. He didn't want to disclose the fact to the US authorities and there was nothing we would do to assist him in this regard. He was disappointed and so were we.

That night, we were back as scheduled. 'Breakfast at 8 sharp?' Kapoor asked me as we wished each other good night. He was a stickler for punctuality. His early upbringing probably had a lot to do with it. His father had been in the army and had initiated some of those strict measures even at home. Kapoor had a specific breakfast routine during our hotel stays. He would have no meat at breakfast. He would first bring to the table two packets of butter, which he would keep on a warm plate for it to melt a bit. He would order an omelette and would help himself to a plate of fruits while the omelette was getting ready. Then he would get two slices of toast on which he would spread the butter—hopefully, by now melted to the right degree—and eat it with the omelette and about a ton of tomato ketchup. He'd finish it off with a cup of 'strong tea with hot milk' that he would specifically ask for and insist on mixing himself, because no waiter has ever managed to get the colour of the tea to match the exact shade that he likes.

Immediately upon our return we were at a clothes store, much to my extreme relief. I had called the airport but after being transferred to three different people, there was no confirmation of my suitcase having been received at Dar.

The next morning, we were at Kirit Desai's office. It was a dingy place in an old building. There were two small rooms there, which were shared by a staff of about seven. Kirit and his accountant worked in one and the rest of them in the other. There was one spare plastic stool intended for a visitor. Both Kapoor and I kept offering the stool to one another and in the end both of us remained standing. It didn't seem to worry Kiritbhai very much, because he made no move to remedy the issue.

'This office is little small,' Kiritbhai told me 'but it is coming very cheap. Too cheap. Why to pay more? In Africa, people don't have enough to eat,' he said. Especially if they come to your house for dinner, I thought to myself.

'Which will go up more, gold or diamond?' Kirit asked Kapoor. 'My wife wants to go on holiday next week. But better I buy her jewellery, so that it becomes investment.' Then, looking towards me, he explained, waving his index finger 'Because, holiday is waste, jewellery is investment.'

I hung around standing to one side while Kapoor told Kirit where to sign and where he would need to get Sushma's signature. I wouldn't mind standing all day, I told myself as long as I didn't have to meet his wife.

'Good morning, Sushmaben,' Kapoor said, looking behind me. I turned with a jerk. To my absolute horror, Sushma was walking into the shop with a stony expression on her face.

Kirit asked her to sign. She seemed reluctant. 'Why should we open with this bank?' she asked. 'Kapoor saheb does not work there. We are just dependent on this youngster, who does not seem smart enough to take advantage of opportunities,' she said, in an obvious reference to our previous meeting. I squirmed and shuffled my feet, saying nothing. 'Don't worry, this boy will do good job,' Kirit said. 'Kapoor bhai will help us. Also, I want to diversify and have one or two more banks. Sign quickly! Otherwise, you will have to pay for parking.'

That was done and Kapoor put the documents securely in his briefcase. 'I will send funds in one month,' Kirit said 'but, please, minimum charges, Jai bhai. Otherwise, all my money will go away in charges. Please make minimum charges. Every dollar is important for minting money. Charges are like drops of blood. If it is too much, the portfolio will become anaemic. But if there are no charges, the portfolio will grow like little drops of water to make ocean.' He had taken me completely by surprise with his imagery. Perhaps, I thought, underneath even the most earthly or materialistic of men, there lurks a little poet, crying to be let out.

# 25

## A MAIDEN, A LONG LEG AND A CATCH!

'What's up, dude?' I asked Kitch, who was sitting at his desk in office, staring at a letter, looking slightly dazed.

He threw up his hands and shook his head. 'Take a look at this,' he said, 'I have never seen anything this dumb. They have changed my name.' It was the welcome letter for a frequent flier enrolment from an airline which flies Dubai-Chennai on its way to its destination. It began with the words 'Dear Bobo'. The letter itself was addressed to Mr Bobo Krishnan.

'Bobo? I asked. 'Where did they get that from?'

He wrote his name on a piece of paper in explanation and we both burst out laughing simultaneously as I realized what had happened. Kitch fancied himself as being rather artistic in the way he wrote and sometimes tended to do his dots as a small circle rather than a plain and simple dot. The airline had mistaken 'B.B. Krishnan' for 'Bobo Krishnan' and no doubt in an attempt at being chummy with their customers, had chosen to address him by his 'first name'.

It was 20 September, 2007. We were flying the same airline to Chennai the next day. Kitch was to get married in three or four days' time. He had initially planned to be there earlier to help out with the arrangements, but as he himself put it, his family had decided he would be less of a nuisance in Dubai. So, we were to go together, Kitch, Galiya, Linda, Melissa and myself. Peggy, Rebecca and Rachel were to join us the next day. This time, it was a bigger contingent from the office than it was for Kitty's wedding.

Rebecca asked me if we would have Indian food or Kazakh food.

'What's Kazakh food?' I asked, never even having considered the possibility of the existence of such a thing.

'I've just been browsing the net,' she said. 'It's mainly horsemeat'.

I stared. I wondered if she was being serious. Based on my limited interaction with her, Rebecca didn't rank very high in my esteem. She seemed to behave a bit weird at times. 'You can bet your bottom dollar there will be no such thing,' I told her. Kitch's family are hard-core vegetarians. They won't even eat a cookie shaped like a horse.'

Just before we got on to the flight, I heard the girls discussing plans to buy 'Indian sarees' to wear at the wedding. They had apparently been looking forward to it for weeks. It suddenly struck Kitch that some arrangement needed to be made to get blouses stitched as well. Much as he (or I) would have liked to see the girls draped just in sarees, this was not the occasion for it. After all, he was the host. So, he called up home to ask them to make prior arrangements with a tailor to ensure that the half a dozen blouses could be stitched at very short notice.

Galiya's parents were already in Chennai, along with—I was told—some twenty relatives from Kazakhstan, UK and France. More were on their way. Galiya was the youngest among six children and most of her close relatives were planning to be there. For almost all of them, this would be their first visit to India.

Kitch, the proud frequent flier member of the airline, and the rest of us took our seats. His issues with the airline hadn't ceased just yet. He opened the meal packet which they had placed on his tray and stared suspiciously at its contents. 'What is this?' he enquired of the steward.

The steward peered at it. 'I don't know,' he said simply.

Kitch was in no mood for this sort of thing. 'How can you not know?' he asked, aggrieved.

'This looks like meat.'

'It is not meat,' the steward replied, picking up the stuff and sniffing cautiously at it.

'I need to know what it is before I eat it,' Ketch persevered. 'If it's a vegetarian meal, then what is it? Is it potato, cauliflower, beans?'

The steward shook his head. 'No,' he said, this time subjecting the contents to a closer scrutiny. 'Not potato, cauliflower, beans.'

'Then, *what* is it?'

'I don't know.'

Exasperated, Kitch almost shouted, 'Then how do you know it's veg?'

'Ah!' said the steward, looking pleased. He could answer that one. 'Because, see here,' he said, pointing to a scribble on the top cover of the packet. 'V–E–G, veg.'

Melissa, who was sitting next to Kitch, went into peals of hysterical laughter and the rest of us too, laughed so much, a couple of other passengers walked across to see what was so funny.

If looks could have killed, the steward would have collapsed right there in front of Kitch. As it turned out, he merely maintained his stoic demeanour and even proceeded to bravely explain to Kitch. 'It looks like meat, but it is not meat. It is *imitation*.'

Kitch pushed it away and started munching peevishly at the bun. Galiya and Melissa gave him the buns on their plates too, so he made a meal of those, with jam and butter, followed by some unnamed dessert of an unusual green colour.

It had not been a great week for Kitch. I hoped things would get better for him. First, he had gotten into some trouble at work for inadvertently trading in a 'restricted stock'. Shortly after that, he and Galiya had their first tiff. At least the first one that I know of. She had asked him to shave off his moustache for the wedding and Kitch, who had always prided himself on it, had neighed like a horse and reeled back, shocked to the very core of his being. There had been a cold war brewing for a day or two until I took Galiya aside and explained to her that to a hard-boiled south Indian like Kitch, a moustache was not simply facial hair. It was almost a sign of masculinity, one that was treasured and carried on as a tradition from generation to generation. Not quite true, of course, and probably a grossly exaggerated version of the facts, but as Kitch's unnamed 'best man' I had to quickly get them back on track. 'So, asking Kitch to shave off his moustache,' I told her, 'is almost like asking you to . . .' I stopped short. I was going to say 'asking you to cover your belly button' but thought the better of it. 'Like asking you to dress shabbily at the wedding,' I concluded lamely. It worked anyway and filled with remorse, she was all over Kitch the next couple of days.

The wedding was at a place not far away from where I lived. The previous afternoon, one of Kitch's sisters had taken the girls out to one of the city's famous saree shops, from where each of them bought a silk saree or two. She had fixed up with a tailor beforehand for the blouses and had arranged for an aunt to be available the next morning to help them wear the sarees. After all, for our colleagues, unused as they are to this beautiful garment, *buying* a saree is only the start of the battle. The bigger issue is to wear it, with its twists and turns, its numerous pleats and folds. Once it was in place, the other issue was to keep it in place and not allow it to 'disintegrate'. After the 'success' of their attire at Kitty's wedding, they were all very enthusiastic about being appropriately and exquisitely dressed and win another round of appreciation from everyone.

That night, Kitch took us all to see—on the big screen—the most recent blockbuster of Tamil celluloid kingpin, Rajinikant, now possibly in his sixtieth year or thereabouts, but with no less appeal to the masses than he was twenty years ago.

The next day, we were all smiles, nicely decked up and ready for some good fun. We entered the gates of the *mantapam* (the marriage hall), which was adorned with full-grown plantain trees on both sides. Above it was a large blue board, on which jasmine flowers had been arranged to form the words 'Kitch weds Galiya'. Melissa giggled. As I looked at her enquiringly, she pointed to the bottom of the board. Some budding copywriter genius had put up a tag line in white thermacole. It read, 'A moment in love when time stands still'. Laughing heartily and making a mental note to rag Kitch about it later, we walked into the hall. Three young girls clad in shiny silk paavadais and blouses enthusiastically sprinkled rosewater on us—more particularly on the girls—and offered flowers, sandalwood paste, and chunky pieces of sugar.

Most of Galiya's relatives were already there, dressed in a variety of costumes. The word *costume* here, is I think, the *mot juste*, because that is pretty much what it was. It was everything except what was most appropriate. Some were wearing skirts, some were wearing some frilly traditional-looking stuff that had layer upon layer of material, some were casually dressed, some were wearing designer gowns and some were wearing suits.

Peggy and Co. caught everyone's attention as we walked in. The tailor, perhaps inspired by the youth and the charm of the girls and their willingness to experiment, had given vent to all his creative urges and had practically gone berserk. Peggy's blouse had a V-shaped neck, with a sleeve that was loose, almost like a shirt but shorter. At the back was a large heart-shaped gap. Linda's blouse had a high neck, but practically no back, just a couple of strings. Rebecca's had what I think is called a halter-neck. Melissa's blouse had no sleeves, a low neckline and a sort of noodle strap to hold up whatever was left of the blouse. The photographer loved it all and for a while, forgot all about the bride and the groom, who were sitting on the smoky stage. They were—prompted by the head priest—pledging in Sanskrit, a language that neither of them understood, to live together and care for each other all their lives.

My parents were already there. Soon, Kitty and Shree landed up too, and it was all fun and games for us even as poor Kitch was rubbing his smarting eyes and trying to figure out what the priest was telling him. Galiya, looked all excited and was looking around everywhere, waving to her relatives and winking at her friends and colleagues. A few minutes later, however, I saw her seemingly in a spot of bother. She had sat cross-legged, probably for the first time in her life and appeared to have inadvertently knotted herself up. With a look of anguish on her face, she seemed to be trying very hard to extricate herself. Later on, she told us her foot had turned completely numb from sitting on it and that she just couldn't move it. As the bride, she had been made to wear not a regular six-yard saree, but a longer, heavier garment that measures nine yards. It is also draped in a more complicated way. If you don't get it quite right, it will not only restrict your movement, it will also make you look like a brightly coloured penguin. Even many of the south Indian women from the younger generation cannot wear it properly without help.

There was a tubby, moustachioed gentleman sitting near me wearing the trademark white véshti and a white kurta. He remarked to the guy sitting next to him—in Tamil—something to the effect that this bride seemed very different from normal Indian brides, who look demure and coy. This one, he said, looked like a war-horse, waiting excitedly for the sound of the bugle. I must confess I found it rather funny. So, it appeared did *he*, because over the next couple of hours, I heard him repeat the same thing to at least three more people.

After the main event, which involved Kitch tying the sacred 'thaali' around Galiya's neck, everyone applauded. After a few prayers, the priest signalled that the ritual was over and people started walking to the stage to offer their congratulations.

'You may now kiss the bride!' Rachel shouted, startling everyone around. There is no such custom, of course, and would have been considered scandalous in traditional Chennai. The tag line on the board outside spoke of time standing still. That phrase could have been said of the city. While other Indian cities had evolved—for better or for worse—Chennai had steadfastly remained the bastion of conservatism.

'Yeah, *Kitch* the bride!' I shouted, not wanting to let a potentially comic situation slip. It caught on. Some of the youngsters among the crowd, including a few from Galiya's family, picked up the refrain. Even as Kitch stood there bewildered and confused, Galiya leaned towards him and kissed him on his cheek. Kitch bent back awkwardly, not sure of how to react. It was accompanied by cheers, claps and wolfwhistles. I don't know about time standing still, but I rather suspect many elderly hearts almost stopped beating that morning.

We were soon filled to the brim with a tonne or two of rice, sambar, mor kozhambu, rasam, three different vegetables, payasam, curd, papad, and pickles. Over lunch, Kitch tried to get us to say kozhambu the right way. His father joked that only a true-blue Brahmin could say it the right way. The syllable 'zha' apparently does not exist in any other language in the world. It isn't pronounced the way it is spelt. Not as in the 'su' of treasure. Nor is it 'za' 'sha' 'ra' 'da' or 'ya', all of which sounds came out from the Myers' gang in an attempt to get it right. It is pronounced by curling the tongue upward pointing towards the throat and bringing it down when you say it. I was the only one who got at least reasonably close to it, though Kitch and his father still wouldn't give me a 'pass' on my effort. I might have been a Brahmin, Kitch's father told me jokingly, in my previous birth.

That evening, we had a reception cum sangeet, or musical function. That was at a different venue—on the lawns of a beach hotel close to Mahabalipuram, an hour away from the city. Kitch's mother used to be a Bharatanatyam dancer and so are his sisters. They had arranged a Bharatanatyam programme by a well-known dancer. At the end of it, one of Kitch's sisters also danced to a Kannada song invoking Lord Krishna and a Tamil song which had lyrics addressed to Yashoda, Lord Krishna's foster mother.

Then the programme took on a lighter hue, with some Bollywood songs and dances thrown in. Kitch had been so impressed with Kitty's dance at her sangeet programme that he had requested her to perform here as well. She did the title song from a film called *Aaja Nachle*. That wasn't all. Hold your breath. Kitty, who seems to have made it her life's mission to make a dancer of poor Shree, got him (after a whole month of preparation, I understand) to dance to a recent Hindi song hit '*Dil da maamla hai dilbar . . .*' I applauded her persistence as well as the guy's efforts, but hey! Dance is something where the rhythm, the feel, the movements and the flow have all got to come from within you. There is no 'dance' or even anything remotely resembling it within young Shree. The poor lad was so nervous that while he mechanically did all the steps that were called for, he did them with a tense, menacing look on his face. It reminded me of a puppet show. Besides, the guy put so much vigour into his movements in an effort to do a good job that someone remarked that if anyone had accidentally got in the way, they'd have been cut into shreds. Kitch's grandfather, who was sitting next to me, turned towards me and said, 'You know, that girl's dance was very soft. But this boy's dancing looks very *violent*!'

There was more, apparently, including a video of the morning programmes along with a running commentary explaining the significance of the rituals for the benefit of the foreign visitors and youngsters, but I missed it. And for good reason. It was the final of the Twenty 20 Cricket World Cup, between India and Pakistan.

A match between these two teams is never a mere game. It is an event when all hearts in the Indian subcontinent stop beating and time stands still, like at Kitch's wedding. It is almost as if the question of the entire history between these two countries is decided by twenty-two players on a pitch of twenty-two yards. A neighbouring hotel had thoughtfully put up a big screen on the beach for the benefit of their resident guests—there were over a hundred of them watching it—and one by one, some of the Indian guests attending our function began to creep away from the lawns and sneak across to the beach, much to the surprise of our foreigner visitors.

Soon, I noticed that a few of Galiya's relatives had also joined us near the screen, wondering what it was that was causing such a commotion on the beach. Pakistan were batting and needed fifty-four runs to get from four overs. Five sixes were hit from the next two overs. The crowd began to turn slightly rowdy and some of them started hurling choice abuses at the bowlers. A couple of them also hurled other things at the screen, including shells, a half-eaten ice cream cone and a banana peel.

Suddenly, I found Melissa tugging at my sleeve. 'What on earth's happening? Is it a football match?'

'No,' I said. 'T20 final.'

She stared blankly. 'Well, whatever that means,' she said. 'Kitch sent me here to find out what the score was.'

'Tell him there's one over to go. Pakistan needed thirteen runs for victory, with one wicket in hand. Actually, on second thoughts, don't tell him anything. He might just leave Galiya in the lurch and come running out here.'

Joginder Sharma was the bowler. The crowd registered a murmur of protest. An international novice for the critical last over in the finals of the World Cup? What was Captain Dhoni thinking of?

First ball. Wide. Twelve needed off six. Everyone groaned. Next, dot ball. Twelve now needed off five.

A *six*!

Six runs needed now, off four balls. Dhoni's smile was increasingly beginning to resemble a grimace.

Next ball. An attempted scoop over fine leg is *caught*! Taken halfway down to the fence. It was all over! The crowd went completely nuts. People ran around in circles. Some turned somersaults, some did cartwheels. Others jumped up and down, screamed like animals, danced like people possessed and hugged complete strangers, including some of Galiya's family who looked bewildered, to say the least. Some of them panicked and ran back inside the hotel.

Some fifteen minutes later, the majority of Kitch's wedding party trooped back grudgingly into the lawns. There were only about twenty-five people seated there—Kitch looking anxious, Galiya looking shocked, the two sets of parents, about a dozen or so of Galiya's family, Peggy and an elderly couple or two who were Kitch's relatives. Just half an hour ago, there had been 250.

Kitch's father was on the stage holding a mike in his hand. I heard him announce '. . . a very happy day for me, for two reasons. Firstly, my son Krishnan has got married to er . . . to a wonderful girl' (polite applause mainly from the French/Kazakh contingent.) 'and secondly, I hear that India has just won the Twenty 20 World Cup!' (wild, thunderous clapping and shouting from about 200 others.)

Phew! What a way to get married!

# 26

## FOURSOME FROLIC

Dad, Mum, Kitty and Shree, Badru bhai and I were all seated for dinner at home. I was staying back for a couple of days. 'Its ages since you took any leave, *bhaiya*,' Kitty complained. 'I want you to come home for at least a couple of weeks, not just a day or two.'

'It's not so easy to get away,' I said, in between sending a text message to Madan bhai. 'There are some twenty to thirty deals I do each day. Every deal is money.'

'For whom? You?'

'For the client,' I replied. 'But of course, if a client does well, brings in more money and does lots of deals, the firm earns more, so that does translate to more money for me. I will cross a million dollars of the company's revenues this year. I want to do 2 million next year and maybe 2.5 or even 3 in 2009. If I can do that, I'd be a rich man myself. I'm planning to buy a house in Dubai. Property prices are going up by 40 per cent a year. Maybe I'll take all of us on a cruise abroad. How 'bout that?'

'Yoo hoo!' she cried, waving her spoon and spilling some aamras on Shree who was sitting to her left.

'And I could fund a dance school for you to run.' It was one of her many whims.

'*And*,' she added 'maybe also pay Shree's fees to join my school. Because, for him, there will be *special* fees which will run very high!'

'But Jai, is this kind of growth in revenues possible?' my father asked me, sounding very sombre. 'It seems very aggressive to me. I read in the papers that the US is already showing signs of major problems. They may get into a recession. They say when the US sneezes, the rest of the world gets a cold. They call it contagion effect or something.'

'Not this time I don't think, Dad. Asia is looking very solid. Even Europe is not really affected. There is every reason to believe that decoupling is likely. The US problems may lead to some slowdown in the west but will leave Asia untouched.'

'I hope so, Jai,' he said. 'But just be careful. They say those who forget history are condemned to repeat it.' My father has this tendency to get needlessly serious sometimes. Almost morbid. When he does that with my mum around, it irritates me, because then, she starts off in the same vein as well.

'No worries, Dad,' I told him lightly, with a careless shrug of the shoulders, 'Those who keep looking into the past cannot see the future.'

A family friend I met that day told me he had got a request from a political party to suggest a bank to hold their surplus funds for them. 'They can keep it for at least a year, but will then need to bring back all or most of it before the next elections. If they win the elections, they will again be in a position to fund the account in a big way. Is it suitable for your firm?'

'I don't think so,' I replied. 'It becomes difficult to justify political money, unless they send it in the name of an industrialist. This kind of thing may be easier for a Swiss bank to handle.'

'I think they already have Swiss accounts. It appears they are looking to diversify their banking relationships.'

But I decided to leave it at that. I didn't want to get involved with political parties.

That night, I wrote a long email to Mina. I wanted to tell her all about the wedding, the cricket match, the dance and everything. She would have loved to be here, but her father wasn't keeping too well. Also, he had been working to finalize a property contract in Dubai which was to be partly financed by a guarantee from Myers against his investments with us. Mina had taken over that work from him now and was being assisted by Kapoor.

The next day, Kitty and I spent time together and visited some of our favourite spots—a couple of book stores, our preferred restaurants, drove down to Fisherman's Cove that night and then did an early morning visit to a temple followed by breakfast at Murugan Idli.

Back in Dubai, the holy month of Ramadan was being observed. It is considered by Muslims to be a month for prayer, fasting, introspection and charity. There is a perceptible change in people's lifestyles and hours of work during this month. For non-Muslims too, there are a few restrictions, mainly relating to food. Most restaurants are closed until sunset. Eating or drinking is not allowed in public until after the iftar prayers are finished.

Ramadan is usually a relatively relaxed time, but for me, it seemed a long, hard grind, longer and harder than usual, because our new assistant (incredibly named Queenie) had got chicken pox. She had hardly recovered when she went down with some other infection and was out of action again. Besides, Kitch and Galiya had taken off on a rather long honeymoon to the Far East and it seemed lonely without them. The portfolios though were doing better than ever. I had to take some losses on a few of the portfolios, when the yen zigged against my expectation of zagging. But that apart and the negative flow of information notwithstanding, there was still plenty of money made. My BRIC investments had almost doubled in just a few months. I had a fairly significant chunk of Jaffer's family money on this sector. The State Bank of India GDRs had shot up to over 120, twice or thrice the price I had bought it at . . . The Dow had kissed 14000 and the Bombay Sensex had jumped from 14000 to 18000 in a matter of weeks. The positions that I had taken in oil were also looking good and rising steadily. But, work was getting just a little too routine and the follow up and documentation relating to the number of phone calls and number of deals were getting a bit too much to handle, with both Queenie and Galiya not being around. But they were back finally towards the end of October and with Mina also scheduled to come to Dubai for a couple of days, I was all buoyed up.

Meanwhile, I was surprised to see a somewhat unusual email from Cyrus addressed to the whole office, which touched upon 'responsibility'. It was the first time I had seen a note of this nature from him. 'The firm treats its employees like senior professionals,' he said in his note, and he expected them to behave accordingly. 'In several areas, our Financial Advisors are expected to exercise judgment,' he wrote. 'Whether it is about accepting or giving gifts, about adherence to compliance norms, or about incurring costs that are being reimbursed by the company, we expect you to exercise prudence and good sense at all times. The company gives its employees a lot of leeway to handle their clients and their book. It does not expect irresponsible use of that freedom.' Then, in a somewhat typically cryptic Cyrus twist, he concluded, 'Let us not misuse the trust that is reposed in us. The office gives us a mile, but let us not—unless it is entirely appropriate—take even an inch of that space.'

Soon enough, I found out the reason for this message from John. In addition to his Ops duties, John assists with administrative work as well, which includes payments of bills. Apparently, there had been an issue about one of Philippe's bills. He had gone to some island in Europe and had submitted a bill for a six-day stay, which had included several bills from the hotel's spa. Upon enquiry, he had initially refused to give any explanation, but had later claimed he had been working on a prospect who was based there and that the expenses were legitimate business expenses. Cyrus had wanted Rebecca to treat the matter as a compliance issue, but Rebecca had said that it was a business decision to approve or turn down an expense that was supposedly in pursuit of business. Cyrus had apparently taken up the matter with London, but no one had really wanted to bring the matter to a head since it involved a star performer. In the end, they stopped with a verbal warning. Cyrus had decided to send out this email to the whole office, though it was actually intended for Philippe.

When Mina came to Dubai, banking work took up a lot of her time. My client Bharat Saxena was very helpful in arranging for the loan. But we still managed to visit the Dubai museum (it was my first time in there) and also made time to go on a long drive one early morning to Hatta, where we had a leisurely breakfast. We did a double date with Kitch and Galiya. We went out bowling and then to the Mall of the Emirates, where Mina and Galiya shopped while the two of us sat and ogled at some of the passers-by. We had dinner at home, with Kitch and Mina doing the bulk of the cooking and Galiya and I pitching in with the cutting and washing. Before that, we spent some time in the pool in the building. Neither Galiya nor I could swim. Kitch had tried to teach me, but I had made little progress. Kitch himself was as much at home in water as he was on land—practically a human amphibian. He told us that in his native village, there was a pond in front of the local temple, where young boys would routinely be flung into the water by anyone who happened to be around. After swallowing a pint or two of murky, greenish water, every kid invariably learnt to swim.

I had learnt enough to swim the length of the smallish pool, but always ended in a state of panic, gasping for breath. I was getting ready to show off even this little bit to the group who were all in the pool. Kitch jokingly warned Mina and Galiya not to stay towards the left end of the pool. He knew from past experience that whenever I swam, I ended up swimming diagonally to my left, since I tended to use my right arm more strongly than my left. The last time Kitch and I were in the pool, I had surged unexpectedly like a torpedo towards the left end, much to the shock of a young lady who happened to be standing there peacefully, leaning against the corner, her arms spread out and resting along the sides of the pool. Worse, I reached her just at the point when my lungs were about to burst and grabbed at her somewhat inappropriately, making her scream and sending the kids nearby into raptures.

Just before Mina left, she managed to finalize all matters relating to the property. Kapoor helped co-ordinate with the developer and Saxena assisted with the bank loan. Between the two of them, they managed to wrap up things for her. Kapoor drove her to the airport along with me. On the way, Mina decided to needle him a bit. I had told her about his strong views on animal safaris and camera-toting tourists. 'You must go on a Kenyan safari sometime, Uncle,' she said, 'You will enjoy seeing the animals.'

Kapoor exploded. 'I have *seen* animals!' he said, almost shouting in his exasperation. 'How many times should we see animals? Why should we keep seeing animals? Do they have names? Do they talk to us? Do they have characteristics that we know? Faces that we recognize? *No!*' he thundered. 'If you have seen a potato in Dubai, would you go all the way to London to see another one? You would *not*! So why should you travel miles to see a zebra or a hippopotamus when we have already seen one? Meaningless! Today's generation of people have forgotten about their own parents, their family. But they go to another continent to see a gorilla! *Jaanvaron ka zamana hai.* This era belongs to animals!'

For five full minutes, Mina managed not to laugh and kept it suppressed. Just as we were about to reach the airport however, she burst into an extraordinary fit of never-ending giggles that had Kapoor worried stiff.

'I hope she is all right,' he told me on the way back, sounding concerned. 'Crazy girl. I wonder what came over her.'

# 27

## PHILIPPE BIDS ADIEU

November to March is the best part of the year in Dubai. To start with, there's the weather. It's a relief to be able to step out any time without worrying about it being too hot. It's the time when migratory birds descend on the city. For the city's residents starved of some of nature's bounty, it's a lovely sight—hundreds of these white, pretty things basking in the sunshine, sitting close together on the patches of green that are scattered around. It's also the time of the year when celebrities flock to the country, whether it's sportsmen looking for training under conditions of guaranteed sunshine or actors or singers looking to provide entertainment and enhance their fan base.

It's a very festive and *happening* part of the year. There's a lot going on. To start with, there's Diwali in November. Although Diwali in Dubai is a sober and muted version of what happens back home, it still makes its presence felt, quietly but strongly, in the form of lights on the balconies of hundreds of apartments all over town. This Diwali was a special one for Kitch. His parents had come to Dubai to be with them as both Kitch and Galiya had exhausted all their leave for the year with their extended honeymoon. Galiya wore a dark violet and gold saree that day to office. Diwali that year happened to be on a Friday, an optional weekend holiday for our staff. So, to make sure everyone saw her in a saree, she wore it on the previous day. Then, in December, it's the UAE National Day, the Christmas season followed by the New Year celebrations and the Dubai Shopping Festival, which is an annual event. Later on, there's the Dubai Golf Tournament, the Dubai Tennis Open and of course, the Dubai World Cup, the richest horse race in the world.

It was the middle of December 2007. Around this time each year, everyone in the industry has made plans for the forthcoming holidays and have mentally switched off from work. But there were simply too many things happening around me.

My asset book had grown further. It was now at USD 120 million, aided by a 7-million funding from Sudhir Shah. Sudhir was an aggressive investor. Much of his initial investments had gone into BRIC equities and that had raked in good money for him in a very short period of time. 'Jai bhai,' he told me, 'you are great! Better I just leave it to you to manage.'

Madan bhai's money in the meantime had been invested in a whole range of mutual funds and ETFs (Exchange Traded Funds) which tracked various sectors' asset classes. He had no particular bias towards India and I accordingly gave him a wide-ranging exposure. The only thing that I couldn't get for him was an off-shore fund that invested in East Africa, something he was very keen on. There was none in the universe of funds that Myers dealt in.

The clear problem areas for the money already invested were Infosys and Citi. Infosys had corrected sharply for two reasons. A good portion of its revenues were from the US and with increasingly clear signs of a recession in the US, Infosys's share price had been tending down for six months. The other reason was the continuing strength of the rupee, which meant fewer rupees for the company's dollar export earnings.

Citi, like Merrill and several other US and international banks, was in serious trouble on account of its mortgage lending in the US as well as the deteriorating quality of the portfolio of its investment banking arm. Liquidity was proving to be a major issue.

Raj and Dan made another trip to Dubai, where they made a presentation to many of our Dubai-based clients and those who were able to make it from the nearby cities. Jaffer was there. So was

Sunny Singh. He seemed to love coming to Dubai and needed only the merest excuse to do so. Among other things, clients were strongly urged not to increase holdings in US financials and in particular, to reduce holdings in Citigroup. That didn't go very well with some of the clients, though. 'What rubbish is he talking?' Jaffer asked. 'Six months back, he told us to buy Citi at 50. Now, he is asking us to sell it at 30. Is he mad?' I arranged a one-on-one meeting for him with Raj, who justified the decision to sell by pointing out that a lot of information had come out in the last six months, which put the industry and possibly Citi in particular, in a difficult situation. The expectations were that the prices would go further down and hence the sell recommendation. But Jaffer wasn't convinced. 'Abu Dhabi has shown faith in Citi. Prince Al Waleed is still holding on. Does this man Raj know more than them?' Jaffer countered. I, too, felt that Raj was being too hasty. So, we decided to ignore Raj's view by and large and sold put options in large quantities for Jaffer. That meant he got paid a premium upfront. However, if Citi dipped to 26 or lower on the date of maturity (which we didn't think was likely) he would be contracted to buy Citi at 26.

Bharat Saxena had dropped in at office to meet with them. I took him to my room. Rebecca had pointed out to me once that clients were expected to remain in the area meant for them, but I chose to ignore her comments. A man with a hundred-million book could get away with such things. I was always tempted to bring the clients inside, ever since I got my own room.

He entered the room and stopped short. 'You're facing the wrong way,' he said. 'You should be facing north-east, you are actually facing south-west. Just shift the table this way and put your chair the other way.' I suppressed a smile. I had no time to move furniture around. I could do half a dozen deals during that time.

'It won't take much of your time,' he said, almost as if he could read my thoughts. 'It's not just mumbo jumbo, Jai. These are just basic beliefs based on the earth's magnetic pull and the impact of space, light and sound on positive or negative energy. Call it

Vaastu, or Feng Shui or what you will . . . Small things, maybe. But I have seen that sometimes it helps.'

Meanwhile, I got a call from someone I hadn't heard from for quite some time. 'Is that Pat?' he asked, as I answered the phone.

*Pat*? Who on earth was Pat?

'This is Jack,' I replied.

'Hello, Pat. This is Stuart Wilson. We met at Vinoo's house.'

'Oh, hi, Stuart. Are you back in Dubai?'

It was the first time I had spoken to him since I opened his account a few months ago. He had got a temporary assignment in Russia or somewhere and had told me to keep things on hold till then. It was also the first time someone had called me Pat. I made a mental note to ask him to call me Jack, I thought. I couldn't possibly answer to four different names, surely? Apart from Jai and Jack, John always called me JP and that had caught on in Ops. And now, *Pat*!

Stuart wanted to buy UK banking stocks. The prices of blue chips like Barclays, Royal Bank of Scotland and Lloyds were about 25 per cent to 30 per cent down from their twelve-month highs, partly because of the collapse of the mortgage bank, Northern Rock. They were now offering dividend yields of 4 to 5 per cent. These were the kind of stocks he wanted to accumulate for his retirement. Over the long run, along with a modest capital gain, it could provide him with double digit returns. It seemed a good idea to me. He said he hoped to be able to retire in about two years time and was planning to settle down in a place called Banff somewhere among the Rocky Mountains in Canada, where he owned a couple of cottages. He kept one vacant for him to stay in and went there at least twice a year.

He also wanted to buy some bonds with a short maturity and a decent credit rating. I suggested to him a senior note of Kaupthing Bank, the largest Icelandic bank, one that carried an investment grade rating. It had a yen-denominated note that matured end of 2009, less than two years away. Its price had come down to about 96 and it paid a coupon of 1.8 per cent p.a. giving him a yield of about 4 per cent p.a. compared to a deposit which would give him less than half of that. If he borrowed yen for the period at a cost of about 1 per cent p.a., it would go to further enhance his returns.

Having tied it all up satisfactorily, I headed towards the pantry for a chat and a cup of something. On the way, I saw John jabbing away at the punching bag. John did it quite regularly. Not really to de-stress—John never got very stressed about anything—I think he just liked the feel of it.

There was Rachel in there, talking to Charulata, or Charu as she was now being called by some of us. Rarely was the pantry vacant. They were talking about Harry. Rachel was saying she found him cute. *Oh no*! I thought, I hope Rachel and Melissa have not gone and started liking the same guy. Even as things stood, there was more than just a bit of animosity between them.

Ahmed walked in. 'So, what's happening, guys? What's the topic?'

I didn't want to say anything to Ahmed about Harry. Rachel mightn't mind saying a few things with me around, but she wouldn't want Ahmed involved in it.

'We were discussing the ideal man,' I told him.

'Oh, come on yaar, I know exactly what these girls would have said. All of them say the same thing. The ideal man,' he said mockingly, mimicking a female voice, 'must be sensitive, caring, well-groomed and must have a sense of humour. Ha!'

'Well, what's wrong with that?' Rachel asked. 'Why, what do you look for in a lady?'

'I want a mix of Pamela Anderson, Jennifer Lopez and Angelina Jolie,' he said. 'I don't care if a woman is not sensitive or doesn't have a sense of humour. I know exactly what I want and I'm not shy to say it. It's a personal choice. Look at Jack here. Everyone knows he is running after a rich client's daughter. That's *his* choice.'

Even if he had head-butted me in the gut without warning, I couldn't have been more taken aback. I was so shocked I couldn't find any words to respond. He couldn't have found a more demeaning way of putting it. Even as I opened my mouth to give vent to my feelings, he took his cup and left.

Rachel tried to play it down saying, 'Oh, don't attach any importance to what he says, Jack. You know what he is like. Just ignore him.' Well, she was right in a way. Of course, I didn't have to attach much importance to what Ahmed felt about Mina. 'No noble gentleman was he, nor he my friend'. If anything, seen through my eyes, he was an 'eternal villain, some busy and insinuating rogue'. Still, he had hit below the belt and it hurt. To quote the great bard again, was 'the unkindest cut of all'. I was still trying to recover when Melissa walked in.

'Have you heard the latest?' she asked, breathlessly. 'Philippe has been sacked.'

# 28

## UNO!

The first quarter of 2008 was bizarre to say the least. It had a bit of everything—the good, the bad, the ugly and the entirely unexpected.

To start with, Sunny Singh called me from London to tell me that he had planned a yacht party for me in Dubai the following week. He said it was to thank me for the returns that I had given him in 2007. His account, which now exceeded USD 25 million in assets had yielded some 32 per cent p.a. for the year and that was in spite of a sharp drop in INFY and C towards the end of the year. His rather large exposure to SBI (State Bank of India) had more than doubled. Oil had done well too and likewise, the BRIC investments. These, combined with some structured notes linked to blue chip equities, had contributed substantially to his returns. Of course, the use of borrowing at low cost helped to enhance his returns as well. He was leveraged to the extent of about 40 per cent.

The party had to be postponed by a day at the last minute, because a public holiday had been declared in Dubai on account of the visit of President George Bush. I had been to London for a week and was not quite abreast of the latest in Dubai. Lost in my thoughts and driving down the creek road that evening in my new car, it did vaguely occur to me that there was hardly any traffic on the roads. Had I been more alert, I would have noticed that the only cars around were police cars. I would have also noticed the sign board and possibly a cop or two waving frantically at me. As it turned out, it was only when two policemen surged ahead and stopped their bikes in front of me that I realized something was wrong. One of them walked up, opened the door and shouted. 'Fool! What you doing? You have gone mad? Why you coming here? You think you are Bush?' I stared blankly at him.

'You want to go jail?' he asked.

'No!' I replied quickly. I was sure of that one.

'*Quick*!' he said, looking here and there feverishly, 'I park the sayyarah here. You go inside that. Go, go *go*!'

I didn't stop to ask questions. I realized now that I had committed some major *faux pas*. 'That' turned out to be a toilet. I locked myself in and immediately realized that for the second time in two years, I had ventured into the ladies' room. And then I remembered! Of course, President Bush! How dumb could I get? No wonder the cop was furious. I must have driven right through a no access road. Probably an entire motorcade was scheduled to come by anytime now. I could hear voices outside now and the sounds of cars. I hoped there was no function scheduled anywhere in the vicinity. I shuddered. I wondered if the First Lady would be there too. I had a sudden nightmarish vision of Laura Bush finding the toilet locked and banging the door. I huddled against the wall nervously for a few minutes, expecting any moment that the policeman would order me to come out and face the consequences. Suddenly, I was gripped by panic. Islamic law! A shiver went through my spine. My pulse was thundering so loudly, it sounded like it came from outside my body. Small pools of sweat formed on my body. I tried to take a few deep breaths to calm myself down and almost immediately stopped. I sounded like an asthmatic horse. Nothing happened for about twenty minutes. I peered out cautiously. It was all quiet. No policemen, no Bush, nothing that shouldn't be there. A wave of relief swept over me. I got into my car, drove home and collapsed on the sofa.

The story went well at the party the next day. Sunny joked, 'I would have invited Mr. Bush to the party, but then we would have to talk in English all the time. Besides, he might find our food too gassy. We don't want him farting around the place.'

Someone else said rather irrelevantly, 'Arre, nahin! Bush is a farm owner in Texas, so I'm sure he would have liked this tandoori chicken.'

'*Oye* brother' Sunny replied, 'forget about what Mr. Bush would have liked. Let us now enjoy our meal.'

'Yes' I agreed, 'After all, a bird in hand is worth two in the bush.'

Sunny had invited almost all his Dubai-based friends to the party. He made a special announcement about me and how I had given him the best returns that he had ever made on his investment portfolio. Earlier that day, I had taken a trading position in Pound Sterling and come out of it within three hours with a profit of USD 4,800. Having grabbed a microphone—specially arranged for by him to allow revellers to belt out Bollywood numbers—Sunny announced to the group that I had made his party entirely 'free' by that deal and requested the guests to keep it flowing. He himself was in full flow, aided by several repeats of his favourite beverage. 'I recommend,' he boomed, slurring slightly, 'opening accounts with this young man. Jai Patel. He's the king. He knows *everything*. Everything . . . except the names of capital cities.' He looked around at his audience, who were staring at him, not knowing quite what to make of this statement. 'All of us know,' he continued 'that the capital of Australia is Sydney or Melbourne. But this boy,' he said, pointing at me accusingly, as I stared at him, aghast. 'This boy thinks it is Kandoora!' He snorted and then broke into a chortle, which lasted for what seemed like an inordinately long time. He then resumed what—much to my embarrassment—was turning out to be a full-fledged speech. 'You will not regret, ladies and gentlemen. Any account with him carries my guarantee. The Sunny Singh guarantee!' he said, tapping his chest with his fingers.

During dinner, I happened to casually mention to a group that included him, that my fate seems to have inextricably got linked to

US Presidents or presidential aspirants. At Kogelo, I missed Obama by just a few months. And now, I had come within a whisker of bumping into President Bush.

Shortly thereafter, I regretted having brought up the subject at all, because after the meal, Sunny Singh, now completely sozzled, took over the mike again. 'My friend Jai will go very far,' he announced, 'Past, present and future American Presidents are chasing him everywhere. He works for an American company. Already, they have made his name fifty per cent American. They call him "Jack" Patel.' By now, he was slurring distinctly and Pammi was trying to gently dissuade him from going on. She managed to, but not before he had one last go at the mike. 'Jack Patel' he bellowed, raising a clenched fist. 'Jack Patel for President!'

I shut my eyes and moaned silently. I reached home at 3 a.m. after helping Pammi deposit Sunny safely on his bed.

At an office meeting the next day, Cyrus confirmed the news about Philippe, though most of us already knew it. He told us Philippe had to leave because of a misdemeanour and just left it at that.

John told me he had forged the signature of a client in order to catch a deadline for a large investment. The client had approved it verbally, but had not been able to sign the document. Based on the verbal confirmation and confident about the client signing an original one subsequently, he had chosen to forge the signature, possibly as a temporary measure. The investment, which was connected to 'Northern Rock', the British mortgage bank, turned sour owing to the sudden collapse and subsequent nationalization of the bank. The client claimed he had never signed any document pertaining to the terms of the investment and said it had been mis-sold to him. That was when the truth about the forged letter came to light. Though Philippe tried using the verbal affirmation of the client in his defence, the company decided that forgery could not be tolerated under any circumstances.

I don't think many tears were shed over Philippe's leaving. There were many in the office—me included—who were hoping that his assets would be transferred over to them, but the office chose to transfer it across two or three Europe-based advisors. While Cyrus seemed pleased that Philippe, with whom he had always had a cold war was out, he seemed a little concerned about the fact that without his assets, the office had effectively shrunk to just a little more than half of its earlier value.

I was now the number one producer and also had the largest asset book. It was a great feeling. Towards the end of February, I got my bonus for the year. The amount was USD 138,460. I was on cloud nine. A 100,000 dollars was something I had never seen in one place at one time except in the accounts of my clients. It felt unreal. I loved the feeling and kept thinking about it several times that day. I had always dreamed of having that kind of money, but had never seriously thought it would actually come my way, so soon. My bank account now had more than USD 150,000 in it. I decided I would use the bulk of it as a down payment to buy an apartment in Dubai and asked Kapoor to suggest one for me. He now owned three.

It was a big month for me for another reason—2008 was a leap year. A non-centenary leap year. Consequently, it was my birthday on the last day of the month. My father's familiar voice woke me up that morning. 'Jai Sri Krishna, beta,' he said. 'Wish you a very happy birthday!'

At office, I was just about to walk into my room when I stopped short. It was filled with balloons, floating around, bumping into the ceiling. Six of them. That was Rachel's idea, I learnt later. It was the sixth leap year since my birth, one each on my fourth, eighth, twelfth, sixteenth, twenty-fourth and twenty-eighth birthday. That afternoon, I received a bouquet from Mina. I was beginning to think she had forgotten. It came along with a card and a poem written by her. I read and re-read the rather babyish rhyme that she had written. Good Lord! If this was the kind of stuff she wrote, I could jolly well show her some of mine. Five minutes later, I nearly fell off my swivel chair as she walked into my room. She had asked Linda to send in the flowers just to make me think she was still in Kenya. She looked radiant and lovely. Having accepted her birthday kiss, I proudly showed off my room.

In March, Dubai was host to the richest horse race in the world, the USD 6-million-dollar Dubai World Cup. The ruling family in Dubai has always been well known for their love for horses and their efforts to promote the sport. This year, we decided to invite our clients to this instead of the tennis tournament. The FAs were asked which event their clients would prefer and the majority seemed to think it would be this one.

It went well with the clients, the ambience in particular. It was interesting to see an Ascot-like scene right here, in the heart of the Gulf; fashionably dressed women wearing all kinds of hats— exquisite, pretty or downright atrocious.

Lalwani told me he enjoyed it. 'This is the kind of thing, what we like. We come, we relax, we enjoy,' he said. 'I have account with another bank. They invited me last month for customer get together. I thought okay, I'll go, maybe I get good dinner. But they had *poetry* session! Some former Royal English poet reading out poems! Reading, reading, reading. For more than an hour. Then they gave us cake and scone and cucumber sandwiches. What nonsense is this! Who is interested in poetry? Last poem I read was "Jack and Jill". After that, I lost interest.'

It was just as well that we had paid for a stall sponsorship well in advance. If we had waited till March, the approval for the expense would have probably never come through. We had been asking Cyrus for an off-site this year. It didn't happen in January, because the Philippe episode was still too raw. He told us we would have it early March.

It didn't happen in March either, because Myers York had discovered and disclosed serious valuation issues with its holdings of mortgage-backed securities. Six months back, it appeared that we would have little or no write-offs. Now, we were told the company would have to make provisions for close to USD 6 billion. It could increase. Worse, the company had a significant holding in the equity of Bear Stearns, another large American investment firm, one that had been voted the 'most admired' US securities' firm according to a Fortune poll in two out of the previous three years. In March, Bear Stearns had to be sold off to JP Morgan Chase at less than 10 per cent of its share price high in 2007. It was a double whammy for Myers. Till recently, Myers York had been seen as the one saint in the den of vice. We had been issuing downgrades, underperform and sell recommendations on all other financials and brokerage houses. Suddenly, we were just the bad guy found out. It was like someone had rudely snatched away our angel masks. We were in it with the rest of them, sharing a bed of thorns. HO issued instructions to cut down drastically on costs. Apart from anything else, this meant—for the time being, at least—no off-sites, no impromptu parties and no business class travel.

# 29

## UNCERTAIN TIMES

In a meeting in May that year, Cyrus told us the only way to retain the Dubai office was to reach the 1 billion mark in assets again, preferably by 2009. When Philippe's book went away, we had come down to just below USD 600 million. We were still there. A few new accounts had been opened. More money had come in, but those additions got lost in the overall valuation because prices of assets had come down since the collapse of Bear Stearns.

My father had been asking me to meet an old friend of his called Deendayal Sharma who lived in Uganda. I had been postponing this trip—and in fact, all travel—as I hated the idea of travelling economy class. Somehow, the fact that I had travelled only economy the first twenty-plus years of my life didn't seem to matter. Twenty-plus months of business class travel and I had begun dreading the thought of travelling economy. I tried talking to Cyrus about it.

'Clients expect us to travel well,' I told him. 'Besides, I generate over a million a year. Give me one good reason why I shouldn't travel business?' I asked him.

He stared at me, expressionless, and said, 'How about because *I* travel coach?'

I turned away, went straight to my room and glowered. Cyrus didn't earn a dollar of revenue. He only cost the firm money. How did it matter to me how he travelled? He could travel by a bullock cart for all I cared. I walked to the punching bag, wrote his name on it and went at it.

Kapoor offered to come with me as he knew Uganda well . . . We landed at Entebbe airport.

'It's good that we are coming here now,' Kapoor told me. 'Many new hotels have been built from the time the country hosted the Commonwealth meet.'

At the airport, there were two large dogs sniffing for drugs. Both were about the size of small elephants. They ran up and down the conveyor belt and all over the bags and suitcases, sniffing. Suddenly one of them stood on mine. My heart went cold as he seemed to bend down and sniff sharply. Thankfully, he bounded away after only a brief dalliance with my suitcase. But for several seconds after that, my heart was pounding. What if someone had slipped something into the side flap? It was a scary thought. I breathed freely only after I came out of the airport.

Entebbe is on the shores of Lake Victoria, the largest freshwater lake in the world. Sharma lived in Kampala, the country's capital city and main commercial centre. He had a couple of businesses there, but he also owned a hotel by the lake, which is where we met him.

I took an instant dislike to the man, which only intensified over time . . .

He had a round face which sported a multiple chin on its southern border. Within the first five minutes, he had told me that he was the best golf player in Uganda. He had a very unique vocabulary and I came across several new words that day. He informed us that he was a highly respected businessman and not just some 'Tom or Dicky'. He said business was something that could never be done in a straight-forward way and that it always involved 'inky pinky'. Throughout our conversation, he had a man standing by his side, whom he referred to as his 'General Manager'. Every time he needed an ego boost after a statement, he would turn to the man who would promptly nod his head vigorously. Sharma told us proudly that the guy had quit his job as a 'male air hostess' for the privilege of becoming his employee. In between, from time to time, he would keep raising his hip and adjusting his underwear in an obscene kind of way. In a nutshell, he was an eminently dislikable chap.

He left us for a while to attend a phone call and Kapoor and I looked at each other. 'I think he will open the account,' he said, enthusiastically. 'I don't want his account,' I responded, vehemently. When Sharma returned, he told us me something else, almost bursting with pride as he did. 'The land on which I have built this hotel was originally only half this size. Little by little, I began reclaiming land by the lake. We worked secretly at night. For a long time nobody found out. When they did, I just bribed the municipality officials. Over the years, I added on almost one square kilometre. If it had not been for me, Lake Victoria would have been even bigger,' he said, simpering smugly. What a sicko, I thought. What on earth did my father think, pushing me to meet this pompous ass. I got up somewhat abruptly and signalled to Kapoor that it was time to leave, much to his dismay.

Later that day, we hired a car and drove around. I got a glimpse of the area where my family used to live many years ago, some two hours drive away from Kampala. My grandfather used to trade in foodstuff, I am told—mainly cashewnuts, fruits and tea. He also had investments in some plantations.

Back in the aircraft the next day, we were waiting for the flight to take off and Kapoor was lecturing me on how and why I should learn to separate business from my personal preferences. I was quite relieved when my phone rang. It was Kitch. 'Jai!' he said, 'I wanted you to be the first to know. I'm going to . . . we are going to have a baby!'

'*What*!' I shouted. 'You're one hell of a fast worker, dude!' Then, realizing I was surrounded by several hundred people, my fellow economy companions, I lowered my voice. 'Kitch! Wow, man! But it's just like a few weeks back that you got married.'

'It's eight months,' he said 'Time enough for us to have already had a baby. Kutti Kitch is due in November.'

'Or little baby Borat,' I added. 'But just make sure the baby's not born on the final of the next international cricket tournament,' I told him. 'Otherwise, poor Galiya and the baby will be in there all by themselves and the doctors and rest of the family will be out in the lounge watching the match.'

I had been hoping to spend a day in Nairobi with Mina, but had to get back to attend another of Raj and Dan's visits. They were now quite regular visitors and came every six months.

Barack Obama had just been elected as the Democrats' nominee for President. Incredibly, it had just been a little over a year since I first heard of him in Kenya. Now, there was no one who didn't know who he was. Most people spoke of him like he was someone they had known for a long time, whether in Nairobi, Dubai or Chennai. There was even—so I read somewhere—a small village or town in Japan, which was growing in popularity and reaping significantly higher tourism rewards simply because it shared his family name.

Dan mentioned Obama in his speech as a symbol of hope and change. He spoke about the steady rise in unemployment and how falling property prices were likely to erode consumer confidence even further. There is no quick fix, he told us, and there is little choice but to wait for the cycle to run its course. He felt it may take another couple of quarters.

The Dow Jones was back at 12,000, down from the peak of 14,000 it had touched just a few weeks ago. Citi had crashed to below 20 and Raj told us its fair value, according to him, was 11. There was a howl of protest. Most of us were holding huge quantities of Citi shares for our clients, bought over the last few months at prices starting from 50 downwards. Citi's new CEO Vikram Pandit had not yet been able to win over the confidence of the markets and the stock, after showing signs of some stability in the mid-twenties was now once again falling like a stone.

'How can you say that, Raj?' Rachel asked, echoing all our frustrations. 'I mean, I do understand that most of these institutions, including us, are holding a lot of non-tradable toxic assets, but Raj, how can we possibly recommend a stock at 50 one year and then say next year that it's too richly valued at 17? We can't keep contradicting ourselves to our clients. We need to do a better job of valuing these stocks!'

'That is precisely the problem, Rachel,' Raj replied. 'We are unable to value financials accurately this year, because the banks are not in a position to get a fix on the real worth of their investments. Something acquires a clear value only when it trades. If it doesn't trade, what do you value it at? At cost? At zero? Or an implied value somewhere in between? And if somewhere in between, where? Investments directly or indirectly related to mortgage-backed securities run into hundreds of billions. Most large US and international banks hold them in their books. It's a serious issue we are all grappling with—analysts, accountants, banks, investors, the Fed and the government. The situation is fluid, uncertain and very worrying. We can't wish this problem away, much as we'd like to provide to our clients a value cast in iron.'

'So, what's the best solution? What strategy can we offer our clients?' I asked.

'We need to try and differentiate the stocks that are falling because they are in trouble, from the ones that are falling because others are in trouble. You have Indian clients. India is still a great story, it's got good demographics and its growth has been resilient. Also, it has relatively little exposure to the US. The Sensex is down from 21,000 to 14,000 in six months. In my opinion, without sufficient reason. Then, there's China. In times of recession, consumers tend to buy cheaper goods. That might keep their exports going. Besides, China also has a huge local demand. The government has a war chest of reserves that runs into trillions. For sure, there is a slowdown. Yes, there will be a mild recession. Consumers are cutting down on spending and companies are shutting the tap on production. Demand-supply equations will come into play. Economics will rule. Concern among investors will pave the way to fear and fear may lead to panic. The share prices of companies will consequently bleed. But, remember what John

Rockefeller said "The time to buy is when blood is on the streets".'

It went well. The son of a what-not could certainly talk. But in reality, it was difficult to convince anyone to sell at 18 something he had bought at 40, by telling him it could go down to 10. It was far easier to get him to buy some more at 18 to lower his average cost.

While I stopped any further exposure to Citigroup, I bought plenty of the US Financials shares (Exchange Traded Funds) across accounts at about 70, down from about 114 a few months back.

Some of the new accounts still had cash which could be deployed at the current, lower prices. The earlier ones, while still significantly positive overall, were down from three months back. The one investment I had made, which was still doing really well, was taking a long exposure to oil. I had started with Sunny Singh's account over a year ago. Oil had gone up almost thrice, since then. With some other accounts, it had 'only' doubled as we got bought it a little later, but it was still good to see it in the portfolio. Talking of Sunny, he called me one day in August, all excited about the release of a new Indian film called *Singh is King*. The film's title had apparently been suggested by the film's hero, Akshay Kumar after spotting those words on the back of a truck somewhere in India. 'He must have seen one of *my* trucks,' Sunny told me proudly, delighted that his little whim or gimmick that originated twenty years ago, had got translated into a Bollywood title.

For Dr Chimanbhai Patel, I had bought Barclays, RBS, Lloyds, HSBC and Stanchart, all UK-based banks that he was very comfortable with. These had all dipped 30 per cent from their fifty-two-week highs. For Stuart, I bought more of these. His Kaupthing bank—the one whose yen bond we had bought at 97 had now gone down to the eighties. 'Is it still investment grade?' he asked. It was. We bought more. I did for some other clients too. Opportunity, I thought to myself, knocks but once.

In the meantime, in a bid to take advantage of the situation, I bought a three-bedroom apartment in the 'Downtown' area with a built-in area of almost 1500 square feet. Six months ago, similar apartments were being offered at 1300 dirhams a square foot. Just some six weeks back, I had *almost* bought it for 1550. Now, I was being offered one at 1650. With a little bit of persuasion from Saxena, who incidentally also arranged for a 90 per cent financing from his bank, the broker sold it to me at 1600. 'Only for you,' he told me. 'There is somebody willing to pay 1700 for this today. Property market is booming and zooming.'

# 30

## HELL BREAKS LOOSE

It was the beginning of September, 2008. There was no improvement in portfolios. But at least it didn't go down any further, so that was a blessing. There were still plenty of issues though. There had been talk about Lehman Brothers since a few months now, whether it would be next in line after Bear Stearns. Dan had assured us that Lehman was 'systemic' to the US financial system and that if at all the problems got really serious, the Fed would rescue it or make alternative arrangements just like it had done with Long Term Capital Management and with Bear Stearns.

But still, rumours were rife. About Lehman, about Citi, about Merrill Lynch, about the Washington Mutual Bank and even about us. Many of the big international banks had made huge provisions in their books for investment losses. UBS, HSBC, Barclays, ING, the list was long and diverse.

Peggy had a long chat with me. She told me there was no doubt that many of America's banks and brokerage houses were struggling with the weight of its so-called toxic investments. Under these circumstances, business was not going to be easy. But she was equally concerned that if our assets didn't keep growing, Myers might be forced into selling some of its offices in a bid to consolidate and raise cash.

'Please keep at it, sweetheart. I see you have reduced your travel a bit. Don't let the negative sentiment in the market get you down. Even if the existing accounts are under a bit of pressure, we need to keep pushing for new business. I'm banking on you for another 50 million this year. Oh, and will you please ask Charlotte to come in here for a minute?' she said.

I stared, puzzled. 'Charlotte?'

'Yeah. The new girl from Mumbai. I call her Charlotte. It is pretty close to her actual name, huh?'

Shaking my head in amusement, I went to find Charu. These Americans! Trust them to find an easy way out of everything, I thought. If only they could manage this financial crisis that easily as well. The number of new phrases that had been introduced to the layman in the last few months by the investment world: 'Subprime', 'Alt A', 'Securitization', 'Toxic assets', 'Liquidity crunch' . . . it wasn't funny. I desperately hoped it would stop soon before it engulfed everyone else.

Charu was sitting at her desk, looking pretty and as always, wearing her hair down to her waist. Her long, beautiful hair was the envy of all the girls at work. Ramzi kept touching it every time he walked past her (which seemed quite often) and saying how beautiful Indian women were (which she consciously and consistently ignored) as opposed to Indian men (which I ignored). I passed on my message and went over to do a summary of my accounts and talk to some of the clients.

Kirit Desai had sent in a million and a half initially and another million and a half this week. He was scheduled to meet us in Dubai next week. He wanted to meet Peggy as well.

Stuart came up with one of his own recommendations, the largest bank in Kazakhstan called 'Bank Turan Alem'. He was very bullish on the country, which he had visited on several occasions in his capacity as a consultant in the oil and gas industry. It was very rich in resources, he said and politically stable. The banking industry, too, was well run and growing. Bank Turan Alem had a USD bond maturing in 2010 that was trading in the nineties, giving a yield of around 12 per cent p.a.

'It looks like an extraordinary opportunity,' he told me. I checked with KCP Securities, a subsidiary of Myers which specialized in emerging market debt, particularly in East and Central European countries. They corroborated Stuart's views and sent me a buy recommendation they had issued on the bank some three months ago. Effectively, it is quasi-sovereign risk, their analyst told me. There is a tacit understanding that the government will not let the country's top banks fail.

At the end of the week, I crossed the million-dollar mark in revenues for the second year in succession. My name had, for quite some time, been right on top of both the lists on the scoreboard. Though I rarely looked at it during the working week, I liked to look at it and gloat over it during weekends when there was no one else in the office. To have achieved this in what had not been the easiest of years for the markets, was something I was very proud of. It also assured me of another 100,000-plus-dollar bonus next year. Maybe I would put that in equities, I thought. I also wanted to do a holiday with the family, something I'd had in mind for a long time. I wished Mina could come with us. I had only hinted about Mina to my mum and to Kitty. My father still didn't know.

The following week, Dilip Kochar had dropped by on his way to London. He asked me if I could arrange for some 'entertainment' for him. I knew he usually tended to do a lot of clubbing and drinking when he travelled, but this time he seemed to be asking for something more. I felt a little cheesed off. What did he take me for? I told Kapoor about it and he shook his head, sadly. 'That man has to stop his drinking. Otherwise he will just get into more and more bad habits. Just leave it, puttar. You don't have to do anything.'

When I mentioned this to Rachel about him, she giggled. 'Why don't you invite him to your home tonight, along with the rest of us? He can partner me, can't he? If he tries getting fresh, I'll pour some cold water on his head. That should keep him sober. Horny bastard!'

I had invited some friends home that night for a quiz. There was Harsh and Joi, Peggy, Richard and Rachel. Then there was Omar and Gavas, both banker friends of mine. I decided to take Rachel's advice and invited Kochar home.

He couldn't believe his ears.

'Quiz? Who, me? Have you gone mad?' he asked.

It was only when I told him I would team him up with a pretty British girl from my office that he began to look at it positively. I remembered how Kochar had once confessed to having a very soft corner for white women. At that time, I thought he was saying it in jest, but perhaps not!

So, it came about that Kochar, seeking 'entertainment', was subjected to the ordeal of my quiz. As he sat down, he seemed in equal parts curious and nervous. No man likes to make a fool of himself in front of pretty women. 'The last time I was so nervous was when I was in front of the US immigration officer while applying for my visa,' he told us. But after he elicited the first laugh or two with his comments from the group and downed a quick drink, he became himself and even started humming and singing.

A few minutes later, on his turn I asked who had been the USA's first Vice-president. 'Are there any negative marks?' he asked, before proceeding to incorrectly suggest that it was Abraham Lincoln, amidst a suppressed twitter from Peggy and Joi and open, happy laughter from the rest of them.

'You must thank your stars the US immigration official didn't ask you this question, Mr Kochar!' Peggy laughed.

'The only question that I really want to be asked is "Dilip, will you have another drink?"' he said and everyone laughed again.

Kochar's initial chagrin at the seriousness of the quiz turned to mild enjoyment after a few rounds of the quiz, during which he knocked down several whiskies. An hour down the line, we were halfway through. Kochar was feeling so relaxed that he even made a pass at the leggy Peggy who was sitting right in front of him. From time to time, he broke into old Hindi film love songs directed at her.

Peggy, I could see, was half-amused, half-disconcerted at this ogling, drunk client. But Rachel was enjoying herself hugely, pulling his leg, addressing him as 'partner', trying to needle him and egg him on. She asked him to explain what the songs he was singing meant, but I quickly put a stop to it. I wasn't going to have my quiz turned into a farce. Peggy's boyfriend Richard was already in splits, as Kochar put on this amorous look and continued singing to Peggy, accompanied by Bollywood style filmi actions. Towards the end of the quiz, when asked to name some Indian union territories, Kochar named Goa and in his drunken stupor, got very upset when I told him it had become a 'state'.

'Nobody consults me, they just do things on their own!' he complained, in a weak, whining voice. He continued along those lines for a minute, while Rachel patted him on his back and assured him that she would ask the Indian government to consult him in future. Suddenly, the weakness passed and he turned strong and belligerent. He loudly berated Indian politicians who he said, for political reasons, kept changing union territories into states and names of cities without even bothering to ask for his opinion. Next time, he swore, he would not vote for them.

'Will you vote for *me*?' Rachel asked him sweetly.

Unexpectedly, Kochar snarled at her. 'I will *not* vote for you!' he shouted, belligerently. For a few seconds, he simmered in silent pique. Then he changed tack and simpered. 'I will vote for her,' he added, pointing to Peggy, sending Richard into another laughing frenzy. For the record, Harsh and Joi won by a very comfortable margin.

As Peggy and Richard left after dinner, Kochar sang in the corridor, '*Hum tumse juda hoke . . .*' This time Rachel pinned him down and insisted that he translate the lyrics to English. Kochar closed his eyes and then explained rather laboriously, 'It means,' he said, 'When I'm separated from you . . .' (again pointing at Peggy), 'When I'm separated from you, I just cry and cry and die!' Everyone howled with laughter, except perhaps me. At that time, I really didn't know whether to laugh or cry. But thinking about it later that night, with Kochar safely deposited in his room, I laughed so much, my stomach ached.

Just as well, because I didn't get a chance to laugh for many days to come. Just two days later, we knew along with the rest of the world that all attempts to save Lehman Brothers had failed. The 158-year-old venerable, highly respected company, teetering under the woes of its investments and its leverage, had crumbled. There was complete pandemonium in office. We had millions of dollars of both client investments (and possibly Myers' own) in the company. Some had Lehman's equity, some had perpetual bonds, some (me included) had notes structured by them. In the last few months, we had stopped accepting notes structured by Lehman—post Bear Stearns—as a measure of precaution, but there were several notes which we had done in 2007, which were scheduled to mature only in 2009.

A day later, Merrill gave itself up to the Bank of America, providing a bit of relief. But that was the only bit. The markets were in a state of complete shock. The bears and the short-sellers held the financials in a tight squeeze. Emerging market equity and debt prices tumbled. Iceland went belly up and nationalized their banks. The speculative bubble in oil deflated, sending prices crashing from over 100 to 70 in a matter of days. Several governments across banned short-selling in shares to stop speculators from bringing down prices in shares which they had sold, without ever owning them. AIG, the insurance giant, found itself on the brink of collapse and had to be saved by the government. Morgan Stanley and Goldman Sachs were gifted banking licences overnight in a measure of desperation as the credibility of the investment banking world evaporated. Several instruments stopped trading overnight. Those who didn't have cash struggled for life. Those who did, held on to it with a vengeance. Those who had borrowed heavily got crushed under its weight. Size, business model, growth rate, profit margin, all these ceased to matter. All that mattered was liquidity. Cash had never before been so indisputably *king*!

Phone calls from clients kept pouring in all day. We had a series of conference calls with the guys in New York, but there was little clarity. There were conflicting opinions between Raj, Dan and Ralph. We saw Bloomberg reports about a potential sale of Myers York to one of the other investment houses. Client portfolios

started crashing. Every day, millions of dollars got wiped off from
their account values. Everyone in office was walking around like
zombies, faces white as a sheet and fear inscribed all over . . .

In the middle of all this, Kirit Desai landed up.

'Prices have crashed. This is good time to buy!' he told Peggy
and me excitedly, his eyes gleaming with the light of expectation.
'Very lucky, I have not bought so far, now I can just *mint* money.
I sold off most of my investments in June-July with other banks.
I did very good thing. Very lucky!' It was a little nauseating to see
him there, almost rubbing his hands together in glee, as most others
were reeling from the shock.

'I want to buy UK banks equities,' he said. 'Very cheap. Also,
I want to buy Washington Mutual Perpetual Bond. 'Wa Mu'. Not
the 2017 bond, that is 60 dollars. I want perpetual bond. Only 40.
Very cheap. I know the bank very well. It is that 'Whoo hoo'
bank! One whole month last year, I was seeing their 'whoo hoo'
advertisements when I was in America. I know that bank. My sister
has accounts with them—100 dollar bond at 40! Very good! My
brother-in-law is recommending it. He wants to buy also. I buy for
both now. 1 million each.'

'A million each?' I asked. 'Are you sure? It's a difficult time for
the industry. It could cut both ways.'

'I am too sure!' he exclaimed, looking like a kid with a new toy.
'My brother-in-law is American. He was working with that bank.
This is big tip from him. He wants to put 1 million of his own in
this. If he is not sure, why will he recommend? After you buy for
me, you ask your other clients also to buy. Er . . . let them also
benefit,' he added, completely lacking conviction. I could guess
what his game was. But I was too worried and tired to think about
it too much. In a rather distracted way, I took down the orders and
placed them.

Two days later, the FIDC moved in to shut down Washington
Mutual. They sold the deposits to JP Morgan Chase, Wa Mu's
share value plummeted and the holders of their 7.25 per cent
perpetuals were left with nothing except a line in their bank statement.

I didn't have the guts to call Kirit Desai. I had just spoken to Stuart to tell him about Kaupthing Bank, which had just got taken over by the Iceland government. Its bonds had stopped trading. Effectively, this senior note that we held, could be worth little or nothing. Stuart was in Banff and it was heart-rending to sense his pain and his helplessness. I felt responsible for it in a sense, because I had suggested it to him. It had appeared such a great idea then and no one had seemed to think any differently. Not me, not the analysts, not the client. I had even suggested that he borrow in yen to buy this one. That wasn't all. His Turan Alem bond had practically stopped trading too, like most emerging market debt. There were just no bids.

A few minutes later, Kirit bhai called me himself, beside himself with rage. He seemed to have completely lost it. 'Cancel the trade!' he screamed into the phone. 'I tell you, cancel the trade. I cannot do this trade.'

I was struck dumb. 'Kirit bhai,' I said gently, extremely thankful to have hundreds of miles of water between the two of us. 'I cannot cancel the trade. It's already done. I'm sorry.'

'*Sorry!*' he shouted. 'What good being sorry? I will be ruined. I will be finished. My brother-in-law is not giving me his money now. I will sue him! I have put 2 million of my own money. I am not doing this trade. It is cancel. Cancel. *Cancel!*' he yelled and slammed the phone.

I replaced the receiver in a daze. I folded my arms, put them on the table and buried my face in my desk. A few minutes later, Peggy rushed into my room. 'Jack, what the heck do you think you are doing? How can you possibly cancel that deal? The Wa Mu one for Desai. I know how you feel, but there's nothing we can do, honey.'

I stared at her dumbstruck. 'I didn't cancel anything.'

'Mr Desai says he just spoke to you and that you have agreed to cancel his 2-million deal.'

'*No*! I didn't do any such thing! He called and shouted at me saying he wanted to cancel the deal. I told him it wasn't possible.'

'Sweetie, are you sure? We could have a legal case on our hands, you know.'

'I'm sure, Peggy. It was only he who kept shouting "Cancel". How could I agree to something like that?'

'I'm sorry, dear. I think I just lost my cool for a minute. That guy is a jerk.' She turned to go.

'Peggy' I called. 'Does this mean he loses the entire 2 million?'

'I'm not entirely certain, Jack. I've just had a word with our legal department. Unfortunately, it appears that *could* be the case.' She walked away, looking more serious than I had ever seen her look. I had a sick feeling in my stomach.

That afternoon, we had another conference call. The only thing that came out was that we were in 'a state of flux' and that we should 'remain close to our clients'. 'These are very difficult times,' Dan told us. 'It is impossible to say which way things will go over the next few weeks and months. If you do nothing else, just do these two things: a. Reduce your client's borrowing and b. Smother them with love. Remain in cash as much as possible. Over the next few weeks, we could see some fantastic buying opportunities.'

# 31

## STOCK AND AWE

'My friend, what is happening?'

'Oh, hi, Jaffer.'

'What is happening?' he repeated. 'Is the world coming to an end or what?'

'Er . . . right now, we definitely seem to be in a state of flux,' I started.

'My friend, I know we are in a state of flux. I don't need my private banker to tell me that. What do we do now, what can we buy, what can we sell? That's what I want to know. What are they saying about Citi now? They were right about it last time. It has gone to bloody five dollars now! Should we buy more?'

'Jaffer, I think we shouldn't look at any single share at this time . . . Let's go for broader indices, individual stocks look just too risky at this time.'

'More BRIC, maybe?'

'Maybe. Over a period of time, say three months. Not in one lot.'

The biggest problem accounts were those where borrowings were involved. Stuart was one, Sunny was another. Kochar was the third.

I started getting calls daily from the credit department. So far, in the last two years that I had been in touch with them, they had been pretty much in the background. Seldom were they ever a topic for pantry talk. It was completely different now. In the fourth quarter of 2008, credit took centre stage. Take Stuart's account. His account value had dipped to less than 40 per cent of its value in just a few months. We had bought Barclays at the average price of 3.50. They were down to 1.50 now. Lloyds, ravaged by falling house prices in the UK and the proposed merger with Halifax Bank of Scotland, had fallen to below one pound from about three earlier on in the year. Standard Chartered had moved from sixteen pounds to six in four months. And as for RBS—one of the banks that bought out ABN Amro just a year ago in a high-profile acquisition game—the less said the better. Stuart's bonds in Kaupthing was being valued in the statement at six cents to a dollar. There was no guarantee that he would get even that; there was no activity in the market even at that price. And we had just heard that the Chairman of Bank Turan Alem had left the country. 'Fled' was the word being used by the news agencies. He was being accused by the Kazakh Central Bank of wrong doing. The only saving grace in the account was a few balanced mutual funds that were still at 60 per cent of their cost price. The loan amount in his account was now almost as much as the value of his investments. Forget about growth or even capital preservation. This was wealth destruction on a massive scale in front of our very eyes and there seemed to be little we could do about it.

Larry Tan, the credit officer, had just given me twenty-four hours time to bring in USD 170,000. Else, he told me he would sell.

'Larry,' I pleaded. 'Twenty-four hours is too short. The client is abroad. He is on holiday in Canada. There is no way he can make arrangements to remit in one day. Please give me three days.'

'Two days, can,' he said, in his typically crisp if somewhat cryptic style. 'But don't delay, lah. Any, delay, I cut. Chop! Finish!'

It would be 3 a.m. in Banff now. I decided to wait another four hours before I called. Meanwhile, there was a ruckus going on in the office. Two of Rachel's clients had come to office and thrown a fit. They had also thrown furniture. Flung portfolio statements.

And hurled abuses. Cyrus and Rebecca had been left shell-shocked and Rachel in a flood of tears. Pensioners apparently, they had lost a substantial portion of their wealth. They had wanted investment grade bonds and Rachel had given them a portfolio of ten companies, all of them investment grade bonds. Three of them— Lehman, Kaupthing and Washington Mutual—had gone bust, all in a span of a few days. Four of them had lost between 5 and 30 per cent while the others were being valued at less than half their cost. I tried cheering Rachel up, but with little success. She was inconsolable.

A little while later, I called Stuart. It would still be only 6 a.m. but I couldn't wait any longer. It was already the longest three hours of my life.

'Stuart,' I said, 'This is er . . . Pat. I'm awfully sorry to say this. I don't know if you are clued in to what's happening in the investment world out here—your account value has come down to 540,000. The loan stands at half a million. My credit department will not lend more than 70 per cent. They need another USD 170,000 to be sent immediately, otherwise they will start selling at market prices.'

There was a long pause, when I just hated myself. If only I had never suggested Kaupthing to him. But then, he may have bought more RBS with it. Or maybe Citi. If only I had insisted that he doesn't borrow. If only . . . . . .

'Actually, I was expecting your call, Pat.'

That came as a welcome respite. I felt a wave of relief surge over me. If he was expecting my call, he must have been known what was happening. If I was not the first bearer of bad news, that was good news for me.

'You know what, Pat? My retirement suddenly looks a very, very long way away. I checked the prices on the net last night and I don't think I slept a wink all night. And I've never felt this lonely, Pat. At least not since your . . . not since Jane died.'

'I'm terribly sorry, Stuart. This is like a nightmare, I know. Kaupthing seems down and out, but hopefully, the others will recover in time. I'll pray for you. But for now, can you somehow, please manage to remit the funds, Stuart?'

'I'll try, Pat. I'll call you in a day or two. Tell those ass-holes to wait.'

Sunny Singh was leveraged too, but because initially his account had gone up substantially in value, he was still okay and his credit still had enough cover. 'What to do, Jai?' he asked. 'Like idiots, we sat and watched the rainbow. Now the rainbow has gone and there is only a thunderstorm. *Gadhe hain hum*! Like donkeys, we are caught in it without even an umbrella.'

I decided the only way we could recover within any reasonable period of time was if we bought at these levels.

'Sunny ji,' I said, 'I think this is really a very good buying opportunity. They say one should buy when blood is on the streets,' I ventured.

'Oye, bloody hell!' he retorted. 'That blood on the street is mine. *Ai mera khoon hai*! State Bank was 120, now it is 40. Oil was 140, now it is 50. I cannot let my blood flow more.'

Kochar was just marginally in the safe zone. I called him to suggest he send some funds. I had to tell him his portfolio had given up all the gains we had achieved in the last year and was now down. Any more decline and there would be a margin call as his investment value could become insufficient to cover his loan. He was very quiet and was very curt in his response, like he was talking to a stranger. My heart sank. It was a very dismal feeling. Telling someone their hard-earned wealth left in your care is worth half of what it was three months ago? What could be worse?

Stuart called me after a couple days. 'Pat, I'm remitting the money today,' he said.

I closed my eyes, summoned up all my courage and said, 'The prices have gone down further, Stuart. I'm sorry, but we need USD 215,000, now.'

'I'm sending 300,000, Pat. I know how these things work. I've been through the Nasdaq crisis. Bankers can be bloodsucking bastards at times like this. But equities seem very attractive at these levels now, Pat. What do your analysts say?'

'That there are some fantastic opportunities out there. This is a great time for those lucky enough to be in cash.'

Meanwhile, the other FAs were having a much more difficult time. Some accounts were very heavily leveraged. A few cases, where clients couldn't bring cash immediately, had got completely wiped out. Charu was fuming because the credit department had gone and sold off all the securities in the account of one of her clients, because his promised remittance had been delayed by a day. As a result, the client had lost almost his entire initial investment of 1.5 million. All that was left was USD 12,000. I took her to Peggy to seek help.

'Peggy, those guys at credit are behaving like monsters. They can't treat us or our clients like this,' I said.

She nodded. 'I know, Jack. I'm fighting them on behalf of all of us. But they have a job to do too, honey, like we do. Their job in this crisis is to try and protect the bank in the best way they can. Some of the borrowed clients are in negative territory. They will start owing the bank instead of them having money with us, because the value of their investments will be worth less than their loans. Myers is not very liquid now and we just can't afford to get into a situation where we have hundreds of such cases. That'll be the end.'

Kochar called me the following week. It was almost 10 p.m. He had not answered my calls the last couple of days. Now he was drunk and abusive. 'Bloody fellow, what advice have you given?' he shouted. 'Damn your advice! You like quiz? You want quiz? I ask you quiz! Question number one! Is Jai Patel my friend? Answer, no! No! Not my friend.'

I remained silent. This must be a bad dream, I was thinking. Surely such things don't happen in real life. They can't possibly happen. Just a few months back it looked like I could do no wrong. And now, this?

'You understand, Mr Patel? Not my friend.'

'Dilip bhai, it's just a question of time,' I told him, gently but unconvincingly, even to my own ears. 'These are ridiculous, unreal values. They will definitely recover in the long run.'

'*Ghanta*!' he raged. 'In the long run, damn it, we are all dead. William Shakespeare himself has said it. William Shakespeare, you *understand*?'

I neither had the heart nor the guts to tell him that the quote was attributed to the economist, John Maynard Keynes . . .

The next day I went through my other accounts. Harsh—down 46 per cent in three months, Saxena—down 41 per cent, Sudhir Shah—down 34 per cent, Madan bhai—down 27 per cent. I spoke to each one of them.

Sudhir Shah was livid and insisted on meeting Peggy. He came over to the office and complained to Peggy that I had invested in highly 'speculative' shares. Peggy brushed off his complaint and asked him point blank why he did not tell her earlier if he was not happy with the handling of his portfolio. The incident left a bitter taste in my mouth. He called me too, and asked me why his investments were not capital guaranteed.

'But . . . but they are equities, Sudhir bhai' I stammered. 'How can they be capital guaranteed?'

'How can you risk my capital?' he said angrily. 'Do you not know that I am a conservative investor? And why did you buy that Lehman note? You did not tell me Lehman will collapse and I will lose my money!'

'Sudhir bhai, I *didn't know*. I had no idea this would happen. None of us did.'

'Then what is the difference, you and me, can you explain?' he asked. I had no answer to give. Many clients allowed their bankers to trade on their behalf. Often clients were advised subsequently. As long as the going was good, no one had an issue. But now . . .

'Better I go to that monkey!' he screamed.

For a moment, I thought I hadn't heard him right. Then I remembered. I had mentioned to him a few months ago that an American newspaper had actually taken the trouble of getting a monkey—Adam Monk—to pick stocks every year. It did this by marking randomly on a newspaper with a pen. Mr Monk's record has not been too bad in some years. That story had seemed very funny then. Now, it did not. I wished I had never mentioned it. I remained silent. How does one reply to something like this?

'Also, I am hearing bad reports about your company. I don't want to take so much of risk. I want to transfer USD 5 million to another place. The question is where? Everyone is covered with shit.'

'Maybe to the monkey,' I said. Not to him, of course, just to myself.

I suggested my friend Omar. His bank was not untouched, but at least they were big.

'I don't want any Pakistani bankers,' he said, hurriedly.

'He's a good guy, Sudhir bhai,' I told him. 'And it's a big bank. Besides, if you just want to leave it in cash, what's the problem?'

Then there was Mina's account. That was down 24 per cent. I heaved a sigh of relief. Under the circumstances, that almost seemed like a profit. Mina had been talking to me every evening after dinner. She knew it was a difficult period for me and kept reassuring me. The hedge funds were reasonably stable—most of them—though a couple had temporarily stopped redemptions. About half a million was still in cash. Two bonds were down badly, but most others were still at over 70 per cent of cost. The guarantee issued against the account could be a source of concern, but only if the portfolio fell by another USD 200,000.

Which it did. The very next day.

On 12 December, Peggy came to me. She looked shaken. 'Jack dear, I want you to be strong. None of this is your fault. It's just a bad time for all of us and for our clients.'

'I can't take any more, please, Peggy. Don't give me any bad news.I assure you, I am not strong enough.'

'You have to keep your chin up, darling. And don't forget, I'm with you in all this. I'll help you talk to your clients. Listen.You have clients in Fairfield Sentry, including USD 500,000 for Mina. Our office has USD 9 million in it. Well, I think that's all gone.

The fund was entirely invested in Bernie Maddoff's fund. He has just confessed it was one big Ponzi scheme.'

'A *what* scheme?

'A Ponzi scheme, named after a guy of that name. It's a fraud scheme, where earlier investors get paid high returns often with new investors' capital. As long as new investors keep coming in and the redemptions are limited, the party goes on. If there are too many redemptions, it comes unstuck. That's what's happened. The whole thing's a fraud, Jack! For 50 billion dollars! Probably the biggest ever. It's not our fault, Jack. Don't worry about this, I'm on your side.'

I remained silent, staring at her, speechless at first.

'Hell!' I said, shutting my eyes and covering my face.

She put her hand on my shoulder.

'Peggy!' I whispered, turning to her, 'This is the *worst*, frigging nightmare I've ever had.'

I couldn't believe what I had just heard. Were these the regulated markets of the twenty-first century or some kind of free-for-all gambling den? In a daze, I moved to the television and joined the small crowd of standing corpses there. Some of these corpses soon sat down, but beyond that, there seemed no sign of life.

I came home that evening in a state of complete shock. Sitting on the sofa, I clutched my head and shouted out loudly. This could not be real. I went into the kitchen and raided the fridge. I was feeling very unwell. I finished a whole tub of ice cream as I stared blindly at the financial channel. At the end of two hours, after having read and heard the word 'Ponzi' about a hundred times, I must have somehow fallen asleep right there. When I woke up, it was about midnight. The television was still on. The name of Maddoff was being flashed again and again. I walked around like a caged animal for some time. Then I called Mina. She had just gone to bed. I spoke to her for half an hour. I was probably rambling, incoherent. But I was clear on one thing. I told her I needed to meet her dad in person. The next morning, I was on a flight to Nairobi. To disclose to my future father-in-law, that unknown to him, amidst all the other bad news, he had just bid goodbye to half a million dollars and now owed my bank money.

Mina met me at the airport and drove me to hotel. She said her father had come from South Africa only that morning and she hadn't been able to discuss it yet. She was planning to do it now and asked me to come by in an hour. She wanted to tell him about it before he met me. To be honest, I didn't mind. A bit of buffer would do no harm.

I indulged in some positive thinking on the way. I visualized Ashok bhai patting me on my arm and telling me it was okay. 'These things happen, Jai bhai. It's all in the game. A son-in-law like you is worth much more.'

As I entered the house, I saw him rush out, a maniacal look on his face. Mina was clutching his arm, trying to pull him back.

'*Chor*!' he cried, with feeling. '*Ye chor chhe*! This man is a thief! *Main iska Ponzi bana doonga*. I will make a *Ponzi* of him!'

A distraught Mina motioned me to go away. I hung around for a while outside but it was getting embarrassing. I could hear shrill Gujarati cries emanating from inside the house. The driver and the houseboy were staring at me curiously. As I turned away and went back to the hotel, I could feel my heart beating like a drum. It was like someone was hitting it with a hammer. Mina's mother called me a couple of hours later saying Mina had been locked up in her room and was not allowed to leave home. I wanted to rush in there to help but Sarojben forbid me to come, saying it would simply make things worse. She asked me to give him a week's time, by which time she said things would settle down. The man seemed to have gone completely off his rocker. In a state of trance, I took the flight back home.

So much for positive thinking, I told myself. If private banking involved being branded a thief by your future father-in-law in front of his driver and houseboy, I would rather be a driver or a houseboy.

Back home, I entered my apartment and switched on the lights.

At least, I attempted to. It remained plunged in darkness. What the hell is happening, I wondered. Has the city gone on the blink? Has the power line tripped? Or . . . when was the last time I paid the bill? It had not been in the last month or two for sure. Nor had I paid my landline bill at home since quite some time. I had practically lived off my Blackberry for months. I picked up the receiver. The line was dead. I washed my face in the dark. I lit a lamp and prayed for a while. Then I cried a bit, as I wallowed in some self-pity. For several minutes, I chanted a mantra, which my mother had taught me. Feeling a wee bit better, I decided to check into a hotel. I came down to the car park and glared at my Porsche. Walking across the car park was a young couple, pushing a pram. It was Kitch and Galiya and the pram they were pushing contained the only piece of good news I had heard since 15 September. A beautiful, doll-like baby they had named Olga, after Galiya's paternal grandmother. Olga Dharini Krishnan, *poora naam*.

'Hi Jack!'

'Yo Kitch, hey Galiya. And *hey, little thing*! The prettiest member of the family!'

'Dude, you're back? I thought you left just this morning.'

'I did, Kitch . . . its a long story. I am just moving into a hotel. They've disconnected the power. I forgot to pay the bill last month.'

They wouldn't hear of it and insisted on taking me home. 'I'll have dinner ready in half an hour,' Galiya said.

'Oh, it's okay about my dinner. I've already had dinner of sorts on the flight.'

'Ah, it's okay, da, Jai,' said Kitch. 'Don't worry, she won't give you horsemeat!' We both burst into laughter. It felt good to be able to laugh.

After dinner, Kitch shared some of his woes. Luckily for him, while most of his accounts were down more than 50 per cent, only one got into a margin call situation. 'That fellow Larry is a real sadist,' he said, with feeling. 'I told him the client will take a few days to bring in cash and that he could not sell his securities.'

Apparently, Larry had just bluntly told Kitch that no power on earth could stop him from selling anything he chose to and even as they were talking, he promptly went and sold his Microsoft shares at a 40 per cent loss.

'There!' he had said, 'I've just sold Microsoft, lah. I can sell anything and everything. The client is in margin call. I have full authority. You understand?'

Kitch also showed me an email he had received from a client. 'I didn't know whether to laugh or cry when I got this,' he said. 'So, I did both.'

It read 'Dear Mr Krishnan, We are greatly aggrieved and upset at the deep discount in our portfolio. We gave you the account to make it grow, not to make it shrink. Your mismanagement has given us sleepless nights. It is shocking that everything you have bought is showing a huge loss. You are not fit for your job. WISHING YOU THE WORST OF LUCK.' The last sentence was in capital letters.

I shook my head. How could people behave like this? 'Don't let it worry you, Kitch. These are difficult times we are going through. We just have to keep our balance, remain focused and wait for it to pass.'

I then told him about Mina and what had happened there. I was expecting sympathy. Instead, the hound burst into laughter. Galiya joined him and very soon, I was laughing too, almost hysterically. It was almost as if we were using this as an excuse to give vent to the tension that we had absorbed over the last three months.

'He will be fine in a day or two,' Kitch assured me, once he recovered. 'In any case, Mina understands. That's the main thing.'

# 32

## NOWHERE TO HIDE

New Year came and went. The only reason we even realized it was there was because it gave us all—bankers and clients alike—an opportunity to switch off our mobile phones and computers as the markets remained closed for a good part of the final week of the year. Between September and December, I had received calls at all hours of the day or night and all days of the week, from panic-stricken clients, senior managers, compliance officers and credit officers.

That last week, it was as if everyone wanted a break from everyone else. Collectively, we went into our respective shells and sat there quietly licking our wounds and whimpering.

Come 2009 and we slowly limped back, hoping against hope that the dawn of the New Year would have changed the fortunes of the markets. On the very first day, I changed the position of the desk and chair in my room. If Saxena felt that could help, there was nothing wrong in giving it a shot, I felt. My ego would not stand in the way of a fair trial. There was little ego left in me anyway. With the kind of bruising it had taken in recent times, it would be a long time before it could come back, if at all it did. I also started praying regularly, a habit that had, in recent times, taken a bit of a back seat.

If we were anticipating a sudden and miraculous turnaround in fortunes, we were mistaken. Lloyds dipped from about a pound in December to half of that. Barclays crashed from 150p end December to about 60p. The price of Bank Turan Alem's bond kept falling further. Stuart's account went into margin call again. State Bank of India moved from USD 60 to less than 50. There was a slight recovery in oil prices briefly, but Citi fell to below USD 3. Infosys remained well below 30. My favourite BRIC fund seemed to have stabilized at 10. A year ago, it had touched 30. *Decoupling*? Far from it.

Five of Ahmed's clients had complained about indiscriminate handling of their accounts. In two cases, recorded telephone conversations proved that they were just opportunists trying to cheat the bank out of money in a difficult situation. Or else had suffered from selective amnesia. One case was in dispute. In the other two cases, the bank decided to compensate the client and Ahmed was issued a letter of warning.

Peggy herself was under a lot of pressure. A client of hers had authorized her to buy the bond of a Russian company called 'Finance Leasing' at a price of 98. Peggy had gone ahead and bought it at 98.35. The company subsequently went into default and was trading at 15. The client had had no issue at the time of purchase, but now threatened to sue and go to the press, as the purchase price was above the limit he had set. He claimed the bond should never have been bought in the first place.

Rachel told me she hadn't slept properly in weeks. She'd collapse out of exhaustion at around 10 or 11 p.m., but wake up at around 2 a.m. After that, she just couldn't go back to sleep. The doctor had put her on some tablets for a month to calm her down. He told her he had seen several such cases—from both the banker and the investor community.

At our New York office, a client had threatened to commit suicide by jumping off the top of the office building and had to be physically restrained. The police had to be called for.

One of Melissa's clients had had a heart attack. The client himself had been advised not to meet his bankers but his wife called up Melissa and blamed her for his illness. She had told Melissa that if anything were to happen to him, she would be responsible.

Another client whose portfolio value had dropped to a quarter million from 1 million blamed her for losing '400 per cent' of his money. 'The market has dropped by only 50 or 60 per cent,' he told her, 'but my portfolio is down 400 per cent!' When she tried convincing him that he was calculating his losses the wrong way, he accused her of trying to trick him by playing around with numbers and threatened to complain to the central bank.

Harry was ploughing steadily on, grim-faced, but stoic. Ramzi submitted his resignation in the second week of January.

We continued to be under pressure for new business and revenues. But I just did not have the motivation to work on new business. Nor did I have that sunny confidence so essential for a successful sale. I was worried about Mina. Twice when I had called her home, her father had picked up the call and had slammed the phone on me. Kapoor had once spoken to her mother. He told me Mina's phone had been taken away from her and that she was not allowed to step out of the house. I was furious. I suggested a police complaint, but Kapoor reminded me that they did not live in the UK where such things could work. Besides, Mina would not want her father to be hauled up by the cops. I was deeply distressed, just like the portfolios of all my clients.

I called up Madan bhai. He still had lots of cash in the account. I asked him if he would like to look at equities at current levels. 'Opportunity knocks but once,' I mumbled, hesitantly.

'Opportunity may knock only once, Jai bhai!' he retorted. 'But we have got knocked down many times. I don't want to fall again. We are not interested in taking any more of this nonsense . . . The capital market seems to be nothing but a casino. We are not gamblers, we are investors.'

My clients were treating me like a pariah. As someone had mentioned to me on an earlier occasion, 'In this business, you are only as good as your last trade.' It didn't matter if you had made money many years in a row. If you screw up big time this year, your client will not look at you. And in my case, I didn't even have the track record of many years. Just a couple, at best.

The atmosphere in office resembled that of a morgue. It was like a war zone, some dead, some bleeding. But all hurt, all stupefied. There was fear, worry, uncertainty. Everybody had questions, no one had answers. There was one positive, though, in all this. There were no more heroes, no villains. No ego, no halo. Suddenly, you found everyone was willing to lend a comforting shoulder or hold a needy hand. The crash had been a great leveller.

From time to time we read reports about investors and bankers committing suicide. We received tons of emails ridiculing the banking community. Jokes on the subject abounded. 'Why would a pigeon find it easier to buy a BMW than a banker? Because a banker can't afford to make a deposit on the car.' 'Why did the banker take up the job of a zoo cleaner? Because bankers can't be choosers.' 'Are there any Lehman sisters around? I'd like to do to them what the brothers did to us.' 'What is the difference between a bunker and a banker? One gives you protection when you go underground. The other goes underground when you need protection.' 'What is happening in the rarefied world of Private Banking? It has become so rarefied it will soon cease to exist.'

Job cuts had begun in right earnest. For the guys who would still be left after the mauling, the G8 countries had already decided to crack down on bankers' bonuses.

But worst of all, my Mina had gone. I tried to convince myself it was meant to be. Maybe, my father was not destined to have a three-fingered samdhi, I told myself, trying to make myself smile. But it only made me feel worse. I decided I had to go back to Kenya to make one last attempt. Kapoor promised to come along.

That night, Peggy came home. She gave me some very disturbing news. She told me the Dubai office was going to be pruned down considerably. It might remain for another year and then would get wound up. She would lose her job. So would Cyrus. So would most of the others. Harry had given in his resignation that morning. He was planning to join a local bank. Peggy had recommended to James Ackermann that he should retain me, Kitch and Linda to run the office for the time being and co-ordinate with the Dubai-based lawyers and with the London office. Most clients would be handled out of London. Peggy was leaving Dubai the next day and was going to take a break in Thailand. She hoped the markets would recover soon and was sure that I would find another job within the year. She looked a pale shadow of the girl she used to be, but I admired her sincerity and her commitment. For the last several weeks, even months, she had been working until very late every single day, making calls, doing trades and trying to increase revenues and bring in new clients even as she was trying to persuade NY to give us more time.

I slept little that night.

The next day was Friday. I didn't go to work. I wanted to avoid the office as much as possible. I switched off my cell phone and spent the day with Kitch. I also went over to visit Rachel. She had heard the news too, but in a sense, it seemed to have actually brought her relief. She looked better than she did when I saw her last.

Cyrus called Kitch and asked him to meet him at 9.30 Saturday morning. He also left a message with him asking me to come over at 10. I assumed it was to tell us about the change. It was, but it wasn't quite what I had heard from Peggy. The *entire* office was being closed with immediate effect. All matters relating to the office in Dubai would be handled by the lawyers. Cyrus himself would be based in London and would control matters relating to the closure of the office from there.

'Is there anything else you need to know, Jack?' he asked.

I hesitated. 'I thought the office would remain for a year?' I asked.

He smiled. At least his lips did. His eyes remained the way they always did. Cold, hard and stony.

'That was Peggy's little game,' he sneered. 'If she had succeeded, I would have been out of a job. This is a crisis, Jack. In a crisis, there are some winners and some losers. I wanted the job. So, I played my own game. And won. This letter gives you all details about the compensation to be paid to you, Jack. You get a three-month salary based on your average earnings over the last six months. Most others have already left yesterday. You can remove your things at your convenience. You will not be required at office any more.'

I walked out of the room. My head was clouded and my knees wobbly. I was not able to think clearly. I went to my room and stared out of the window. I must have been there for a long time. Suddenly, the phone rang. I noticed there had been several missed calls. I picked up the phone. A not unfamiliar voice spoke. It was Hitesh, Dr Chimanbhai's son.

'What have you done to my account, you bastard?' he asked. 'It's all bloody *shit*. You bought Infosys at 40, it's at 26 now. Barclays is 60 per cent down, Microsoft is 50 per cent down . . . what the *fuck* have you been up to, man? This is just rubbish. We're holding *shit* in this account. And you called up Dad and told him it will recover in a year's time? That old fool doesn't have the brains to know that you're just shamming. Recover in a year? You must be out of your fucking mind, man! What the hell do I do now with this buggered up account? This is *raddi*, just complete *shit*.'

No one had ever spoken to me like this before. No one ever. Every cell in me was smouldering. I had nothing to lose.

'I'll tell you what to do,' I told him. 'First, you take a *dubki* in this shit. Dip your head in it. That will make your face look a lot better. Then, you remove all those dumb rings off your face and go and get a decent haircut. It will make you look human. Then maybe you can stop sponging off your dad's money and go and do some work for a change. Your dad's a great man. Do something to make him proud of you. Stop being a bloody parasite. *Ass-hole!*'

I slammed the phone, put a few things in my bag and started to leave. The phone rang again. It was the same number. I walked away. I was done with that call.

For a while, I walked around the office, stopping here and there. I don't know why, maybe I was just taking in the smells and the memories. I wondered whether I should have one last cup of tea in the pantry, but decided against it. Instead, I went to the corridor and put on the boxing gloves. Fifteen minutes later, I was so tired I could hardly stand. But in my mind, I was feeling a little better. As I came out, I noticed that the television was on. As usual, it was playing the financial news channel. Two analysts were aggressively debating between a 'V-shaped recovery' and a 'W-shaped recovery'. A third was pitching his case for a long-drawn-out recession featuring an 'L-shaped recovery'. The anchor was alternating between each of them, obviously trying to generate maximum excitement. I picked up the remote and hurled it on the screen with all my strength. It crashed into it and fell softly onto the carpet. I surveyed the ruin with smug satisfaction. Then I walked out to the reception.

From there, I called Kitch. He sounded down and out. 'I suppose this is the notorious American pink slip,' he said morosely. 'Never thought I'd experience it so soon in my career.' After trying to cheer him up a bit, I decided to make a quick call to my clients to let them know. I didn't want to go back to my room, so I called them from the reception.

Sunny Singh told me not to worry. This is a game, he told me. 'We win some, we lose some. You will get another job, you will come back to us. We will again open account with you, you will again make money for us. That is life.' I was grateful to him for his kindness, but I knew he was wrong. I would never do this job again.

'Keep close to your family, Pat.' I don't have to tell you who that was. 'Keep close to your family, keep close to nature. If you can do that, everything else will become manageable.'

'Thank you, Stuart. I have much to learn from people like you. By the way, do you know you are the only one in the world who calls me Pat? With the others, it's either Jai or Jack.'

Stuart paused briefly. 'Did I tell you I had a son?' he asked.

'Yes, I know. In Australia.'

'He died four years ago.'

I was stunned. He had never let me on to that. He had always spoken of him as if he was there.

'He was about your age and your build. His name was Pat.'

I was dumb-struck. 'I . . . I am sorry, Stuart,' I told him. 'Sorry about . . . sorry about everything.'

I called Saxena. I needed his advice desperately. I needed to sell my apartment and liquidate the loan. But the broker said the apartment would fetch nothing more than 1200 a square foot. I had paid 1600 for it. Dubai had been badly hit in the crisis and the real estate had got badly squeezed. At a selling price of 1100, that price, I would still be short even with my savings, the sale proceeds of my Porsche car and the three months' salary that I had just got. Saxena called me home over for dinner that night. He had invited the broker as well and fixed a price of 1200 a square foot. He said he would take care of the loan closure for me. I apologized for not being able to achieve with his account what I had set out to. He smiled ruefully.

'Remember what I told you when we first met, Jai?' he asked, drawing a line along his forehead signifying destiny. '*Jab kismet hai gandu, to kya karega pandu?*' he said smiling. '*Koi muqaddar ka sikandar nahin hota, Muqaddar hamesha sikandar hota hai.* You cannot conquer destiny.' The crisis had made everyone philosophers.

After settling the loan, I was left with 2,400 dollars for my thirty-eight-month stint overseas. What irony, I thought. Perhaps that was my kismet. I would leave the next day itself, maybe. I just wanted to get away from it all. I was eager, even anxious to get back home.

The only thing that was bothering me now was the thought of Mina. I would talk to Kapoor. If he suggested it, I could fly over from Chennai and somehow make her father understand. What an unmitigated disaster he was. As if he was the only one in the world who had lost money. And what a shame that poor Mina had to contend with a *bandar* like him for a father.

It was past midnight when I reached the apartment that night. Sans job, sans house, sans money and sans girlfriend, I thought to myself, paraphrasing my close companion of these days. Every night I read Shakespeare. It seemed to transport me to another world. Under the circumstances, what could be better?

As I stood in the lift waiting to reach my floor, I felt a huge weight on my drooping shoulders. My head was bowed. I was very tired and lonely. A few feet away from my apartment door, I stopped. There was someone sitting on the floor just outside, leaning against my door, a forlorn figure, face covered with her hands. It looked like . . . could it be Mina? *Here*?

It was. She looked pale, tired and haggard. She got up, staggered slightly from the numbness of sitting there for goodness knows how long and fell into my arms. She cried for a long time and I don't mind confessing that I did, too. Tears came easily those days.

She said she had been trying to get me on the phone for two days. To tell me that she, her mother and Kapoor had finally managed to sober her father down and make him understand that Jai Patel was a victim rather than a villain. She had tried my cell phone, my office and my home number and couldn't get me on any of these. Finally, she decided to take a chance and fly down to Dubai along with Kapoor. She had gone to the office but found no one there. She had checked with my neighbours and had been told I was still in town. So, she had just sat down in front of the door and decided to wait.

Suddenly, things looked a whole lot better. In fact, they looked terrific! She didn't want to go back to Kenya for the time being. Would I consider staying back in Dubai for a few days, she asked. Or if I was going to India, could she come along with me? *Could* she? I was delighted. *Oh boy*! *What a girl*!

We visited Kapoor and thanked him. Unknown to me, he had gone to Nairobi and pleaded my case with Mina's father . . . I didn't have words to thank Kapoor. Raising a toast to him I said, 'Kapoor uncle, I think . . . I really think . . .' and paused, groping for the words that could precisely convey my gratitude for everything he had done for me in the last two years. Even apart from the business. If it had not been for him, I would never have met Mina. If it were not for him, I may never have got her back.

'Don't think, Jai bhai,' he responded. 'Just drink!'

The next morning, while Mina went to a beauty parlour, I

shopped around for a few things for Mum, Dad, Kitty, Shree, Murugan, Aadhilakshmi, the maid and others. Mina and I did some shopping together. And then, we turned the time back two years and went to the bar at Burj Al Arab.

From the airport, I called up Saxena again to thank him for his help. I called to say one final good bye to Harsh and Joi and to invite them to Chennai. And also to request them to settle my landline bill, which I hadn't yet paid.

Just as we were waiting in the lounge, I noticed a familiar face smiling at me. At first I couldn't quite figure out who she was. Then, with a shock it came to me. It was Sushma, Kirit Desai's wife. *Damn* the woman. And *Mina was with me*! I felt like my heart had been ripped from its moorings.

She walked up, still smiling. An icy mist had enveloped my body. I was numb all over. What was she going to say?

'I just want to thank you,' she said softly. 'Kirit is a different man these days. We had gone on a pilgrimage for two weeks, just the two of us. It was the first time we have spent so much time together ever since we got married. He is at work nowadays only in the mornings. He comes home for lunch. We see movies together, he comes for walks. All thanks to you, Jai Patel.' I didn't know what to say. I didn't even know what to think. She walked away. I heaved a *huge* sigh of relief.

I had told my parents three days ago that they were in for a surprise. I had meant my coming back to India for good. Now, they were in for a much bigger surprise. I was being accompanied by the girl I had chosen as my life partner. I hoped they would like her. After all, she was pretty, soft-spoken, respectful, a Gujarati and one from 'chhe gaam' at that, our own little group of six neighbouring villages. What more could they ask for?

It was 20 January 2009. Barack Hussein Obama had just been sworn in as the President of the United States of America. For Mina and me, it was as if a personal friend had triumphed. Somehow, it seemed symbolic of the way we ourselves had overcome the challenges of the last few months.

# 33

## HERE AND NOW

My Tamil has improved by leaps and bounds. Even Mina can now manage a simple conversation with the maid Thilaka, with Kannan, the man who looks after the cash crops or with Murugan, our driver. Murugan is now only a part-time driver. His main responsibility is something else. He is in charge of the farm. We brought him down with us from Chennai. For him, it is actually something of a homecoming. He used to be a farmhand before his father pushed him into learning to drive and going to the city to try and make his fortune. When he heard about our moving down here and getting into agriculture and farming, he pleaded with us to let him come along. He is a much more confident man nowadays and handles both animals and people with panache . . . He has received a further boost by the release, a few weeks ago, of a new Bollywood flick titled *Quick Gun Murugan* and can't wait to see it. 'I very lucky, saar!' he told me. 'Fillum coming my name. That too, Hindi film—national release. Nobody else has fillum coming their name. Not you, not madam, *nobody*.' So nowadays, he alone walks around with a swagger.

Actually, there's little doubt in my mind about who is the one who is *really* in charge over here. It's probably Mina. She is completely clued in. I have never seen anyone learn anything so quickly. She is quietly in control, now here, now there, messing about, mucking around, getting her hands dirty without a second thought, giving orders and ensuring that the work is done. Perhaps

I realize this all the more because I myself have been a relatively slow learner here at the farm—ponderous, tentative and hesitant. The very first time Mina tried milking a cow, within a minute or two, she was doing it like she had been doing it all her life. I've tried it as well, but I seem to have my eye more on the cow's hind legs—for the fear of getting kicked—than on its udders. Also, the feel and texture of the thing . . . it's rubbery and rather awkward to touch. On one occasion, when I was sitting on a stool trying to follow instructions, I happened to get in between the cow's tail and a fly on its back. I ended up getting whacked on the side of my head.

These things tend to prey on one's mind. I also have of a horror of lizards, which have this knack of creeping into the house sometimes. My response to this is simple, swift and unwavering. I jump on to the nearest sofa and holler for Mina, Thilaka or Murugan who then come by with a stick and guide the thing out.

But these are small things. Looking at the brighter side, we are 'sir' and 'madam' of the place and have a caring, conscientious staff. Mina and I do a lot of things together. Or more accurately, she does, while I watch and suggest ways to do it more efficiently. The one thing that I have managed to do well, though, is to handle the dog. We have a Doberman, whose name is 'The Boss'. Nothing to do with the legendary American singer Bruce Springsteen. Initially, we just named him 'Boss' because of the way he would sometimes sit and survey the place around him. But our neighbour, who is heavily into astrology, numerology and such, told us it would be good for him if his named started with 'T'. So, we changed it accordingly.

There is a waterfall nearby. Sometimes, we go there for a 'shower'. We often bathe in the river, which passes by just half a kilometre from the farm. It takes us less than six minutes to get there. Initially, we were considered 'outsiders' by fellow bathers, who would get a little self-conscious, huddle together and stare at us. Gradually, we became one of them. More than me, Mina has been quick to make friends. I once asked her if she ever thought of London or Nairobi. 'Sometimes,' she replied. 'But my mother has taught me to focus on what is, rather than what isn't.'

We enjoy the relative tranquillity, the clean air, the pristine beauty of the landscape nearby. We rarely use a cell phone. More out of choice, really. Kannan always carries one. After several years of using it almost non-stop, even now, I occasionally seem to hear, or sense that once familiar ring tone of my old cell phone. When that happens, I shudder. I like my new life and to a large extent it's because I share it with Mina. Like Stuart had said, being close to nature and to one's family brought a certain balm to one's heart. It is a soothing, calming influence. But to be completely honest, in one corner of my heart, there still does remain that little feeling of having left a task unfinished, a job incomplete, a puzzle unsolved back there in the investment world.

Mina and I got married eight months ago. It's been a wonderful experience. The wedding itself went through without a hitch. My parents were floored from the day they first met her. Kitty and Mina are so friendly that when the two of them are together, it is I who feels like an outsider. Mina's mother has been—she always has—very sweet and helpful. Quite a 'brick' as Emma would have said. Even her father has come around. I can't say I've quite forgotten the incident of that awful day, but I've been quite willing to put it behind me and look ahead.

Much water has flowed under the bridge since 20 January, when Mina and I came to Chennai. We didn't go straight home. We first went to the Hotel Woodlands, which is just a step away from home. We left our things there. I left Mina there as well, while I went home. There was a lot of hugging and crying. It's true that you never really appreciate home till you live on your own. Coming from where I did, having gone through what I had, I have never experienced as much warmth, security and a sense of belonging as I did that day. Kitty too, came within a few minutes of my mum's phone call to her and flung her arms around me.

'I hope you have not come here for two days,' my father told me. 'We have been missing you so much. We just long for you to spend time with us, get married and give us the pleasure of playing with our grandchildren. After all, you are almost twenty-nine, Jai beta. Please do consider.'

'I think I will be able to do all of that now, Dad,' I told him. 'I have not told you much, but I have gone through a lot of difficulty in the last six months. My office in Dubai has closed down. I have lost my job. I have lost my savings. I have had to sell my apartment in Dubai. But . . .' I paused, 'I have one piece of good news for you. There is a wonderful Gujarati girl whom I have met and like. If you and Mum can meet her and give us your blessings, we can start work pretty quickly on the grandchildren.'

I must say he took it rather well. I think Kitty's marriage had made my father a little more flexible.

Two days later, all of us—my parents, Kitty, Shree, Mina and I—went out and watched *Slumdog Millionaire* on the big screen, just like one big, happy family. As we watched the quiz-themed movie, I was reminded of Rachel, Peggy, Harsh, Joi and of course, Kochar.

Over the next few days, I took Mina out to all my favourite restaurants. She and I watched the Shahrukh Khan hit *Rab Ne Bana Di Jodi*. 'Mina *ji*,' I told her, I am going to change my name to 'Punjab Power'. After all, my motto too, is going to be "Lighting up your life, *ji*".'

Her parents came over the following week and the wedding was celebrated a month later. Both Mina and I were anxious to get it done with early and without any major expense to either set of parents. We had already purchased the land for the farm and had started renovation of the house we were going to stay in. Post 2008, I think we had both acquired a cautious streak as far as spending went, whether it was our own money or that of our parents. So, there was no 'big, fat, Indian wedding'. We had had a smallish affair attended by about 150 people and celebrated on a modest scale. There wasn't much of a sangeet either, but Mina and I had choreographed and put up a little ten-minute thing which I thought was really cool. Unfortunately, not too many others did.

Few rave reviews came our way. About fifteen of Mina's relatives had flown in from Kenya or elsewhere. Kapoor was a very special guest and received a warm welcome.

The purchase of the farm and the adjoining lands was funded partly by my father and partly by Mina's. My father had intended to fund all of it. When Mina's father offered to share the cost, I had initially put my foot very firmly down. I had no intention of accepting any largesse from my father-in-law. I have no issues accepting money from fathers-in-law, generally speaking. If I had married Warren Buffett's daughter and he had offered me a billion or two, I would have lapped it up without a second thought. My problem was this man in particular, who had, almost in public, called me a thief. He should have remembered that if he points one accusing finger at me, his *two* remaining fingers point back at himself. But to come back to the er ... point, my stand seemed to upset Mina a bit. She saw it as an olive branch being offered by her father and felt that it would be best to accept it gracefully. So, we did and that went to fund a portion of the purchase.

The entire cost of the farm house renovation and the purchase of livestock was funded by my mum. She, of course, insists that it is *my* money, but I don't look at it that way. The month I was born, she had signed up with a local bank to pay 5,000 rupees every month into a recurring deposit scheme. She had been doing it for years and finally encashed it when I got married. It had accumulated to 5.7 million rupees, or about USD 110,000. The thought occurred to me that to invest money sensibly, you don't have to be a genius, or highly educated. You don't have to use the latest in technology, live in Silicon Valley or be a Nobel Prize winner in economics. Maybe all you need is discipline and a long-term perspective. It was a sobering thought.

~

It was some time in January, 2010. Mina and I were relaxing after a hard day's work. I was checking out the 'Cricinfo' website for some updates. Mina had just had a bath and was drying her hair and Murugan was reading out an account of the farm expenses for the day. He had bought bird feed from our regular supplier in Pattamadai. He had repaired the fence. He had paid the 'cow doctor' (as a vet is referred to in Tamil) for six tubes of ointment. He had paid a supplier in Tirunelveli for earthworm vermicompost. Also, was madam okay with paying the gardener his next month's salary in advance? There was going to be a ceremony at his house next week to announce and celebrate his daughter's coming of age . . .

The phone rang. Murugan put it on speaker, as he usually did.

'Hello,' he said.

'Hi!' said a voice with an American twang. 'Is that you, Jack, darling?'

I jumped. So did Mina.

I picked up the phone. 'Hello, this is Jack.'

'Oh *hi* honey, it's Peggy!'

'*Peggy!*' I almost yelled. 'How nice to hear your voice! How on earth did you get this number?'

'Oh, I got it from Kapoor. I'm back in Dubai now, Jack. *Hey*! Kapoor told me you have got married to Mina. Please accept my congratulations, Jack. I am absolutely delighted to know that. I'm *really* happy for the two of you.'

'Thanks! Yeah, we got married in March. And we're here now, tucked away in the interiors, far away from the big bad city, growing organic crops and stuff! Chilli, primarily. Also peanuts, like Jimmy Carter! You really ought to visit us, Peggy! One week here, wading knee-deep in cow dung and you won't need sanitizers for the rest of your life!'

She laughed. 'That's so epic. Organic farming . . . Can't get any better, can it? That's really awesome, Jack!'

'I couldn't grow portfolios, but am doing pretty well with earthworms, Peggy!'

'*Earthworms*! No one grows earthworms, surely?'

'Not like crops! But it's good to let them breed. They aerate and enrich the soil.'

'You're pulling my leg, Jack. I mean, earthworms are pests!'

'Far from it, Peggy. In fact, they are referred to as the farmer's friend. Take it from Farmer Jack!'

'Well, I mean! *Really*! One lives and learns, huh, Jack? If earthworms are where the momentum is, I guess you must follow it. As they say, the trend's your friend! Hey! What's Chris up to, Jack?'

'Oh, Kitch! You'll be surprised, Peggy. He's started a small restaurant, called 'Kitcha Hut' that serves south Indian fast food. He says he's going to start another one for north Indian snacks and one for ice creams. He plans to name them 'Kitcha Inn' and 'Kitcha Corner'!'

'Oh my God!' Peggy exclaimed. 'I just can't believe this! Ask him to make sure he doesn't get sued.'

'I did! But he says if the Americans can try to patent yoga and basmati rice and make a film called *Avatar* he sees no reason why he can't start a 'Kitcha Hut'. After all, Kitcha is his pet name at home!'

Peggy laughed. 'Wow! I mean, I just don't know what to say! It's phenomenal, you guys are so enterprising! By the way, Jack, did you know Cyrus has got married to Rebecca?'

'*No!*' I nearly dropped the phone. '*Really*? I had no idea!'

'Apparently, they had a thing or two going even then. They married in February.'

'I just can't believe it somehow. And how's Richard, Peggy?'

'Oh, that's over, Jack. We're not together any more.'

'I'm so sorry, Peggy ... I ... didn't know that.'

'It's all right, Jack. I've moved on. Er ... I'm with Dan, now.'

'Dan?'

'*Yeah*! You remember Dan Streep surely?'

'Dan in New York?'

'Oh, he's in Abu Dhabi now. He's a consultant to Abu Dhabi's Sovereign Wealth Funds. He's here during the weekends and I try and go there at least once during the week. He's great. But Jack, all this organic farming and fast food stuff has left me slightly unsure if I should ask you this question. But I think I still will. Would it be of any interest to you to know that I have just joined Abbots Bank in Dubai? Things are looking distinctly better now, Jack. Many clients have recovered a good portion of their money. Those who continued investing in the first quarter of this year have, in fact, *made* money. The Dow has crossed 10,000. The Indian Sensex has more than doubled in the last year. Most markets have recovered big time. Dubai's looking up too, Jack.'

'Looking up? Are you kidding? Some time back, even the earthworms here were discussing the Dubai crash.'

'I think that's over, Jack. Everyone's moving on. Real estate appears to have turned the corner. The Burj Khalifa got launched quite spectacularly early this year. One of the Metro lines has been in place for months now. I'm looking to build a team here, honey. I was hoping my star performer would be in a position to come back to my team. The G8 still keeps talking about cutting bonuses for bankers, but there are enough players willing to pay good money to attract talent. I can make it attractive for you, Jack. Is there any hope in hell for me? *Huh*? Please tell me there is.'

I was struck dumb. This was completely out of the blue. I didn't know what to think. I looked at Mina. She stared back at me.

'Jack? Honey? Are you there?'

'*Woof!*' barked The Boss. '*Woof, woof!*'

# ACKNOWLEDGEMENTS

The thought of writing a novel had always been tentatively scheduled for 'after retirement'. The swift kick in the pants needed to propel me into immediate action came in the form of the 2008 financial crisis. For the final output of my efforts—which you are now gingerly holding in your hands—there are many I need to blame. Or thank, depending on how you see it.

My colleagues Mani, Asad, Varun and others who gave me the initial push. My friends Sanjeev, Harshit, Mazher, Juzar and Venkat who threatened to publish the book themselves, if no leading publisher did. Ujwal, Bhagyashree, Anantha and Juhi who egged me on. I must also point an 'accusing' finger at Kumar and Pammi, Visalakshi and Shankar. Then there's Patrick Michael, S.M. Patel, Vana, Anju, Manu, Uma, Dhiraj, Mukul, Padma, Janaki and others. They are all party to the crime.

My parents and my in-laws. My sisters Shobhana and Sheela who encouraged me blindly in a way only sisters can. Kaarthik, Kshama and Kaushik, my seeing-eye pals to the world of the young, the mad and the reckless.

Ravi, Vaishali and Paromita of Penguin India for seeing potential that even I wasn't sure about. Shankar Mahadevan for taking time off from his incredibly tight schedule to read this book in its entirety.

My wife Anandhi who has approached this book with a mix of trepidation and girlish enthusiasm; and finally my son Roshan who, in all his innocence, assured me when I started, that my book would 'win the Booker prize'. Love you all.

I enjoyed writing this book. If it brought you some joy, I consider my job done. Or on second thoughts, maybe just started.